What Goes on Tour

The Texan Quartet #1

Claire Boston

BANTILLY
PUBLISHING

First published by Momentum in 2014
This edition published in 2017 by Bantilly Publishing

What Goes on Tour: The Texan Quartet 1

EPUB format: 9780995391871
Mobi format: 9780995391888
Print format: 9780995391895

Cover design by XOU Creative
Edited by Elizabeth Cowell
Proofread by Laurie Ormond

DEDICATION

To Mum and Dad for teaching me I can do anything I set my mind to, and to my husband, Luke for his support and encouragement - I love you

Chapter 1

Breathe.

Libby Myles' heart was doing its best rock concert impression, thudding hard enough against her ribs that she thought it was going to break through.

She was going on television, not to face a firing squad.

Hurrying alongside the keep-up-or-be-left-behind production assistant, Libby figured it amounted to the same thing.

If she messed this up it was the death of her fledgling career. One wrong word, one misinterpreted sentence, and she'd be *that* sound bite on tomorrow morning's radio. The one that was played over and over again while the DJs asked each other, "What *was* she thinking?"

Suddenly the blond-haired assistant stopped and directed her into a room. Libby braked, wobbled on her four-inch heels, and took a couple of quiet, slow breaths to stop herself panting. God, she was unfit.

"This is the Green Room. You can wait here with the other guests and I'll be back to get you when it's your turn." The woman turned and strode away before Libby could ask for introductions. Libby cursed the fact she had missed the earlier rehearsal due to her book signing and snail-like traffic.

Who had her publicist said would be on tonight's show? An English comedian, Tony someone, and American rock god,

Kent Downer.

Stepping into the room, she noticed there wasn't any green in sight, rather the walls were painted a pale beige reminiscent of a doctor's waiting room. Two men sat on a retro red couch, turned toward each other, deep in conversation, perhaps mid-forties in age. Manager and comedian, Libby decided as she heard their English accents. No point trying to get a seat there.

The other red couch had a single occupant. Not the kind of person you wanted to meet in a dark alley, late at night.

Kent Downer stared straight at Libby, one hand in his lap, the other over the top of the couch, his long, rangy legs crossed at the ankles. She smiled, but he didn't respond, staring but not seeing, his attention somewhere far more interesting than these four walls. She took the opportunity to study him. Short, spikey black faux-hawk, pale skin and the thickest black eyeliner she'd ever seen on a man. His clothes were black too. Skinny-leg jeans, plain, fitted T-shirt and a waistcoat that hung unbuttoned at the sides. Stereotypical rock star. She'd never be able to use him in one of her books – she'd have to make him different in some way. Otherwise she'd get the comment from her editor – "Don't make him a cardboard cut-out."

Libby moved across the room and sat on the couch next to the rock star. He must have felt her movement, as he blinked and looked at her briefly before returning his gaze to the spot he'd been staring at.

Obviously a charm school dropout.

But then again, a rock star of his reputation wouldn't be interested in talking to an author. She pushed aside the twinge of self-doubt. It was his loss.

Libby had a moment of regret for insisting her publicist have the night off – and then shook her head. She didn't need to be babysat.

She poured a glass of water, grabbed a handful of chocolate from the bowl on the glass coffee table and scooted back on the couch to relax.

It didn't happen. The couch was as comfortable as its color was subtle.

Shoving the chocolate into her mouth, she took her notebook and pen out of her bag and opened to a blank page.

She was about to be interviewed in front of a live studio audience and broadcast all over Australia.

Libby's skin grew clammy and she shook her fingers briefly to release some of the stress.

This was a huge opportunity. Struggling writers didn't get this kind of thing. Someone must have owed her publicist a favor. Big-time.

Libby knew if the viewers liked what they saw, they'd mention her to friends, maybe go out and buy her books. If enough people bought them, she'd finally be able to give up her day job and write full time. And prove to her parents she could make it as an author.

Right now, though, she'd settle for a decent royalty check. The repairs on her car had used up every last cent of her savings, and if she didn't get a new temp job when she finished her tour, she'd have to survive on whatever she could harvest from her vegie patch.

There was no way she would ask her parents for help. She couldn't face the 'I told you so' she'd get.

She couldn't stuff this up.

"Tony, you're up." The efficient assistant was back, motioning the comedian toward the door. The two Englishmen rose and followed her out of the room.

Nerves clenched in a death grip in Libby's stomach. She ignored them, taking some more chocolate, then shifted her weight, lifting her knee so she was sitting sideways on the couch.

All the better to observe the rock star.

She needed the distraction.

He was attractive, if you went for the bad boy type, with his designer stubble and dark brooding eyes. Libby imagined some women would get a thrill to have those eyes focused on them, even for a moment.

The man was so still, so absorbed, he almost looked like a wax dummy. Then his fingers twitched, a minute movement, almost indiscernible, the tiniest drum of his fingertips against the back of the couch. A pause. Then the drum again.

Nerves?

From the television in the corner came the sound of applause as the comedian was introduced.

She was next.

Libby swallowed hard.

Making a note in her journal, she heard laughter from the set and stifled her urge to fidget. She was a writer, not a performer. She wasn't used to being the center of attention.

At least the producers had got it right – start the show off with a laugh, end it with a rock star and allow the young adult writer to sag in the middle.

Her stomach danced a tango with her nerves.

No.

She knew how to fix a sagging middle. It was all about being friendly, chatty and enthusiastic about her new book. That was the easy part. She straightened her spine.

"Didn't your mama ever teach you not to stare?" The deep Texan drawl took her by surprise. The rock star had come out of his trance and was now watching her with intense brown eyes. His whole body was rigid, as if waiting to pounce if she said the wrong word. She was the baby antelope coming face to face with the cheetah. Adrenaline zinged through her veins.

"I, ah, no." She stopped babbling, took a deep breath and smiled. "Sorry, I was visiting my muse. I wasn't really staring at you." She held out a hand. "I'm Libby Myles."

He looked at her hand as if she had something contagious.

"Libby, it's your turn."

Saved by the efficient assistant.

Libby dropped her hand, stuffed her notebook and pen in her bag and tucked it next to the couch, hoping her face would return to its normal color quickly. Then she jumped up and hurried after the woman.

She didn't need rock stars and their egos.

They reached the edge of the set. She was about to be on television.

Dread smashed into Libby like a wrecking ball and her breath came faster. Oh, God. She hadn't checked a mirror.

She could have chocolate all over her teeth. She ran her tongue across them, prodding at the spaces in between, then gently patted her hair to make sure it was in place and smoothed down her knee-length skirt. The television make-up that had been caked on earlier was thick, but the make-up artist had assured her it would be fine on screen. She breathed deeply, once, twice, willing the dread away.

She forced herself to stand still as someone attached the microphone to her.

"You look fine." The efficient assistant gave Libby a smile. "This is your intro."

The chat show host's voice rang out. "Our next guest is the author of much-loved young adult series, the Jessop Chronicles. The latest book, *On Winter's Edge*, is out now. Please welcome Libby Myles."

The assistant led Libby toward the set and gave her a gentle push in the direction of the stairs.

Stairs.

She hadn't thought about stairs when her publicist convinced her to wear the highly impractical four-inch heels.

Libby's legs threatened to turn to jelly, but she couldn't let them. The crowd was clapping and she had to make her entrance. Placing her hand firmly on the bannister, she slowly descended, ensuring one foot was firmly planted before moving the next one, smiling at the first couple of rows of audience members.

At the bottom she gave herself a mental pat on the back and walked toward the host, Brian Lowry. His infectious grin made her smile back. He wore a dark, pin-striped business suit buttoned over a white shirt and his short, brown hair was gelled into position. She clasped his outstretched hand and kissed his cheek before turning and greeting Tony, who had moved down a chair. Finally she sat down, crossing her legs and placing her hands in her lap.

The applause died down and her hands shook.

"Welcome to the show, Libby. Your latest book in the Jessop Chronicles series has just been released and you've become an overnight sensation. Why do you think that is?"

Libby smothered a smile. Her success had hardly come overnight and she didn't think her sales really counted as a sensation, but she'd go with it.

She took a breath. "The series has been out for a while now. Word of mouth has been building slowly." Her voice quavered and she swallowed down the nerves. "*On Winter's Edge* is the fourth book in the Jessop Chronicles, and readers are keen to find out what's going to happen next to Shannon, Melissa and Jill."

"So what is going to happen to them?" Brian asked.

Libby laughed. "You'll have to read the book to find out!"

The audience tittered.

Libby's hands stopped trembling as Brian said, "It's on my bedside table." He grinned at her. "I'm sure many people are wondering where you get your ideas from. Some of the creatures in your world are weird and wonderful."

Libby leaned forward slightly. "Ideas are all around. They're everywhere." The brick in her stomach dissolved. This was what she knew. She could talk about her writing until the cows came home. "It's a matter of recognizing how they can be used."

Ten minutes later Brian wrapped up the interview. "Everyone is going to rush out and buy a copy of *On Winter's Edge* now." He turned to the audience. "Please thank Libby Myles."

Libby smiled out at the audience as they applauded. It was over.

She barely remembered what she'd said but she was pretty sure it had gone well.

"My final guest tonight is the devil of rock himself, Kent Downer."

A section of the small studio audience went mad, screaming and shouting. Libby stood and moved down a chair to make way for Kent, who sauntered down the stairs, acknowledging the screaming girls with a salute and shaking Brian's hand with gusto.

Obviously Brian's hands weren't contagious. Libby smirked.

The girls finally calmed down and Brian was able to speak. "Sounds like your fans are pleased you've finally decided to tour Australia. What can they expect at your concert?"

"The best time of their lives," Kent drawled.

Someone in the audience shrieked, "I love you, Kent."

"Love y'all," Kent called back, blowing a kiss.

Was this guy for real? Libby forced herself not to roll her eyes. His arrogance reminded her of her ex. Her heart twinged and she pushed the thought away.

Kent launched into the details of his show.

Then everything went dark.

Blackout.

***

Kent's breath hitched as darkness filled every space. He struggled to hold back the fear surging up and his pulse raced.

"There's no light," he whispered to remind himself that he was still there.

The crowd murmured and Brian's voice called out, "Don't panic, folks. Just a little power outage. Our technicians will have it fixed in a jiffy."

Kent gripped the arms of the chair he was sitting in. He had to fight it. He couldn't give in to the hysteria building inside him. He wasn't trapped, he wasn't alone, he wasn't afraid of the dark.

"Let's play eye spy," Tony called and the audience tittered, a nervous response.

Kent's chest was tight, his breaths short and sharp as his windpipe closed over. He couldn't go to pieces. He had to focus on something. He had to remember his tricks for fighting the fear, but his brain wouldn't cooperate.

Something warm and soft covered his hand. He flinched, and then, recognizing it as the writer's hand, he clutched on to it, holding it tight. He wasn't alone, she was next to him, grounding him to the now.

Her other hand covered his and she stroked it, trying to soothe him.

Kent forced back tears. Forward stroke, breathe in, backward stroke, breathe out.

"Why don't we all sing a song?" the writer asked loudly.

"What about 'Waltzing Matilda'?" Brian suggested. "Everyone should know it. On the count of three – one, two, three."

The audience started a very noisy, very off-key rendition of the Australian folk song. Kent didn't know the words, but some of the fear drained out of him as he listened to the raucous voices.

The writer ran her hand up and down his forearm, stroking

it gently. Kent closed his eyes and focused on the sensation, visualizing her face; her emerald green eyes, her small nose, her hesitant smile and the straight, chocolate brown hair that fell past her shoulders. She was attractive, in an unassuming way, and he concentrated on that hum of attraction he'd felt when he'd first noticed her in the green room.

His hand trembled but little by little the fear receded.

He took a deep breath in and opened his eyes as the song was ending. Off set a light appeared, bobbing up and down, and a crew member walked out carrying a torch.

He was safe.

Kent snatched away his hand and shielded his eyes from the light, resisting the urge to jump up and hug the man.

He turned to the writer, hoping to thank her, but she was looking down at her hands in her lap.

She'd saved his sanity.

He couldn't thank her now, couldn't cause a fuss in front of an audience full of smart phones. He took a deep breath in and then out, his body weak with relief.

He would thank her afterward.

**

Libby ran a thumb over her aching hand. Kent had a strong grip. She checked for signs of bruising and flexed her fingers, trying not to wince. She needed a bag of ice.

She turned toward Kent to see if he was all right. He lounged in the armchair as if he didn't have a care in the world, but one hand clutched the armrest tightly while the other was fisted. He was still recovering. She tried to catch his eye to give him a reassuring smile, but Kent didn't acknowledge her. Not even a glance, a nod or a smile of thanks.

Disappointment flashed through her and she was annoyed with herself. What had she expected, a rush of gratitude? It was typical of a man not to admit to any weakness. In her experience, men had little time for women. It would probably ruin Kent's image if he was seen talking to a writer.

The crew member gave Brian the torch and left. Brian raised his voice. "It's going to be dark for a few more minutes, folks. They've found the problem and are working to fix it. Now we have some light, why don't we have some questions from the audience?"

"Will you marry me, Kent?" a woman yelled.

The crowd laughed.

"I'd hate to put Kent on the spot," Brian said and shone the torch over the audience. "Any *other* questions?"

Hands sprung up, and they spent the next half an hour answering audience questions. To Libby's surprise, there were a number of questions for her as well. Kent had completely recovered and he flirted with the crowd, showing no trace of his anxiety.

Finally the lights came back on and the audience cheered.

"Where were we?" Brian put a hand to his ear and then turned to Kent. "I'll repeat my last question to you before the lights went out and we'll go from there."

The interview began and Libby cradled her bruised hand in her lap. It was throbbing and she desperately wanted to ice it so it would be fine for her book signing tomorrow. She should have said she'd knocked it in the dark and got the efficient assistant to bring her something.

Brian wound up the interview. "Now, folks, we've got a treat to close the show. Kent is going to sing something from his latest album." He motioned Kent to the stage and Kent rose and strode to where a microphone was set up.

"Ladies and gentlemen, all the way from Houston, Texas, here is Kent Downer with his latest song, 'To Be Hurt.'"

The applause was thunderous and then died down. Libby was expecting a loud, thrashing tune, but instead it was low and melodic. A ballad.

Kent's voice was soft and wistful. Libby listened to the words.

"If only it stung,
If only I hurt,
Then I would know
What it is to love."

Kent barely moved. There were no theatrics, no gestures, he just clutched the microphone as if it was the only real thing in the room and sang.

Libby was mesmerized. His voice flowed over her and

resonated with the part of her that knew what it was to hurt. The part of her that had known love and had it thrown back in her face. Kent didn't know what he was asking for. That kind of hurt shouldn't be longed for, it should be shied away from.

The words and melody entwined around her.

Maybe Kent wouldn't treat a woman as she'd been treated. Maybe he would be gentle and kind. Her heart reached out to him.

What the hell was she thinking? Men like Kent weren't interested in women like her.

Libby ripped her gaze away to see how the audience was reacting. They were equally entranced. No one shifted in their seat, no one murmured to the person next to them – they all sat still and silent as this magician weaved them into his world.

The song ended and for a moment all was quiet before the audience came back to life and applauded, shouting and whistling their approval.

Kent blinked, took a small step backward and smiled, saluting to the frenzied listeners.

"And that's all for tonight, folks," Brian shouted above the noise. "Please thank all of my guests – Tony Giuseppe, Libby Myles and the amazing Kent Downer. I'll see you again the same time next week. Goodnight."

None of the audience heard him.

"I've got to hand it to him, the man has presence," Tony said to Libby and stood up. "I'm off." He strode off stage as she rose from her seat.

"Thanks for coming on, Libby." Brian was all smiles, holding out his hand.

She took it and then winced as he shook it. Her hand had already begun to bruise.

"What's wrong?"

"It's my hand. I bumped it on something when the lights went out," Libby said, removing it from his grasp. "It's a little sore."

"Let me get someone to check it for you." He motioned behind her and the efficient assistant strode out. "Can you get some ice for Libby?"

The woman's eyes widened as she saw the hand. "Come with

me."

Libby glanced to where Kent was surrounded by the crowd before following the woman off the set and back into the maze of beige corridors. They passed the green room and Libby ducked in to grab her bag on the way to a first-aid station.

The first-aid attendant pushed her into a chair and gave her a cold pack. "How'd you manage to do that?" he asked.

Libby shrugged. "Hit it against something when the lights went out."

"Against what?"

"No idea. I couldn't see a thing." She looked down at the cold pack as she spoke. She didn't know why she was covering for Kent. He'd not acknowledged her help in any way. But somehow it didn't seem right to mention it to anyone.

"Sit there for a minute with the pack on." The attendant turned to fill out some paperwork.

To Libby's surprise the assistant was still hovering. "Do you think you could have broken something?" she asked, her eyes fluttering back and forth.

She wasn't worried about Libby – she was worried Libby might hold the station accountable.

"No, I'm fine. Really, I'm sure it will be all right by tomorrow. I can be a bit clumsy at times."

The efficient assistant let out a breath. "Good. Have a nice evening." She was out of the room before Libby could reply.

Ten minutes later Libby was climbing into the taxi the attendant had called for her. She couldn't afford to stay for the after-show drinks. She had work to do.

Kent's song kept playing over and over in her head. There had been such longing in his voice and it tugged at her.

She was being ridiculous. She wasn't lonely. Besides, it was better to be alone than with someone who didn't love her. Her ex had taught her that. Not that she'd ever thank him for it.

Kent was good at what he did, making his audience believe he was singing just to them.

Besides, someone probably wrote his songs for him.

The taxi pulled in to her hotel. She quickly paid the driver with the cab voucher her publicist had given her and got out. She didn't have time to dwell on Kent or his song. The deadline for her next book was creeping closer and she needed to get some words written before she called it a night.

She covered her yawn with her hand. One day she'd be able to quit her day job and write full time, but in the meantime she had to write whenever she could.

Which meant now.

***

Adrian shut the hotel door behind him and leaned back against it. This wasn't home but it was his safe space for the moment. The entrance light was on and down the corridor there was more light and the flicker of a television screen. He bathed in the security of the glow.

"Is that you, Uncle Adrian?" Kate's voice called.

Adrian pushed away from the door, letting out a breath. "Sure is, kiddo," he called. "I'll get rid of Kent and be in." He moved into the bathroom.

Christ, what a night.

He reached for the make-up remover, squirted some on cotton wool and began to scrub at the mascara under his eyes. Normally the routine of removing the traces of rock star Kent Downer was soothing, but not tonight.

He hadn't had a panic attack like that in years and his throat closed over again now thinking about it. He hadn't been prepared for total darkness, and if it hadn't been for the writer, he would have gone to pieces in front of everyone. His tough, rock star persona would have been obliterated. He would have lost everything he'd worked so hard for, everything Daniel and George had helped him to achieve, and let everyone down.

But the writer had sensed something was wrong, or perhaps she had been scared herself and had reached out and touched his hand. It had grounded him, proved to him he wasn't alone in the abyss. Afterward, it had taken him so long to extricate himself from his fans that she'd left before he could thank her.

Damn it. Grown men weren't supposed to be afraid of the dark.

Adrian took some more cotton wool, squirted on the liquid and worked on his other eye.

He'd thought he had it beaten. Every night at every concert

he stood in the darkness before the lights came up and the music began. Every night he fought the hysteria. Every night he won the battle against the demon. But one unexpected blackout and he was right back to a quivering mass of Jell-O.

Turning on the taps, he waited until the water ran warm and washed the remnants of his alter ego away. Patting his face dry, he looked in the mirror.

Hi, I'm Adrian Hart and I'm scared of the dark.

He grimaced and threw the handtowel on the sink. There was no time to dwell now. His ten-year-old niece was waiting for him and her nanny was ready to go home.

He walked into the sitting area of his hotel suite. Kate and her nanny, Emily-but-you-can-call-me-Em, sat on the couch watching an animated movie.

Emily hit the pause button. "How did it go?"

Adrian shrugged. "Fine." He wasn't about to confide in her.

Kate turned around and knelt on the couch, resting her arms on the back and pushing her long, curly red hair out of her way. She grinned. "So who'd you meet?"

Some of the tension in Adrian's shoulders melted. He always had to give her details about which celebrity he'd met and what they were like. But after what had happened tonight, he completely blanked on the names. "There was a comedian who'd just starred in a movie." He paused. "The something Games."

Kate rolled her eyes. "*The Final Games.* That's Tony Giuseppe. Honestly, Uncle Ade, sometimes I wonder if you care at all." She smiled. They both knew he didn't care about celebrities. "So who else?"

Libby's face appeared before him with vivid, alpine clarity. "There was an author, Libby someone."

Kate's mouth dropped open. "Not Libby Myles?"

Adrian looked up at the ceiling, trying to remember. "She writes adventure stories. The latest has just come out."

Kate turned and swiped a book from the table, hurrying around the couch to show him the author picture on the back. "This Libby?"

Adrian took the book from her and stared at the picture. It was a good photo – it made her seem approachable and kind.

"Yes."

Kate slapped him on the arm. "Get out!" She sounded disgruntled.

Adrian took a step back. "What's wrong?"

"You were on a show with *the* Libby Myles and you didn't invite me to come backstage with you? I can't believe you!"

"You're a fan, I take it?"

Kate had both hands on her hips. "Duh. She writes the Jessop Chronicles, my *absolutely* favorite books."

Adrian flipped over the book he held and checked the cover. He'd bought Kate the book last week when it was first released, but he hadn't paid any attention to who the author was.

"Argh. I can't believe I missed my chance to meet her!" Kate stared at him, her face full of the anguish only a pre-teen could pull off. "Thanks a lot." She snatched the book from his hand and stormed toward her room.

"Where are you going?"

"To bed." She didn't turn around and slammed the bedroom door behind her.

Adrian rubbed at the ache in the back of his neck. He'd let Kate down. He'd been too busy battling his own anxieties to strike up a conversation with the woman. If he had, he might have remembered buying Kate the book. It wasn't a mistake Kate's father would have made.

The pang of sorrow was as strong as the stab of guilt. Kate had been so good on this tour, not complaining about the constant travelling and the hectic schedule. He'd had a fabulous opportunity to do something nice for her and he'd blown it.

Maybe he'd made a mistake bringing her on tour with him. What did he know about being a parent? He was making it up as he went along.

Perhaps Kate should have gone to summer camp like Kate's aunt Susan had suggested.

Emily switched off the television and stood. "Don't worry about it. She'll get over it."

That wasn't the point. Emily didn't understand. He strode over to the dining table where his laptop sat and switched it on. He had to fix this. If Libby was promoting her book, she might be doing a book signing somewhere around Melbourne tomorrow. He sat down, already focused on his task, when he realized Emily was standing next to him. "Why don't you go to bed?"

He needed a nanny to care for Kate while he was performing or doing publicity, but he didn't like having a stranger in his space. Emily was nice enough and definitely competent, otherwise he wouldn't have let her near his niece, but she wasn't family, or a friend, and he wanted to be alone.

Emily came around behind him and massaged his shoulders. "You look tense."

He shrugged her off and half-turned in his chair. "I'm fine. I'm sure you're tired. I'll see you in the morning."

"You know, I could help you release some of your worries."

She wasn't referring to a massage. Christ, he didn't need this now.

He should have gone for the older woman he'd interviewed, but she'd seemed too spacey, so he'd chosen the younger, highly organized and far more attractive Emily, who came recommended by one of Susan's friends.

"That's not necessary. I'm going to see if Libby Myles has a book signing tomorrow and then go to sleep myself." He kept his tone polite but distant. He wasn't interested.

She didn't take the hint. She leaned forward, her scent wafting toward him thick and cloying. It was like being ambushed by a rose bush and just as thorny.

"Come on, Kent. We both know it's inevitable. I've seen the way you look at me. Why don't we stop denying this attraction?" She glanced over her shoulder at Kate's bedroom. "Kate will be asleep by now, and if we go to my room we won't disturb her."

Her first mistake was using his stage name. Anyone close to him, anyone who knew him, called him Adrian. Her biggest mistake, though, was the suggestion he leave his niece alone in a strange hotel room. He stood slowly, keeping his eyes on hers. She must have seen the anger in them, as she stepped back.

"I'm not interested, ma'am." His tone suggested she was anything but a lady. "I suggest you leave now."

Emily pouted. "Don't play games with me, Kent. It's not nice."

"I'm sure as heck not playing any games."

She stepped back, her face flushed – with embarrassment or anger, he didn't know which. "You've been leading me on all this time. I don't have to put up with this treatment." She turned and stalked to the door. "I quit."

Just like Kate, Emily slammed the door behind her.

Chapter 2

Adrian stared after her in disbelief before sinking back into the chair. He acknowledged the hint of relief that she was gone but what the heck was he going to do now? He had no nanny and tomorrow morning was filled with radio interviews and sound checks before his concert that night. He ran his hand through his hair thinking frantically. He should call George.

There was a noise behind him and he turned. Kate stood at her bedroom doorway, her pajamas on, holding Sebastien Bear, her ever faithful teddy bear. "Was that Emily yelling?"

He wasn't going to lie to her. "Sure was. She's decided not to look after you anymore." He stood and walked over to her.

"Why not?" She squinted up at him, suspicion all over her face.

Neither was he going to tell her the whole truth. "We had a disagreement." He put a hand on her shoulder and steered her back toward her room. "You need to get some sleep if you're going to be coming to my radio interviews in the morning."

Her face lit up like a carnival. "Really?"

"Yep."

"Awesome!" She hugged him tightly before leaping into bed and snuggling down, pulling the sheet up to her chin.

Just like that he was forgiven.

Adrian leaned down and kissed her forehead. "Sweet

dreams, kiddo."

"Same to you."

He brushed her hair off her face and gave her a wink. When he reached the door her voice called out, "Uncle Ade."

He turned.

"Did I do something wrong?" Her eyes were full of concern and she looked younger than her ten years.

"Of course not." He came back into the room and sat down on the edge of her bed. "She liked looking after you. The disagreement was between the two of us."

"Did she kiss you?"

Where the heck had that come from? "No."

"She wanted to."

Adrian frowned. "What makes you say that?"

"I heard her talking to a friend one night. She said it was only a matter of time before she got you in her bed."

Adrian cursed Emily but kept his voice light. "Well, it's not going to happen, kiddo. Why don't you forget about it and go to sleep?"

Kate turned over on to her side, hugging Sebastien Bear. "I won't miss her. She wasn't much fun."

Adrian closed his eyes briefly. Kate had never said anything about her nanny before now. He cursed Emily again. "I'm sorry." He rose and walked to the door.

"Will you turn the stars on?"

He turned at her voice. "Sure thing." He walked over to the star night-light and switched it on. Stars appeared on the ceiling. He blew her a kiss, not allowing the anger to cross his face until he had turned away.

Damn that woman! Kate had been doing so well during the last few months. Sleeping with the light off, no more nightmares – and now with this one upset, she was back to needing the comfort of her stars. He couldn't blame her, but it was a step back in her recovery. He would have to be vigilant and make sure the next few weeks were as settled and easy as possible.

At least he knew one thing he could do to make it up to her.

Adrian sat down at his laptop and typed "Libby Myles book signing" into the search engine.

He could introduce her to her idol.

***

Libby needed coffee. There was still another half an hour of the book signing to go, but it was becoming increasingly difficult to stay focused. There was no air movement and the heating was turned up to drowsy warmth. The droning voices in the bookshop as well as the cars on the street made it hard to hear.

The bookshop owner had set her up on a tiny table at the front of his store, almost as if she were part of the display. He'd gone to the effort of throwing a white tablecloth over the table, dragging a plastic chair from out the back and even splashing out for a bottle of water. Libby's publicist had left after making sure Libby was set up, as she had an urgent meeting she had to attend. Libby hadn't minded, because the other signings she'd done had been fine, but she hadn't realized until now the little things her publicist had done for her, like topping up her bottle of water and talking with the bookstore owner.

Libby checked her watch. She'd been here almost three hours.

She'd only planned on writing a couple of pages of her latest manuscript after the talk show last night, but the story had flowed, and before she knew it, it was two in the morning.

Now she was desperately trying to stay awake, ignore her aching hand and show her fans the attention they deserved. She handed a blank notebook to the young girl standing in front of her. "Write your name, there so I'll spell it right when I write in the front of your book."

The girl's mother snatched the pad out of her daughter's hands and scrawled a name down before thrusting it back at Libby. "Jane is not difficult to spell."

Libby put on her best polite-and-pleasant smile. "I've seen three different spellings of Jane so far and it's often hard to hear over the din when people spell it out. I'd hate to get it wrong." She turned to the young girl. "Who's your favorite character, Jane?"

"I love Shannon. She's so brave." The girl jigged up and down.

"You'll love what she gets up to in this story," Libby said as she wrote in the front of the book. She handed it back to Jane and flexed her sore hand. "I hope you enjoy it."

As the girl and her mother turned away from the table, Libby applied the now warm cold pack to her hand and checked the line. Another ten people and she was done. She loved meeting her fans, but today her hand ached like she'd hit it with a hammer. There was only the slightest tinge of bruising, though – nowhere dark enough for the pain it gave her. She swallowed a yawn as the next person stepped up.

Half an hour to go.

***

An hour later, Libby was getting desperate. The line wasn't any shorter, her water bottle was empty and the pain in her hand was terrible. The bookshop owner was oblivious to the time. He stood to one side, grinning at the never-ending line of paying customers.

Libby waved him over, but he didn't meet her gaze. She turned her attention to the next child, wincing a little as she signed her name.

"How long have you been here?" the child's mother asked.

Libby cleared her dry throat. "A few hours."

The mother noticed the empty water bottle on the table. "And they haven't provided you any refreshments?" She looked around. "Is he the owner?" she asked, gesturing to the man.

"Yes."

"I'll make sure he brings you something to drink."

Libby was too relieved to refuse. "Thank you. I can't get his attention."

"It's my pleasure. Your books give me hours of 'me' time while Jenny reads. I should be thanking you."

Some of Libby's tiredness evaporated and her smile was sincere. "I'm glad to help."

Boosted by the praise, she turned to the next child while the woman went to speak to the owner. Within minutes, the owner was offering her a fresh bottle of water. Before he could leave, she touched his arm, indicated that he should wait, and finished signing the book in front of her.

"I need you to make sure no one else joins the line."

The man smiled a big fake smile. "But surely you don't want

to disappoint your fans?"

Be polite. "Of course not, but I do have other commitments and I've already stayed for longer than planned." He didn't need to know her commitments were to herself. She needed to do some more writing.

"But your publicist said this was your last signing in Melbourne."

Libby fixed a smile on her face and inwardly cursed her publicist. "Book signings aren't my only commitments. Besides," she smiled harder, trying to make it seem genuine, "I haven't eaten since lunch, and with the water I've had, I'll need to visit the ladies room soon."

The man scowled at her as if she should be superhuman.

"Don't be so inconsiderate," the woman next in line told him. "She's been here hours and the poor dear looks exhausted. If you don't stop people lining up, I will."

Bless her, Libby thought as she waited for the owner's reaction.

"Fine," he said and stormed off.

The woman checked he was doing what she'd asked of him and then grinned at Libby. "Not many to go, love."

A pang of guilt whizzed through Libby's stomach. "I normally wouldn't mind – "

The woman held up a hand. "No need to explain. You can't be expected to sit around until there's no one left. You've got far more patience than I have. I would have been bored hours ago." She scrawled her name on the notepad and handed over her book. "My name's Myrtle."

Libby opened the front page and wrote her thanks before handing it back.

Myrtle read the message and grinned again, hugging the book to her chest. "My pleasure."

The next few people went by in a blur, and when Libby checked there was only one person left in the line. She let out a slow, soft sigh of relief and greeted the young boy. She signed the book, answered his questions and then put down her pen.

"What do you mean Libby's finished? She's sitting right there." The voice was loud and incredulous, but it was the Texan drawl that caught Libby's attention. It sounded very much like Kent Downer.

She said goodbye to the young boy and his father and waited until they left so she could see who was making the fuss.

He was the same height and build as the rock star but that was where the resemblance ended. His dark hair was combed flat, and his white muscle T-shirt and blue jeans made him look like the boy next door. He was staring down at the owner. "My niece has been waiting all day to get her book signed." The man shifted and Libby spotted the young girl behind him. She had the most gorgeous deep red, curly hair Libby had ever seen. The girl held the man's hand and was looking up at him with wide eyes.

"Then you should have come earlier." The owner puffed out his chest.

This was not going to end well.

"It's all right," Libby called before the uncle responded. The three of them turned toward her. She beckoned the young girl closer. "Come over here."

The owner huffed and moved over to the counter, but Libby paid no notice. It was the girl who captured her attention.

The girl's smile was electric. She peeked up at her uncle and he nodded. She hurried over, clutching her book to her chest. In front of the table she paused as she looked between the pile of new books waiting to be purchased and the one in her hand. "Uncle Adrian already bought me the book," she said.

"Then your Uncle Adrian was clever to get in early," Libby said, reaching out her hand for the book with her sore right hand. As she closed it around the book, it cramped and the book fell to the ground. "Oops, sorry." She wrapped the useless cold pack around her hand as the girl picked up the book.

"What did you do to your hand?" the girl asked as she placed the book in front of Libby.

"Oh, I hurt it last night," Libby answered as she passed the girl the blank notebook. "Could you write your name down there for me?" She gazed up at the uncle. He was staring at her hand, his mouth slightly ajar. Libby shifted in her chair and his intense brown eyes met hers. Her heart jolted. He looked slightly horrified, though much friendlier than the cheetah last night.

Though he barely resembled the rock star, Libby was sure it was him. "Hello, Kent."

The surprise was a shooting star across his face.

"You recognized him!" the girl said as she handed back the notebook. "No one does when he's not in costume."

Libby took the notebook and checked the name. "I met him last night, Kate." But this man was nothing like the one she'd met yesterday.

He hesitated and then held out his hand. "When I'm not in costume I'm Adrian."

Libby gingerly took it.

He held her hand gently, his touch warm and his eyes narrow as he examined it. A flutter started in her stomach as his thumb gently ran over the tender area. When he let go, his eyes asked the question.

She nodded slightly – yes, he had done it last night – and turned her attention back to Kate.

"I was so upset when he told me he'd met you, he made sure we came today, even though it meant we had to leave rehearsal early. George was fit to be tied, wasn't he, Uncle Ade?" Kate's enthusiasm ran on like only a child's could.

Adrian smiled down at his niece. "He sure was."

Kate laughed. "He's such a grump. Especially since Emily quit."

He compressed his lips and hummed an agreement.

Obviously a sore topic.

"I see you've started reading the book," Libby said to Kate, touching the bookmark. "Where are you up to?"

"The bit where they've arrived at the camp. I'm not sure whether they're goodies or baddies."

"Which way are you leaning?" Libby gripped the pen and wrote in the front of the book.

"Baddies," Kate said decisively.

Libby raised her eyebrows. "Interesting."

"Am I right?"

Libby handed back the book. "You'll have to keep reading to find out."

Kate gave a playful pout. "Awww."

"I'd hate to ruin the story," Libby said as she packed her

pens away.

"Kate, why don't you have a look around for a book to buy before we leave?" Adrian said.

Kate stuck her bottom lip further out. "I was chatting with Libby."

"I need to talk to her about the show last night. You can come back and chat after you've found a book."

Kate sighed. "All right." She turned to Libby. "Please don't go before I say goodbye."

Charmed, Libby answered, "I won't."

When Kate had left, Adrian turned to Libby. "Are you finished now?"

"Yes." She was dying for some painkillers and a coffee. She retrieved her bag from the ground.

Adrian shuffled from foot to foot. "I'm sorry about your hand. I didn't get a chance to thank you last night for what you did." There was no trace of the arrogant rock star in his demeanor now. If anything he was bashful, almost shy. The contrast was intriguing. This was a man Libby could see writing the song he sang last night.

Libby waved a hand. "I didn't do anything."

"You saved my career and my sanity." He checked on Kate, who was kneeling down, browsing the books. "Can I buy you a coffee ..." He shrugged uncomfortably. "As thanks?"

There was something unusual about the man standing in front of her. It wasn't just that he was so unlike Kent Downer of last night. No, there was something about him that had Libby's story sense tingling.

"Throw in some painkillers and you have a deal," she said as she stood and placed her bag over her shoulder.

"There's bound to be a drugstore around here." His smile was uncertain as he gazed over his shoulder – it wasn't the easy grin that had made his fans crazy in the studio last night, but Libby's heart still sped up a little.

"There is," she said. "I just need to say goodbye to the owner."

"I'd better check how many books we're coming home with. I really need to buy her an e-reader."

"And miss the fun of lugging tons of books around?" Libby

laughed. "I'll see you at the counter."

She walked over to the owner, who was standing with his arms crossed watching her. "Thank you for your hospitality today," she said as she held out her hand.

"You're welcome." He shook her hand.

He was one of those men with an overly firm handshake and Libby winced. She extracted her hand as Adrian and Kate came over carrying a pile of books.

"You sure you can carry all of those, kiddo?" Adrian asked.

"Absolutely." Kate dumped them with relish on the counter.

The owner's demeanor softened slightly as he rang up the total. Adrian paid and gave Kate the bag of books. "Come on, I'll buy you a cup of hot chocolate."

As Libby fell in step beside them, Kate asked, "Is Libby coming too?"

"Sure. I owe her a cup of coffee."

"Yes!" Kate whooped.

***

The coffee shop was relatively quiet and Adrian was glad. He didn't know what had possessed him to ask Libby out for coffee. Yes, he was grateful she'd helped him last night, but he didn't do coffee dates, especially not as Adrian. He never knew what to say.

Kate led them to a table at the back and took the seat by the wall. He sat next to her with Libby opposite. Seeing her hand, the guilt washed over him again. He'd been so caught up in his own fears he hadn't realized how tightly he'd gripped her hand. He'd hurt her without thought and hadn't even thanked her. He didn't know how he could be so oblivious.

Perhaps hurting people was part of his genetic make-up.

Before he could examine the idea a waitress came over to take their order. Libby ordered a slice of pecan pie to go with her coffee.

After the waitress left they sat in silence for a moment. Adrian glanced at Libby, then at Kate. What did he say now? *Sorry I was such a jerk last night. Sorry I didn't notice your pain.*

"Do you have a concert tonight?" she asked.

"Yes." He checked his watch. "I've got a couple of hours

before I have to be back at the venue."

"Are you going, Kate?"

"Yep. George is going to look after me now Emily's gone."

"George, the grump?"

Adrian drew his brows together and then remembered Kate had called George a grump in the bookstore earlier. George had not been happy about Emily quitting. He and Kate shared a smile.

"George is my manager. He's looking after Kate at the concert tonight, as Kate's nanny had to leave us and I haven't had a chance to find a new one." He shouldn't be telling her this. Usually when he met a woman he would stick to basic information, but then again, he didn't often meet a woman as Adrian who also knew he was Kent Downer.

"It must be exciting to see the concert from backstage. I've always wanted to see what goes on behind the scenes," Libby commented.

"Nuh-uh," Kate said. "It gets boring after a while, which is why Emily used to look after me in the hotel while Uncle Ade worked."

His anger at Emily surfaced. She'd really left them in the lurch. He couldn't keep taking Kate to his concerts. Susan was right about that.

Suddenly Kate sat up straighter and grinned. "You could come tonight. Can't she, Uncle Ade?" Kate looked up at her uncle, pleading. "It would make it more fun."

"Oh, no, I couldn't." Libby shook one hand in a no motion.

"Libby might have other plans," Adrian said to Kate. He regarded Libby. Though he didn't often invite people backstage, perhaps this was a way he could make up for his rudeness the night before. "You're welcome to come if you want. It's not very exciting." He didn't want to get her expectations up. Watching from backstage was different from being part of the audience.

"Please." Kate drew out the word as if it had four syllables.

Libby blinked. Then she smiled, warm and genuine. "I'd love to."

Kate clapped her hands. "Yay! I can show you backstage and then you can watch Uncle Ade perform. Then we can go to his dressing-room and play games. We have computer games, or board games or cards. And there's lots of food. I never have dinner before a concert."

Adrian chuckled. "Slow down there, Kate. You're going to overwhelm her." Kate was so much like her mother, Penny. Always positive and eager, ready for an adventure. He understood why Daniel had married Penny.

"Sorry." Kate's eyes flittered down, contrite, and then she looked up and grinned. "We'll have so much fun."

He hoped he wasn't making a mistake inviting this woman he didn't know backstage. But she already knew his secret – when he wasn't in costume he was a plain, ordinary man with anxieties.

And it would make Kate happy.

That was the main thing.

It was too late to worry about it now.

Maybe Kate was right. Maybe it would be fun.

**

Libby was ready when Adrian and Kate picked her up just after six. They were staying in the same hotel, though Libby's room was several floors lower than theirs. Libby had checked in with her publicist, confirmed the details for her meeting tomorrow and taken a short nap before she had to get ready.

She hadn't fussed with her appearance, not that she had many options from her suitcase – jeans, shirt and jacket. As she was going to spend the evening playing games with Kate, she only swiped on some lip gloss and mascara.

She couldn't help the buzz of excitement at the thought of going to the concert, though. It had been years since she'd been to one – her budget didn't run to such extravagant events.

Kate was positively bouncing with energy as they walked out to the car. She carried a backpack, which Libby assumed was filled with books and assorted games. Adrian was still dressed as himself, and none of Kent Downer's fans waiting impatiently outside the hotel for a glimpse of their hero recognized him as they walked past.

Libby was amazed. No wonder he needed an alter ego.

Inside the waiting car she met George. She'd obviously been

watching too many movies, because he was not what she was expecting. Instead of being older, slightly overweight, long-haired, chain-smoking and on the verge of a heart attack, he was young, tall, broad-shouldered, short-haired and wearing a suit. In fact he looked like he'd stepped out of one of the high-rise buildings next door. The one expectation he did meet was that he looked harassed.

His greeting to Libby was perfunctory. As he pulled out of the hotel, he said to Adrian, "After you left this afternoon, the shit hit the fan."

Kate giggled.

"Shoot, ah, things stopped working," George amended.

"What kind of things?"

"Fuse blew, lighting crashed to the ground and the damn –" He stopped himself and his gaze skimmed to Kate. "The support band came down with gastro."

"Lucky I wasn't there," Adrian said.

George snorted.

"Is it all sorted?"

"Of course."

Adrian gave him a lazy smile. "That's why you're the details man. You feel any better?"

The stiffness faded from George's shoulders. "Yeah."

Libby listened to the interchange in fascination. They were obviously close and it seemed Adrian knew George needed to vent.

"George, you can play the shooting game with me and Libby if you like," Kate said. "It helps to let off steam."

"Thanks, Shorty."

They pulled up at the backstage entrance of the venue and piled out. The fans yelled and then decided there was no one interesting in the car and went back to their waiting.

Adrian, Kate and George hustled into the building with Libby hurrying to keep up. Once safely inside George turned to Libby. "So you're the writer."

"Yes. And you would be George the grump."

George lifted an eyebrow as Kate giggled. "You'll keep." He turned back to Adrian. "Do you want to give them the tour or shall I?"

"You do it. I've got to get ready." Adrian turned to Kate. "Be good tonight and listen to George and Libby."

Kate rolled her eyes. "Yes, Uncle Ade."

"George will be able to answer any questions you have," he said to Libby, and with a wave, walked off.

She felt a twinge of disappointment.

"Right then, ladies. This way."

For the next half an hour, George took them around backstage, answering all of Libby's questions and explaining what was going on. Kate stopped to chat with a couple of roadies, greeting them by name and introducing Libby to them. Then the newly hired support act began and it was hard to hear anything. George made Kate wear earmuffs and Libby wished she had some. The band wasn't great.

Kate tugged on her arm and indicated that they should leave. Libby followed her and George to a dressing-room with a Kent Downer sign on the door. Kate knocked and it wasn't long before Adrian answered in his full Kent Downer outfit.

The change was incredible. He stood taller, his chest puffed out and the gesture he made for them to come in was large and theatrical. He caught Libby staring and winked at her.

Libby gaped at him, refusing to step back though she wanted to distance herself. The lovely and shy Adrian of this afternoon had been replaced by this cocky, confident man. A man who reminded her of her ex. She suppressed a shudder.

She couldn't quite believe Kent and Adrian were the same person, despite the fact that she'd seen Kent the night before. Did he have some sort of personality disorder? Which was the real man?

Libby entered the dressing-room with its mirror-lined walls and big, comfortable brown couches. Kate dumped her backpack on the wooden coffee table and pulled out a board game.

"What are you going to play tonight?" Adrian asked her.

Kate looked up. "Are you playing, George?"

"Sure, Shorty."

"Then we'll play Clue. Do you have time for a round, Kent?"

Libby was surprised as Kate referred to her uncle by his stage name. Adrian checked the time. "If it's a quick one."

Kate deftly set up the board game and Adrian waved Libby onto the couch next to her. He and George sat opposite them.

"What time do you go on, Adrian?" Libby asked.

He glanced up. "Call me Kent when I'm in costume. I don't want anyone to associate Adrian with Kent."

It made sense to separate the two – they were so different.

"In about an hour." He scanned through his cards and marked something off on his score sheet.

Kate rolled the dice and whooped as she moved her piece around the board. "I suggest it was Colonel Mustard in the library with the knife."

Libby checked her cards, showed one to Kate and then rolled the dice. She'd forgotten how much fun it was to play board games. Growing up, her family had never bothered with 'bonding activities for the mundane', as her father put it, but her best friend Piper's house had always been full of laughter and games.

She'd spent every free moment she could with Piper, and Piper's family had welcomed her and made her part of their own family. Libby felt far more comfortable with them than she did with her own family. They had wanted her. Libby had been devastated when they'd moved back to Texas.

This game was the same: full of suggestions, jokes and laughter. Libby relaxed and let the mood infect her. If she ever had children, this is what she'd want it to be like. Finally Kate said, "Ah ha! I know who it is. I accuse Miss Scarlet, in the kitchen with the lead pipe." She pointed an accusing finger at Libby, who was using the Miss Scarlet piece.

"Go on then, kiddo," Kent said handing her the envelope from the middle. "Check if you're right."

Kate snatched the envelope and cautiously peered at the contents, one card, then the next and the final one. She threw the three cards down onto the board. "Told you!"

"Good one, Kate," George said as he dropped his cards on the table. He checked his watch. "It's almost game time. We'll play again after Kent hits the stage."

Kate stood. "Kent needs quiet time before he starts," she explained to Libby. "I'll show you the best spot to see the stage."

Kent flashed Libby a grin that didn't quite reach his eyes. He drummed his fingers on the table as she stood.

Nerves again.

She'd not detected any when they were playing the game, but the moment they stopped, they were there. "Break a leg," Libby said, and then paused. "Do they say that to singers?"

"You can, as long as it doesn't come true," George said and ushered them out of the room.

Kate held Libby's hand and moved toward the stage. The support band had finished and roadies raced back and forth to set up for Kent's band. Kate weaved in and out, dragging Libby with her. Libby checked to make sure George was following. She didn't want to get in the way.

"Hold it there, Shorty," George called and Kate stopped so suddenly that Libby bumped into her.

George caught up and pointed to an alcove in the wings. "You and Libby wait there until they finish setting up, otherwise you'll get trampled. I've noticed something that needs my attention. You'll be all right here for a minute?" His eyes were focused on the other side of the room.

"Sure," Kate said.

George didn't wait for Libby's response. He turned and walked toward one of the roadies, calling out as he did. He might be a grump at times, but it was obvious he cared for the young girl.

And why wouldn't he? Kate was a sweet girl. But why was she touring with her uncle? Maybe Kate's parents were like Libby's own, happier when she wasn't under foot. At least Kate had Adrian.

Around her the roadies moved in a sequenced dance, moving equipment, avoiding each other and transforming the stage into a rock star's lair. They were a team, obviously experienced and certain where each item should go and what should be done. Only once did Libby see two men almost crash into each other. They swore at each other good-naturedly and continued on their way.

Libby itched to get her notebook out and write down what she was seeing. It was such a different atmosphere. Though the lights backstage were bright, every surface was black, making it seem dimmer than it was. There was electricity in the air, the hum of expectation and tension. The drone coming from the audience on the other side of the curtain was deep and primal.

Every now and then a chant would start. "We want Kent. We want Kent." It would carry for a moment and then lose momentum. A couple of girls screamed as if they couldn't keep the excitement bottled up any longer.

Next to Libby Kate scuffed the ground with her feet, looking bored.

"Do you like watching your uncle perform?" Libby asked.

Kate shrugged. "It's weird 'cause it doesn't seem like him performing. He's much nicer than Kent."

Libby had to agree. "I wonder why he doesn't go out as himself." She didn't mean it as a question but Kate answered it anyway.

"Dad told Mama it was because he was too nervous to be himself. He needed to pretend to be someone else." Kate looked up at her. "Do you think that's weird?" Her brow was furrowed and her nose scrunched up. She was obviously concerned.

Libby covered her surprise and considered her answer. "There are a lot of people who get stage fright," she said. "They each deal with it in their own way. Besides, isn't that exactly what actors do each time they go on stage – pretend to be someone else?"

"But that's their job."

"Perhaps this is the only way your uncle can do his job. He's a very good singer." She remembered his performance the night before. Very good didn't begin to describe his gift.

Kate seemed satisfied with the answer. "Kind of like when a basketball player suits up to play ball. Oh look. He's ready to start." She pointed to Kent, striding toward the stage.

He was in cheetah mode now. The same intense focus Libby had witnessed in the green room the night before. His gaze was on the stage and he acknowledged no one as he walked by, not even Kate.

Libby checked to see how Kate reacted.

"He's in the zone," Kate said and grinned in satisfaction, not the least bit bothered.

It would seem this was the norm.

He stopped in the wings of the stage and nodded once at something George said to him. One of the roadies handed Kent a microphone and George signaled someone off stage.

The lights went out.

Libby gasped as the pitch darkness swept over her and Kate clutched her hand. The audience roared in approval. Libby's heart pounded in her throat. Shit. Kent was afraid of the dark.

What could she do? She couldn't rush out there to help him. She would likely be more hindrance than help, but this couldn't be happening to him twice in two nights.

The noise from the crowd was deafening. She crouched down to yell into Kate's ear. "We have to find George."

"Why?" Kate yelled back.

"Because the lights have gone out." Kate mustn't know her uncle was scared of the dark.

Kate squeezed her hand. "Wait."

Suddenly the thrum of a guitar rang out over the screams of the crowd. The yells reached a crescendo as the next note played and the lights came on with a bang. Kent's voice belted out the beginning of a rock song.

Libby blinked as her eyes adjusted to the light. Kent swaggered around the stage, singing his song, flirting with the audience.

It was incredible. Libby had been expecting to see him in a quivering puddle on the floor.

Kate tugged on her hand. "Did it scare you? He starts every concert like that."

Libby absently shook her head. On stage Kent was confident, smiling, picking someone out of the audience to sing to. She couldn't quite comprehend it. Kent was terrified of the dark and yet he faced his fear every night at work. She had to admire him.

"Where are your earmuffs, Shorty?"

George appeared in front of her and Libby jumped.

Kate looked guilty. "I left them in the room."

"You know the rules. No muffs, no music."

Kate sighed. "Yes, George. Come on, Libby. Let's go play a game."

Allowing herself to be pulled away from the stage toward the dressing-room, Libby couldn't resist peeking back at Kent.

"He's something, isn't he?" George asked as he followed behind her.

Libby nodded, not able to phrase any words. George must have known of Adrian's phobia. He was Adrian's manager and his close friend.

They entered the dressing-room and closed the door. The music receded to a reasonable level.

"Hell of an opener, don't you think?" George asked as he settled down on one of the chairs.

"I think Libby was scared." Kate laughed.

Libby debated what to say. "No, I was concerned how Kent would get on stage in the dark."

George squinted at her, as if wondering whether she knew something. "He paces it out before every show so he's in the right place."

"It takes some guts." Even without being terrified of the dark.

"Yes, it does." George paused. "But Adrian's that kind of guy." There was obvious admiration in his tone.

"Let's play Snap," Kate said.

"Sure, Shorty. Why don't you deal and I'll get us some food?" George stood and left the room.

Kate held up the pack of cards to Libby, questioning.

Libby nodded, but her thoughts were elsewhere.

What kind of guy was Adrian really?

Chapter 3

"Libby, can I ask you something?" Kate had dealt the cards and they were waiting for George to come back with the food. Kate picked up her pile, tidied them and put them down.

"Sure."

Kate fidgeted, patting her cards into place again. "Is it hard to write a book?" She didn't look at Libby as she asked.

"Sometimes." Libby answered. "Getting started is the easy bit. I get a great idea and I write down an outline and have fun creating characters. Then I start writing."

"So when does it get hard?"

"Some days the story isn't flowing or something doesn't work right and it takes time to work out what's wrong. And sometimes, if I've been writing the story for a long time, I get tired of it and want it to be magically finished." She waved her hand about like she held a wand.

Kate giggled and then became serious. "Do you think I could write a book?" She glanced down at her hands and then back up at Libby with hope in her eyes.

Libby considered her answer. She didn't want to make it sound easy, but she didn't want to discourage her either. "It can be hard work, but I don't see why not. Have you got a good idea?"

"I think so," Kate said. "It's about a kid my age who has

super powers and is able to save people, like if their car is going to crash, I could swoop down and save them." Kate stopped. "I mean my character could save them."

Libby's heart wedged up into her throat. Is that what had happened to Kate's parents? Had they died in a car crash? Libby didn't dare ask because Kate was obviously uncomfortable. "What would your character be called?"

"Lilly Lionheart."

"Great name," Libby said. "And would she wear a cape?"

"Yeah, with a big ferocious lion on it."

Libby reached into her bag and drew out her notebook. "Okay, so name is Lilly Lionheart. Wears a cape." She wrote down the details. "What color?"

Kate gaped at her. "You're writing it down?"

"Of course. There's no time like the present to get started."

"Really?" Kate bounced up and down on the couch. "Hang on. I'll get my laptop." She dashed across the room to her bag and drew out a small laptop, which she dumped on the table and turned on.

Libby tucked her notebook back in her bag as George walked in with a platter of food. "Ready to get your butt kicked at Snap?" he asked Kate as he placed the platter on the coffee table.

Kate waved him away. "Not now, George. I'm writing a book."

Libby suppressed a smile at the surprise on George's face.

"A book?" he asked.

"Yeah. Libby's helping me." Kate pressed some buttons and began typing, her tongue stuck out between her lips.

"Well then," George said and took a piece of sushi from the platter, biting into it. "I'll just amuse myself." He raised an eyebrow at Libby.

Kate was too absorbed to even respond. When she'd finished typing, she asked Libby, "What else do I need?"

"Have you described how Lilly looks? Hair color, length, style, eye color, height, age. You need to be able to picture her completely in your mind."

Kate went back to typing.

Libby chose a smoked salmon hors d'oeuvre from the

platter. She could tell George wanted to say more about Kate's writing, but he didn't dare in front of the child. Libby couldn't see what harm would come of it. It would keep her busy for as long as she was interested.

***

An hour later Kate's yawns were getting bigger and closer together, though she tried to stifle them with her hand over her mouth.

Libby checked if George had noticed but he had his own laptop out and was typing away, oblivious to Kate's yawns. She didn't want to suggest that Kate should go to sleep, in case he thought she should mind her own business.

Someone banged on the door and George went to answer it.

"We've got a problem," a male voice said as George opened it.

George moved toward the man, angling himself to block the view, and spoke quietly, so Libby couldn't hear what he was saying. He looked at Kate, back at the person who was speaking and then back to Kate.

"If you need to go somewhere, I'll be here with Kate," Libby said.

The indecision was clear on George's face. Though Libby had spent the evening with them, she wasn't one of the group and he'd told Adrian he'd take care of Kate.

The person at the door said something, his voice low and urgent.

"Will you be all right without me for a little while, Shorty?" George asked.

"Duh. I've got Libby to keep me company. Go save the world." She yawned.

"If you need me, call me on my cell." He thrust a card at Libby.

"We'll be fine."

George hesitated, then was out of the door.

Kate yawned again.

Now George was out of the room, Libby didn't have any qualms. "How about you lie down on the couch and have a rest? You look tired?"

"But I haven't finished."

"There's always tomorrow."

"But you won't be here to help me."

Libby didn't deliberate. Kate was a delight to be around and with an uncle like hers, she would know how to keep a secret. Libby reached into her bag and drew out a business card. Flipping it over, she wrote her email address on it before handing it to Kate.

"This is my personal email, so make sure you don't give it out to anyone."

Kate nodded vigorously.

"You can email me whenever you have a question and I'll answer you as soon as I can."

"Really?" The girl clutched the card tightly to her chest.

"Really."

Kate yawned and looked between her laptop and the couch, still undecided. "You're my guest. I can't go to sleep with you here. It would be rude."

So that was the problem. Kate had been brought up with good manners.

"How much longer will the concert go for?" Libby asked.

"Another hour or so."

Libby leaned forward toward Kate. "Can I tell you a guilty writer secret?"

Kate straightened and leaned forward. "Yes."

Libby reached into her bag and drew out her notebook and pen. "I carry this everywhere I go so I can write down ideas, or descriptions. Sometimes I jot down a sentence or two and sometimes I write pages." She handed it over so Kate could flick through it. "Tonight I've been itching to write down some of the ideas I've had for stories, but I haven't because I know it would be rude."

Kate's eyes squinted as she read some of the entries in the notebook. She nodded in understanding.

"So we could make a deal. If you lie down and have a nap, I can write down my ideas while you sleep. That way we cancel out each other's rudeness and it's not rude at all."

Kate handed back the notebook. "So I'd be doing you a favor if I had a nap?"

Libby nodded. "But only if you're tired. I don't want you to feel you have to have a nap, because I'm happy to keep working on your story if you want," she added in a rush.

"It has been a long day." Kate paused. "And I can really email you if I have any questions?"

"Of course."

"All right, I'll have a rest." She shut down the computer, got up and fetched a pillow and blanket from a corner of the room.

Libby took the blanket from Kate and waited for her to lie down on the couch. Libby then tucked the blanket around Kate and smoothed back her hair, remembering how Piper's mother used to do that when Libby slept over. "Enjoy your nap."

Kate grinned. "Enjoy your writing." She closed her eyes and snuggled down.

Libby sat on the sofa opposite and settled her notebook in her lap. She hoped Adrian wouldn't think she'd made Kate go to sleep so she could write.

Kate's quiet, steady breathing showed she had already fallen asleep. Libby had done the right thing. The poor girl was tired.

Relieved, she started writing.

***

The door opened, allowing the noise of the audience to flood in. Libby expected George to walk in, but instead Kent stood there, sweaty and hyped.

Their eyes met, drawn like magnets for a split second, and Libby saw his confusion. He'd forgotten she'd be there. He looked to where Kate still slept on the couch, his entrance not noisy enough to wake her.

Kent closed the door quietly behind him and shook his arms and legs, as if shaking off the adrenaline still pumping through him. "Where's George?" He spoke softly.

"There was some problem he had to fix."

"He left Kate alone?"

Libby arched her brows. "I've been with her the whole time. She was tired, so I suggested she have a nap."

"While you wrote down what you observed tonight so you can go to the media?" he asked, pointing at her notebook.

He was still coming off his performance high, Libby told

herself. Still, it stung. She closed the notebook and held it out to him. "I don't like to be idle. Would you like to have a look at what I've written?"

He took it and browsed through the last few pages. His lips quirked upward. "Like a cheetah?" he asked as he handed it back.

Mortified, Libby felt heat flood her cheeks. He was referring to her description of him. She ignored his question, tucked her notebook back in her bag and stood up. "You'll want to get changed. Do you want me to wake Kate and take her with me?"

Kent was still smiling as he said, "Let her sleep. I'll use the bathroom."

"I'll wait outside then." She didn't wait for his response, wanting to get out as quickly as possible.

She should have thought about what she'd written before offering him her notebook, but it galled to have him think so poorly of her. As if she'd go to the media. She wasn't that desperate for publicity.

She should have expected that kind of reaction. It had happened before. Accuse first, without asking for an explanation. Were all men the same? Or did most of them have secrets they wanted to hide?

She sighed. She was used to it. What did it matter? He didn't know her and they wouldn't see each other again after tonight.

George strode over to her. "He's back, isn't he?"

"Yes."

"Darn it. I was hoping I'd be done before he finished." He grimaced. "How mad was he?"

Libby considered it. Kent hadn't yelled but there had definitely been a thread of anger in his words. "Not furious, but I'd definitely say annoyed."

"All right." He let out a breath. "I need to find a new nanny for Kate so this doesn't happen again." He paused and then studied Libby. "You're from Australia. Do you know of anyone who'd want the job?"

She needed a job. "What does it entail?"

"Australia's the last leg of the tour. We're here a month. Basically we need someone to care for Kate when Adrian's working. It would be every concert night, plus when he's got publicity. When he's not working, Adrian spends his time with Kate, so the nanny would be free to do what she wants. I've got a schedule."

The idea crept into Libby's mind. She tried to shake it away, but it was sticky.

"The pay is a grand a week, plus all meals, hotel accommodation and travel expenses." He paused. "And she has to sign a confidentiality agreement."

"I'll think about it. I might know someone." This could solve her financial problems.

"I'll send you the schedule, so you have an idea of the hours." He exhaled a deep breath. "I'd better go face the music. There's a seat down the hall if you want to wait there." He tapped on the door and entered without waiting for a response.

Libby wandered down the corridor to the seat and sank slowly into it. Would the schedule allow her enough writing time? She had been planning to use the month between temp jobs to finish her manuscript, but that was before her car had died and she had used all her savings fixing it. Now she was flat broke and there was no guarantee she'd get another job quickly when she returned home to Western Australia. All she had to eat was a small stock of instant noodle meals, a few frozen dinners and her vegetable patch. And if her fridge finally died, as it had been threatening to do for the last six months, she'd really be in trouble.

The pay George was offering was more than she'd ever earned and would mean she could save a little for emergencies. And she'd probably have time to write when Adrian wasn't working. Surely she'd have enough time to finish her manuscript.

It couldn't just be about the money, though. Kate deserved better than that.

No. It was foolish to think about offering to care for Kate. She'd never cared for a child before, unless she counted the occasional time she'd helped to look after Piper's younger brother when Piper's parents went out. She had very little experience with children at all.

But Kate was a fantastic kid; she was smart, keen and fun to be around. And it wasn't healthy for her to be dragged around after Adrian every night.

Libby looked at it from another angle. It would be great to spend some time travelling around Australia. She hadn't had the opportunity during her book tour to see any of the sights; it had been bookstore after bookstore, with the occasional library talk thrown in. If she was Kate's nanny, they could explore the cities together, fill her writer's well.

She tapped her fingers on her thigh and took a deep breath.

Then there was Adrian.

Or Kent.

She wasn't entirely sure who was the real man, but she suspected it was Adrian. If she was being honest with herself, he intrigued her far too much. He was good-looking, sure, and an amazing singer, but there was that shyness she'd seen when they'd had coffee that was appealing. Was that why he went to such measures to protect his identity? Libby was itching to know more. He'd make an interesting character study. But that's all it was – a professional interest. What kind of person willingly faced their phobia every single night? She was curious to find out more about Adrian – if she could manage to put up with Kent, who just rubbed her the wrong way.

She tucked her hair behind her ears and thought about Kate.

How long would Kate's interest in writing a book last? It had been more fun than Libby had expected, taking her through the different phases of developing a character. If Libby became Kate's nanny, she could continue helping her with her story and potentially have time to write herself. She would definitely have time on the days when Adrian wasn't working, and she was used to working part time.

What was she thinking?

Adrian wouldn't be interested in hiring her. She had no experience.

Dare she risk the rejection?

***

Adrian turned from the sink as the door to the dressing-room opened. He wiped the last of the mascara off and tossed the wipe in the trash as he walked out to see George taking stock of the sleeping Kate.

"You left her alone." Adrian couldn't believe it. Though Kate didn't show it, she was still vulnerable, still scared about losing people she loved.

He'd trusted George with Kate and George had left her because some problem had come up.

"Libby was with her the whole time."

Libby was a whole other problem Adrian didn't want to think about right now. He'd forgotten she would be there and his initial reaction after the surprise had been a very unwanted spear of lust. It was just his body's reaction from coming off the stage high, but he resented it all the same. It wasn't the time or the place. "How much do you know about Libby? She could be anyone." He kept his voice low so he didn't wake Kate.

"I googled her before the concert. She's got four books out, works short-term contracts in administration, is twenty-eight years old and there are no nasty rumors. Every social media site made her seem like she was a nice person." George paused. "Plus she was helping Kate write a book when I left."

That stopped him. "What?"

"Kate wants to write a book with a superhero in it and Libby was helping her develop her character."

Darn it. It was a nice thing for her to do. And it gave Kate something to keep her occupied, but it didn't mean George should have left. "What was so urgent?"

"A fan." George said it as if it was a swear word. "Eight months pregnant and swearing it was your baby. God knows how she got in, but she was threatening to go to the press if she didn't get to see you."

It was then Adrian noticed the exhaustion in his friend's eyes. He gestured for George to sit on one of the stools near the mirror and took the one opposite. "What happened?"

"I told her who I was and said what she claimed could easily be proven with a paternity test. I took her contact details and told her I'd be in touch." He slumped down. "I don't need to ask the question, do I?"

"No." He hadn't slept with anyone in over a year. He'd been too busy caring for Kate and figuring out how to be a parent.

"Good."

Kate was sleeping peacefully on the couch, her red curls

covering part of her face. She shouldn't be here. What if the fan had made it to his dressing-room?

Adrian didn't even want to consider it.

"I need to replace Emily."

"I've asked Libby if she knows of anyone," George said.

Adrian opened his mouth to protest.

George held up a hand. "She lives here. She may know of someone reliable. If she doesn't, no harm."

Adrian didn't know what it was about the writer that irritated him. No, irritation was the wrong word. She made him uncomfortable because she'd slipped into his inner circle without so much as a ripple. He had been himself while playing Clue before the show and it made him edgy. It usually took him ages before he was comfortable with someone new. Few people could be trusted.

Besides, he had Kate to think about now, not just himself. "Let me have a shower and get changed. Then we can talk about it."

He needed to get back to being Adrian.

***

Twenty minutes later Adrian was clean, refreshed and had shed the last of the high from being on stage. Damn, he was hungry.

He walked into the dressing-room. Kate was still asleep on the couch and George was working on his laptop.

"You all right?" George asked.

"Yeah."

"I'll go and scope the crowd outside. Do you want me to send Libby back in?"

Adrian didn't really want to face her, but he'd been rude and he couldn't leave her out in the corridor. "Sure." As George left, Adrian sat down and loaded up a plate from the platter.

At the quiet knock on the door, he put down his plate and stood up to answer it. Libby stood straight, perhaps slightly defiantly, but smiled at him. It was the smile that unnerved him. It was so friendly, so kind, and it made him want to smile back, made him want to drop his defenses, made him *want*. He didn't know if her smile could be trusted and he didn't need the complication.

He waved her inside.

Kate was still asleep on the couch. Libby kept her voice low. "I'm sorry if you're not happy that George left Kate with me. I can assure you I didn't leave her for a moment."

"It was unexpected," he said. Damn, he needed to apologize. "I was still hyped from the concert and wasn't thinking clearly. I'm glad you were here for her."

She softened. "I hope George was able to solve the problem."

"Yeah." They couldn't keep standing like this. He gestured her to a seat. "Do you want something to eat?" He sat back down.

"No, thank you. Kate and I ate earlier."

"George tells me you were helping her write a book." He dipped a carrot stick into some dip and took a bite.

Libby smiled and Adrian almost choked. He'd thought her other smile was good but this one was something else. Her grin was wide, showing a row of even white teeth, and her eyes sparkled. It socked him in the gut like a well-pitched baseball. He took a deep breath in.

"Yes." Libby said. "She wants to write about a superhero her age." She paused. "I hope you don't mind, but I gave her my email address so she could email me if she had any questions."

He put down his plate. "You would do that?" Libby barely knew Kate. What did she want in return?

"Of course. For as long as the interest is there. Tomorrow she might wake up and decide she wants to do something else."

"She's tenacious," Adrian warned.

"It's fine. I'm happy to pass on what I've learned to others. Writing is often a lonely and difficult road."

Was there sadness to her tone? "You've managed it all right."

"I've been lucky."

Luck might be a portion of it but he doubted that was all. If getting a book deal was anything like getting a record deal, she would have put in a great deal of effort to get where she was.

George returned. "The crowd's beginning to thin. By the time you've finished eating we should be good to go."

Adrian turned to Libby to explain.

"Fans wait outside the back entrance hoping to catch a glimpse of Kent leaving. Most nights I get straight off the stage and into a car, but there're always people waiting. I didn't want to expose Kate. It wouldn't be good to have her associated with Kent." Some of his fans were fairly intense, which was another reason he needed to be careful. He glanced at his niece. "She doesn't need to be part of that."

"I imagine it could be a little scary."

"They can get a little wild." Between them and the mothers who thought he was a bad influence, it could get quite messy. It was Adrian's job to protect Kate. She'd seen enough in her short life and he was determined to make the rest of her life as trouble free as possible.

He finished his food as Kate stirred.

"I'll check what's happening," George said and left the room.

Adrian got up and knelt down by the couch. "Hey there, sleepyhead."

"Uncle Ade?" Kate's voice was raspy from sleep.

"Yep. We're almost ready to go, kiddo. Do you want me to carry you out to the car?"

She swiped at her eyes and sat up. "I can walk." She focused behind him. "Hey, Libby."

"Did you have a nice nap?" Libby asked.

Kate nodded. "Did you have a nice write?"

"Yes."

They shared a smile and Adrian felt a pang in his chest. Despite what Kate had been through, she did what he struggled to do – make friends and trust people.

George walked back in. "It's clear."

Adrian packed up Kate's laptop and put it in her bag before slinging it over his shoulder. "You ready to go?" he asked his niece.

"Yeah."

Libby and George waited by the door.

Adrian took hold of Kate's hand and walked through the venue to where his car was waiting. By the time they reached it, Kate had fully woken up.

As they drove out, Kate asked, "Libby, can you help me with

my story tomorrow?"

Adrian froze. No. This wasn't good. Kate was getting attached to Libby, which would only lead to more heartbreak when they moved to the next city in a couple of days. "Libby might have plans," he said. It would be better if they didn't see her again after tonight. He hoped she didn't feel obligated.

"I've got a meeting with my publisher in the morning, Kate, but I should be free by three. Will you be busy then?"

Kate looked to Adrian.

Adrian looked at George.

"Nothing's scheduled for the afternoon."

A whole afternoon free. Adrian wanted to get out and show Kate some of the sights around Melbourne. "Don't you want to go sightseeing?" he asked Kate.

Kate twisted her hands together.

He hated putting her on the spot.

"I tell you what," Libby said. "Why don't you go sightseeing with your uncle and you can give me a call when you get back? I'm staying another night in the hotel, so you can call my room if you want to do some writing."

Kate had hope in her eyes, seeking permission. He couldn't refuse her.

"Sure." Libby was being very accommodating. He couldn't prevent the twinge of suspicion. What did she want in return? Everyone wanted something from him now he was famous. Whether it was to be seen with him for their two minutes of fame or to boost their careers, they were never interested in who he was as a person. They were the same kind of people who had turned a blind eye to his welfare when he was a child. When Daniel died, he'd found out who truly cared for him.

"That would be great!" Kate said.

They pulled up at the hotel and piled out of the car. George handed the keys to the valet. After travelling up in the elevator together, Libby said her goodbyes at her floor and left them.

Adrian let out a sigh as the elevator closed.

"You should have walked her to her door," Kate said.

He looked at his niece in surprise.

"It's late and it's good manners."

George coughed back a laugh.

Kate was right. It was good manners to walk a lady to her door. But it would make it seem like a date, which it wasn't. It was too late now anyway. "I'll make sure I do it next time," he said, sure there would be no next time. The thought of being alone with Libby made him nervous. He wasn't sure what he would do.

The elevator dinged at their floor. He said goodnight to George and waited for Kate to give George a kiss goodnight before bundling his niece into the room. It was way past her bedtime and she needed sleep.

And he needed to put Libby out of his mind.

***

Libby was running late. She'd forgotten to set her alarm the night before and had woken at nine o'clock. Her meeting with her publisher was across town at ten. Leaping from the bed, she ordered a taxi and flung herself in and then out of the shower. She was low on clean clothes but luckily she'd saved her business suit for this meeting at the end of her tour.

Her chest was tight and she reminded herself to breathe.

The phone rang as she finished dressing and the concierge informed her the taxi was waiting for her. Quickly she smeared on some clear lip gloss and grabbed her bag, checking she had all she needed, and then took her room key and raced downstairs.

At five to ten she walked into her publisher's building.

The receptionist greeted her by name and offered her a seat. "Donna and Simone will be with you in a moment. They're just finishing up another meeting."

Libby sat on the navy blue sofa at reception. The wooden coffee table in front of her held a selection of magazines and catalogues, but nothing of any interest. On the walls surrounding her were framed covers of some of the books they'd published. The most successful ones. She was determined one of her covers would be up there one day.

She focused on her breathing, trying to calm down after her mad rush across town.

By the time her publicist, Donna, came out, the residual stress was gone.

"Sorry to keep you waiting," Donna said, her hand outstretched.

Libby rose and clasped the woman's well manicured hand. "No problem. It wasn't long." Her bruised hand was starting to feel better.

She followed Donna along the corridor to a small meeting room where her editor, Simone, was waiting.

"Libby, lovely to see you again." Simone stood and they shook hands.

As she sat down, Donna poured her a cup of coffee and offered her a blueberry muffin, which Libby gladly accepted. Her stomach was telling her she hadn't had breakfast.

"As you know this meeting is to talk over the book tour and find out what worked and what didn't work. It's always good to know how we can improve our tours," Donna said.

Libby retrieved her notebook, where she'd made notes of things she wanted to say, and they discussed each leg of the tour.

Libby was pleased they took her feedback seriously and took their own notes.

"Your next book is due at the end of August. How's it going?" Simone asked.

She'd been hoping Simone wouldn't ask. "The first draft is almost complete."

"Good. We wanted to discuss whether we can change the deadlines for the following two books."

"Oh. To when?" Her books were currently scheduled to be released nine months apart and it was a schedule she was comfortable with. She was working four days a week and couldn't afford to give up temping yet, as much as she wanted to.

"We'd like to release them six months apart."

Six months? Libby's heart pounded like a jackhammer in her chest. "I'm not sure." She didn't want to say no, flat out, but she wasn't sure how she would manage it. She spent all of her free time writing as it was. It had been one of her ex-boyfriend's issues.

She mentally reviewed her writing plan, calculating how many words she would have to write per week to meet the new deadline.

Too many.

But this was what she wanted. This was her dream. If only she could live off the advance she'd been paid, but it wasn't enough, especially with her recent car woes.

"Will that be a problem?"

Libby considered the question. If she wrote faster, she would have more books available, and maybe she could finally give up her day job. It was going to be hard. She'd have to get up earlier and write for longer after work. But she didn't want to lose this opportunity. Her stomach squirmed. She'd make it work.

She had to.

She took another deep breath and forced herself to smile at Simone. "Not at all. I can meet the new deadline."

"Good," Simone said. "I'll get the paperwork."

***

It was three o'clock before Libby arrived back at the hotel. Donna and Simone had taken her out to lunch to celebrate the end of the tour and they'd had champagne and good food.

She pushed her hotel card into its slot and dumped her bag on the floor near the little writing desk. The stress of accepting the new deadline washed over her. She was exhausted.

With the tour completed, her plan had been to take the month off to finish her book, but that was no longer possible. She couldn't survive a whole month on the one hundred dollars and change she had in her bank account. Her car had chosen the worst possible moment to die. When she returned home she'd have to put her efforts into finding a new job instead of finishing her manuscript.

Unless she applied for the job as Kate's nanny.

The money would cover her living costs and give her a nice security blanket in case another unexpected expense came up.

Adrian's schedule might help her to meet her new deadline, too.

She had to focus on the bigger picture. She was a published author and one day she might be able to live on the income from her writing. But right now she had to earn enough to pay the bills.

She wished one day would hurry up.

Turning on her laptop, she waited for it to boot before opening her email. The first item made her pause, her body frozen for a second before she double-clicked on it to make it larger and hopefully change the message she'd read.

It was from her realtor. The lease on her rental property was up in five weeks and the owners were going to demolish and rebuild. She'd have to find somewhere else to live.

She groaned. Could her day get any worse?

Rental properties in her price range were in short supply and had ten or more applicants for each house. How the hell was she going to get a property if she was offered the position as Kate's nanny? Any owner would take a person the realtor had met over someone who applied online. And she'd barely have time to pack her stuff.

Then another bit of reality crashed down on her. She didn't have a permanent job. It hadn't been an issue when she'd applied for her current property as she'd been working full time. Now though … Who'd want a tenant who only had temping jobs?

The thought of asking her parents if she could stay with them flashed out of her head as quickly as it had flashed in.

She was not going to give them the opportunity to lecture her on her bad career choice.

The phone rang, breaking through her thoughts.

"Hello?"

"Is that Libby?" The voice was young and female.

"Yes. How are you, Kate?"

"Great. We just got back and I was wondering whether you could help me with my story?" Her voice was uncertain.

Libby weighed her options. With her new deadline, and now the need to find somewhere else to live, she really should say no – but she had promised. Part of her wanted to pretend she hadn't read the realtor's email. She wanted to forget her problems for a short while and Kate would help her do that. She ignored the little part of her that wanted to see Adrian again. "Sure. I'll be up in a jiffy." She got the room details, hung up and seized the little notebook and pen set she'd bought after leaving the restaurant.

She would push her worries aside for the afternoon and help a little girl with her dreams.

She'd focus on her own dreams and problems tomorrow.

Chapter 4

There was one other person in the elevator when Libby entered it. Libby smiled at her and went to push the button for the top floor but it was already lit. She stood back on the opposite side of the elevator to the woman.

The woman had her phone out and was doing something on it. Libby tapped her foot to the elevator music while surreptitiously taking note of the woman's details. She was tall, a few inches taller than Libby, and her long blonde hair showed just a hint of dark roots. The blue dress she wore hugged her figure, leaving no doubt that she was curved in all the right places. Libby wondered if the woman's breasts were as natural as her hair color and then smirked at her uncharitable thought.

They reached the top floor and the elevator dinged open. Libby walked out, checked the room numbers on the wall and headed in the direction of Kate's suite. Finding it, she knocked on the door and stood back. She glanced down the corridor as the woman from the elevator paused for a second, stared at her and then turned around and walked back the way she came.

That was odd.

The door opened a crack, the security lock in place, and Kate's head poked around. "It's Libby," she called and the door shut again.

The security lock clanked back and then the door opened

wide.

"Come in." Kate beckoned her inside.

Libby entered. "How was your day?"

"It was great. I wanted to go to Luna Park, but it was shut, so we went to the markets and rode in a tram."

"Did you buy anything?"

Kate grinned. "A bit. Uncle Adrian tells me I have to carry anything I buy, so I can't go overboard."

Libby followed the girl into the suite and stared.

It was far bigger than her room, that was for sure. It was almost as big as her beach shack she lived in back at home and a hell of a lot more fancy. The room had a sitting area with big, soft couches, a large flat-screen television and a coffee table. Kate's laptop was set up on a dining table big enough for six. There was even a fancy kitchenette with a full-sized fridge. Two doors led off the main room, probably to the bedrooms.

Adrian stood up from the couch and moved to greet her. "How was your meeting?" He shoved his hands in his jeans pockets.

Surprised he'd remembered her plans, she ignored her rapidly beating heart. She hadn't reacted this way to Kent. "Good," she said, then sighed, remembering her new deadlines.

"Do they want you to write more books?" Kate asked, her hands clenched together against her chest like a prayer.

"They want me to write them faster – a book every six months rather than every nine months."

"Yay! More Jessop Chronicles." Kate pumped the air.

"Can you write a book that quickly?" Adrian asked.

"I have to now." Libby forced a smile. "My next job is only four days a week, so it should give me some more time." Or else she'd go without sleep.

Adrian's frown was so fleeting Libby wasn't sure if she'd imagined it. "Would you like a drink?" he asked.

"Oh, can we have the double choc, whipped cream, marshmallow delight?" Kate smiled with hope.

"What else?" He strode toward the kitchenette. "How about you, Libby?" He turned back for her answer.

"With a description like that, how could I say no?" She smiled at him and he blinked quickly. Libby's whole body warmed. She was so aware of him. It wasn't a good thing. Men weren't interested in her and she didn't have time for them.

"Come and see what I've written," Kate said and pulled her toward the dining table.

Libby allowed herself to be led over to one of the chairs. She retrieved the notebook and pen she'd bought out of her bag. "I saw this and thought you might like it." She handed it to Kate.

Kate took the gift. "Wow," she breathed. "A writing notebook." She flipped it open and paged through it. "It's like yours."

"The perfect size for your bag."

"And it's for me to keep?"

"Of course. Every writer needs a notebook."

Kate hugged it against her chest. "Thank you." She opened it and wrote her name on the front page. Then she jumped up and raced over to Adrian. "See what Libby bought me?"

"That's very kind of her." He smiled at Libby, the pleasure filling his whole face.

Libby's body went hot, head to toe – she felt like she was glowing like a coal.

He had some smile. It was wide-eyed and honest, friendly with a hint of something else. Nothing like the sleazy, I'm-a-rock-god-everyone-should-worship-me smile Kent had.

Kate pinched a marshmallow from the bench and raced back over, turning her laptop so Libby could see what she had written. "I've created a nemesis for Lilly Lionheart."

Grateful for the distraction, Libby bent over the laptop. "Let me see." She read through the description, impressed by the girl's imagination. "This is great."

Kate beamed for a second and then sobered. "What do I do now?"

"Do you know how the story starts?"

"I think so."

"All right. You can do a couple of things. You could dive right in and start writing the story, or you could outline what the story is about."

"What do you do?"

"I'm more of a plotter than a pantser."

"A what-er?" Kate scrunched up her face.

Libby grinned. "A plotter. I outline the whole story first and then I start writing. There are other writers who are pantsers – they write by the seat of their pants, which means they generally only have a vague idea of where the story is going and they let the story lead them."

"Which is better?"

"Neither. It's whatever suits the way you write. You'll have to decide for yourself."

Kate chewed on her bottom lip as Adrian walked over carrying two mugs that could only be described as sinful. The top of each mug was filled with whipped cream, sprinkled with chocolate pieces and small marshmallows, and finished with a swirl of chocolate sauce.

He placed the mugs on the table in front of Kate and Libby.

"Wow."

"Wait until you try it," Adrian said as he went to get his own mug.

Libby shifted the laptop to the side so she didn't spill anything on it and then lifted the mug toward her. She used the spoon Adrian had given her to stir in some of the cream, which was beginning to melt, and then took a careful sip.

It was a chocolate-marshmallow explosion. She groaned. "Oh my God." She lifted her eyes skyward.

"I know." Kate grinned. "It's awesome."

Adrian sat down opposite her and took a sip.

"Where did you learn to make this?" Libby asked.

Kate's smile disappeared. "It was my mama's recipe."

Was. Past tense. Libby checked Adrian's reaction, and there was sadness in his eyes. "Well, that makes your mama awesome too," she told Kate.

Kate took a sip of her drink. "I guess so."

Libby cast her mind about for something else to talk about. "So, do you think you'll be a plotter or a pantser?"

Kate ran her tongue over her top lip to lick up the cream smeared on it. "Maybe a plotter. I know what's going to happen and I'm scared I might forget."

"Then you'd better write it down."

Kate placed her mug to the side and pulled the laptop toward her. She started typing.

The only sound was the clack, clack from the keyboard.

Libby took another sip of the delectable drink.

"What's your day job?" Adrian asked.

Startled by the change in conversation, Libby took a second to catch up. "I do temp work, mainly in administration roles."

"Is that a bit risky?"

It was proving so at the moment, but Libby shrugged. "There's plenty of work around, and it gives me time to write when I need to." She just wished it paid better.

"I don't think I could be stuck in an office all day." Adrian shuddered.

"It's not so bad, especially when the weather's bad," she said. "What did you do before you became so successful?"

"I worked for my brother, Kate's dad, as a laborer with his construction company. We built houses."

"They were the best houses, weren't they, Uncle Ade?" Kate looked up from the laptop.

"They still are," Adrian agreed. "Daniel's best friend still runs the business."

Kate's parents must both have died. Libby's heart went out to the young girl. To be orphaned at such a young age was tragic. At least she had an uncle who cared for her.

Adrian's cell phone rang and he excused himself to go and answer it.

"How's it going?" Libby asked as she sipped the last of her delicious drink.

"Slowly," Kate complained. "I can't find the keys."

"Maybe you should learn to touch-type."

"What's that?"

"It's when you can type without looking at the keys. Shall I show you?"

"Yeah." Kate slid the laptop over to Libby.

Libby shifted the cursor so it was a couple of lines below where Kate had been typing. "It's like this." She kept looking at Kate while she typed a couple of lines of text.

"That's cool. How long did it take you to learn?"

"A few months. I practiced each day until I learned where all the keys were and then it was a matter of getting faster."

"I want to do that."

"There are lots of free typing lessons on the internet," Libby told her. "Maybe your uncle can download one for you."

Adrian came back into the room.

"Libby says I need to have touch-typing lessons," Kate said.

Adrian raised an eyebrow.

"Hang on a second." Libby raised her hands, palms facing outward. "I suggested you might like to learn – I didn't say you had to."

Kate grinned at her and then turned to Adrian. "Can we download something?"

"I'm sure we can find something for you, kiddo." He paused. "George was on the phone. We need to head in a bit earlier tonight."

Kate pouted. "Do I have to go? I'm busy writing."

"Afraid so, kiddo. You can't stay here by yourself."

"Libby can look after me." Kate turned to Libby, her eyes pleading. "Can't you?"

Libby was torn. She had writing she had to do. She should go back to her room and spend a few hours on her own work, but she was enjoying spending time with Kate and Adrian. If Kate wanted to write, perhaps Libby could use the time to write too, especially considering how slowly Kate was typing.

Maybe Adrian would offer her the job if she proved herself.

"Kate, why don't you go into your room and let me talk to Libby?" Adrian's voice was mild but there was something in his tone that cautioned against refusal.

"Yes, Uncle Ade." Kate saved her work and left the room.

Adrian turned to Libby. "I'm sorry she keeps putting you on the spot like this."

"No, it's fine." Libby braced herself. "I don't mind taking care of her tonight – as long as you don't have a problem with it." She paused. "Kate is a delight, and I was only going to spend the night writing." She glanced at Kate's laptop. "I can probably do that here, or wait until Kate goes to bed."

Adrian rubbed his palms against his thighs. "I'm not sure."

It was better than a flat-out rejection. Perhaps he wasn't sure whether he trusted her yet. "I have a couple of friends you can call for character references," she said. Just not childcare references.

"No, it's not that." He sighed. "Kate is getting attached to you. I'm worried she'll be hurt when you leave tomorrow. She's still really fragile after her parents' deaths."

"What happened?"

"Car accident, a year ago." His voice was flat. "Truck driver had been on the road for eighteen hours and drifted to the wrong side. Killed Daniel and Penny instantly. Kate was trapped in the back seat until emergency services pulled her out."

Libby gasped and brought a hand up to her throat. "I'm so sorry."

Adrian had pain in his eyes. "Kate still has nightmares."

The poor girl. To have so much tragedy at such a young age. Libby couldn't even imagine what it would be like. It would have been so difficult for Adrian as well, having to cope with the deaths and help Kate through her mourning.

She glanced down at the words Kate had written on the laptop. Perhaps writing the story would be a form of therapy for her. Maybe Libby could help her heal.

"Would it help if I became Kate's nanny?" The words came out of her mouth before she could think about it.

Adrian stepped back and Libby rushed to explain, the slight panic at what she'd just said speeding up her heartbeat. "I have a month before my next job starts – I could tour with you and Kate. We can work on her story and it might be good therapy for her. It's about a superhero who can save people."

Adrian cursed quietly and rubbed a hand against his face.

Oh, God, she sounded desperate. "Why don't you think about it?" she said. "I can look after her tonight and then you can decide."

He was silent for a long moment. He was going to refuse.

"All right."

Libby had been expecting a no and quickly regrouped. "What time do you have to leave?"

"In an hour."

"I'll go now to give you some time together and be back in an hour." She had to work out how she would manage her writing if he actually said yes to her offer, but she reminded herself that she was flat broke and might need more money for a bond. It was a sensible plan and would benefit them all.

"That's fine," Adrian said and Libby gathered up her things. He walked her to the door, and as she stepped out, he put his hand on her arm.

It was warm and sent a jolt through her.

"Thank you."

Libby couldn't speak. She smiled, nodded once and headed for the elevator.

Maybe this wasn't such a good idea after all.

***

Adrian turned away from the entrance and sighed. He was torn. The pain of his brother's death crept up and blindsided him, making him vulnerable. Was that why he was considering hiring Libby as Kate's nanny?

It was true she was good with Kate. Buying her the notebook had been a lovely gesture and she was patient and attentive. But he saw Kate gravitating toward her in a way she never had with Emily. Emily had been all business – friendly enough, for sure – but always slightly stand-offish. Libby was just Libby, interesting and kind.

And that was another problem. He couldn't deny he was attracted to her and he had to add that to the equation. The nanny he hired had to be the best for Kate's wellbeing and nothing to do with him. He'd promised himself he wouldn't hire anyone he was attracted to. But he also didn't have a lot of choice.

He went to Kate's bedroom and poked his head in. "You can come out now."

Kate jumped off the bed and raced out, looking around. "Where's Libby?"

"She's gone to her room to get ready. She's going to come back and look after you tonight."

"Yes!" Kate did a little happy dance.

Adrian smiled. "Kiddo, we need to have a talk."

"Uh, oh."

He led her over to the couches and they sat down. "I need to find you a new nanny."

Kate slouched down in the seat. "Yeah, I know." She peered up at him. "Can we make sure she's not like Emily?"

"What didn't you like about Emily?" Adrian asked.

Kate shrugged. "She was a bit boring. She didn't really like to play games or do anything except shop."

The guilt was sharp and hot. Adrian pressed his lips together. He should have noticed. "Why didn't you tell me?"

"It didn't really matter. You and I do all the fun stuff."

In other words, when he wasn't around Kate was unhappy. God, it had been a mistake bringing her with him. He'd thought it was for the best – she'd get to see the world, and being in a different place might help her forget for a little while – but maybe he'd been wrong. Maybe Susan had been right. The doubt that was never far away hovered over him. "What's on your nanny wish list then, kiddo?"

"What?" She squinted at him.

"If you chose your nanny, what kind of person would she be?"

Kate sat up straight, screwing up her face as she thought. "She'd have to like to play games like cards and board games."

Adrian jumped up and took her notebook from the table. "Games." He wrote it down.

Kate grinned. "She needs to like to go out and do stuff – but not shopping. Go exploring."

"Exploring," he said as he added it to the list. "Got it. What else?"

"She should be able to cook. Emily wasn't very good." Kate twisted her hands together. She did that when she wanted to say something else but she wasn't sure she should.

"Spit it out, kiddo."

"Well, it would be cool if she knew about writing."

Adrian's hand paused for a second on the notepad. "Writer. Okay, is there anything else?"

"She should be fun and kind too," Kate added in a rush.

"All right. I think I've got it all. I'll see what I can do."

Could he ignore his attraction to Libby for the good of Kate?

He had some thinking to do.

***

Libby took her time getting ready. She'd done it now. She'd

offered to care for Kate and now she had to wait for Adrian to decide. She wasn't sure what would be worse – if he agreed or if he refused.

She fired up her laptop before she headed to the shower and afterward she checked the rest of her emails. The one from the realtor hadn't magically disappeared as she'd hoped. She flagged it and ran through the rest. At the bottom there was one from George with the tour itinerary and the contract.

Her heart jolted. Did that mean Adrian had agreed?

She checked the time it was sent. He'd sent it this morning, before she'd seen Adrian, like he said he would.

She opened the contract first and worked through the legal speak. When she got to the part about remuneration, her jaw dropped. Even though she had a new deadline, being Kate's nanny *definitely* made financial sense. She'd be able to afford the bond on a new place and replace her fridge if it died. She wouldn't have to go to her parents for help. She just hoped the hours would work in her favor.

Mentally crossing her fingers, she opened up the itinerary and scanned it. Adrian had four concerts in Melbourne, four in Sydney and three in Brisbane before heading west to her home state for two concerts in Perth. Every couple of nights he had a break and between cities there were several days free.

Most of his media appointments were on the day of his first concert and of course he had sound checks to sort out as well. Kate only needed care on concert nights and the media day. There would be lots of free time for Libby to meet her writing commitments. She calculated her daily word count and winced slightly. It was still doable.

The breath she'd been holding whooshed out of her. Her impulsive offer wouldn't jeopardize her career.

Besides, she had to wait and see if Adrian and Kate wanted her, and they probably wouldn't. She shrugged away the thought.

Now that she'd offered to be Kate's nanny she realized she didn't really know anything about Adrian or Kent. Giving in to impulse she did an internet search. Scrolling through several gossip websites, she learned that he was either reported as a recluse or a party animal. One site had been created by a group of concerned parents rallying to stop his music being played on the radio. They thought it was a bad influence on children. Libby found some of his music videos and watched a couple. She didn't understand what his fans' parents were so concerned about. The lyrics were meaningful, all about not giving up, fighting for what you believe in and trusting yourself. Libby thought they were inspirational.

Checking the time, she flagged the emails she had to reply to, then packed up her things and went back upstairs to look after Kate.

***

Adrian let her in. "Kate's having a shower." He was slightly tense and his fingers drummed against the door as he held it open.

Was he regretting his decision?

Libby walked through and placed her laptop case next to the couch. She had to be professional and allay his concerns. He didn't need to be worrying about Kate while he was at work. "What does she have for dinner?" she asked.

"The nanny usually cooks but I promised Kate she could order room service tonight. She's not allergic to anything and she can have whatever she wants." He paused. "There's nothing too unhealthy on the menu."

"What time is bedtime?"

"Eight thirty. She's still recovering from the late night yesterday and we're going out exploring tomorrow so I want to make sure she's not too tired." His tone was slightly defensive, as if he was expecting her to disagree.

"Good thinking." Libby kept her tone light. "Anything else I need to know?"

He ran a hand through his hair. "Sometimes Kate sleeps with her stars on. It's a night-light that revolves and projects the night sky on the ceiling. It's in her room and she knows how to use it. I leave it on all night for her."

Kate came out of the bathroom dressed in green flannelette pajamas covered in blue stars and with her hair wrapped up in a turban. "Hi, Libby. Can we do some more writing tonight?"

"Of course." Libby was surprised at how keen Kate was.

Other children she knew would have lost interest when they realized how much work it was.

Adrian's cell rang and he answered it. He listened to the speaker and then said, "Be right down." He hung up and turned to Kate.

"I've got to go, kiddo." He shuffled as if he wasn't sure about leaving.

"Have fun." She gave him a hug.

"You too." He turned to Libby and handed her a business card. "If you need anything, this is George's cell phone number."

Libby reached for it, but she sensed he was still reluctant. "I'll take good care of her. I promise."

Their eyes met and Libby saw the love and concern he had for his niece. She'd never seen that kind of concern on her parents' faces. Her insides melted.

"Hurry up, Uncle Ade. George hates to be kept waiting and Libby and I have work to do." Kate grabbed her uncle's hand and dragged him toward the door.

He grinned. "Okay, okay, I'm going." He swiped his bag and let his niece pull him out of the room. He glanced back at Libby.

She smiled and waved, not at all worried about his reluctance. It was only to be expected. Kate skipped back into the room. "Ready?"

"Yep. Let's get set up." Libby placed her laptop on the dining table. "What time do you want to order dinner?" she asked. It was still early and Libby was full from her double choc, whipped cream, marshmallow delight, but Kate might be hungry.

"We could order now for six. Then we don't have to worry about it." Kate jumped up and snatched the room service menu from the sideboard. Bringing it to the table, she opened it and put it between them so Libby could read it as well.

"I'm going to try the Aussie burger. It's got beetroot in it – that's so weird."

Libby smiled. "Tasty, though. I'll get a salad." At Kate's incredulous look she added, "I had a big lunch. Do you want dessert?"

Kate flipped to the desserts. "Banana sundae."

Libby stood and went to the phone to order. Afterward she turned to Kate. "Let's get to work."

For the next few hours they worked on their stories, stopping only to eat dinner when it arrived. They started with a brainstorming session that had them in fits of giggles, but then there was silence, broken by the clack of keys as they wrote.

Checking the time, Libby sighed. "Time for bed, Kate."

"No, I just have to finish this bit." Kate didn't look up from her typing.

Was Kate going to be difficult? "Five minutes."

She knew how long 'just finishing a bit' could take.

Kate grimaced but continued to peck out the words.

Libby stood and tidied up the dinner dishes, putting the tray outside to be collected by hotel staff.

She stretched, reaching her hands above her head and standing on tiptoes. Writing was such a sedentary job – she felt stiff if she sat for any length of time without getting up.

"Time's up," she said.

"Finished!" Kate said with a flourish.

Libby was surprised. She'd expected to have a fight on her hands. "Make sure you save it."

A few minutes later, Libby tucked Kate into bed.

"Thanks for your help today, Libby."

"It was my pleasure." And it had been. She'd really enjoyed watching Kate's mind work as she plotted and discarded ideas and then wrote down the story. "Will you come and say goodbye before you leave tomorrow?" Kate asked.

Libby's heart compressed at the hope in Kate's eyes. "Of course. You still have my card, don't you?"

"Yep."

"Then it's not goodbye. It's until we meet again."

"Or until we write again." Kate giggled.

"That's right." She gave the girl a hug. "Good night. I'll be right outside if you need anything."

"Night, Libby."

Libby left the room, leaving the door open but turning off the lights in the main room so only the light over the dining table was on. She sat down at her laptop and stared at the screen.

She'd had fun tonight. Kate was easy to be around and Libby had to admit encouraging her to write was a joy.

For someone who had been orphaned, Kate was coping well. Libby put it down to how well Adrian cared for her. For a single man in his early thirties, he was a fantastic guardian.

Libby really wanted to spend some more time with them. Both of them.

And wasn't that a problem? The last time she'd spent any length of time with a man, was when she'd still been with her ex, Clint, and she'd almost lost her book contract. It had doubly hurt when she realized her loss had been pointless – that he had only been using her. She'd never fall for that again.

She needed to focus on her new deadline and forget about men altogether. They weren't worth the heartache.

She stared at the screen, willing words to come, but her mind wandered.

She'd been so in love with Clint.

It had been at one of her mother's charity events. Libby always felt awkward at such events. People assumed she had money to spend because she had multiple books published and when she never bid on anything she felt she was being judged. On this particular night she'd figured her obligatory two-hour attendance was up when Clint had introduced himself. He was a doctor, planning to specialize in the same field as her parents. That should have been her first warning.

He'd made her laugh with his assessment of the people around them: those who were there to be seen, those who were sure their social status was locked up in how much they bid for an item, and those there to have fun.

Libby had been relieved to have someone to talk to. They chatted mostly about his work and for the first time Libby was glad all her family were in the medical profession, because she could understand what he was talking about and could empathize.

Before she knew it, it was the end of the night and Clint had asked for her phone number.

He'd called the very next day and they'd met for coffee. Libby had listened while Clint told her about his dream to be neurosurgeon like Libby's father.

After that they spent as much time together as they could, but his long working hours made it difficult. Libby stopped writing so she could meet his schedule, and when they didn't see each other he would call. She introduced him to her parents and then endured a dinner at which the three of them spoke about surgery. Afterward her father had been impressed by Clint. Libby might not have followed the family tradition, but she could marry someone who did.

She knew Clint's roster by heart and was thrilled when the phone rang – and disappointed when it didn't.

She told herself to be happy with the time he gave her, though it wasn't much. Part of her worried that his job took so much of his time. Any children they had would miss their father like she had. But at least they'd have her.

Libby had been so caught up in the dream that she'd been late delivering her second manuscript and almost lost her contract.

Then she'd cancelled a dinner with her parents and Clint had been angry. He had a scholarship opportunity he wanted to discuss with her father. She'd told him to go without her and he had. From that point the phone calls were fewer and further apart. It was her mother who had told her that Clint had won the scholarship, and when Libby had mentioned she hadn't seen him recently, she was told not to be needy. Training to be a surgeon was hard work.

Finally she found out the real reason she'd seen so little of him. Her mother had rung to tell her all about the wonderful scholarship dinner she'd attended the night before, and to ask why Libby hadn't told her she'd broken up with Clint. He'd been there with a charming woman and they were engaged.

Libby had felt as though she'd been sucker-punched, but she asked her mother for all the details. Finally her mother seemed to realize that Libby hadn't known about the fiancée. "Are you all right, Elizabeth?"

"Fine." It was all Libby had been able to choke out. She hung up and let the tears flow.

It had taken her a day to get through her tears and then she buried herself in her writing, immersing herself in another world, a world where Clint didn't exist, where she hadn't been dumped by the man she'd loved, where *she* decided the fate of others. She understood what her mother did not. Clint hadn't loved her.

He had used her. Used her to get the scholarship he so desperately wanted.

He hadn't found Libby interesting enough to want her or love her.

She'd so desperately wanted to be loved that she'd ignored all the signs.

Even after the truth came out, Libby had never confronted Clint. She never demanded an explanation.

The fact that she'd rolled over without a fight irritated her still.

Reviewing their relationship now she'd realized she'd made all the sacrifices. She'd run to him when he'd called, she'd not questioned his desire to take the relationship slow. He'd never invited her to his place, was always too tired for a physical relationship, had barely even kissed her.

Even now the pain was still there. She held her hand to her heart. Clint had reinforced what her parents had taught her – she wasn't loveable.

She wouldn't forget it, just like she wouldn't allow herself to walk blindly into a relationship again. And she certainly wouldn't put a man before her writing again. She was stronger and wiser now.

Her offer to be Kate's nanny was a good financial decision and nothing to do with Adrian.

She sighed, stretched and focused on her screen. She really did need to get some words down. The climax to her book was right around the corner and she just had to get there. The rest would flow from that point.

She scrolled back a couple of pages and read where she was up to. Then she wrote.

***

There was a click from the hallway, the sound of the door opening. Libby got up and walked a few steps toward the entrance as Kent came in. His hair was damp from sweat, his clothes clung to his body and Libby imagined other women would find him sexy as hell.

She took a step back.

It was going to take some getting used to seeing Adrian as Kent. "How was the concert?"

"Great. How were things here?" He glanced toward Kate's room.

"Great," Libby echoed. "Kate had a burger and sundae, then she finished the first chapter of her book and was in bed by 8.30 without complaint."

"Good. I'm glad." He shifted his stance, more Adrian than Kent. "Give me a second to clean up." He motioned to his face and ducked into the bathroom without waiting for her response.

She should pack up and be ready to leave. Should she ask if he'd considered her offer or would it seem pushy?

She saved her work, backing it up to a USB stick, then shut down her computer and packed it away.

"I've had a chat to Kate about her nanny," Adrian said quietly.

Libby turned to see he'd come out of the bathroom, his face now clean of make-up. Despite the black clothes he was much more like Adrian now. She had a sudden urge to run her hand over his cheek to feel the dampness of his skin.

She clenched her hand as he went over to the sideboard and picked up a piece of paper. He handed it to Libby. "These are Kate's requirements."

Libby took the note, and when he signaled for her to read it, she opened the list. It was remarkably short.

Games. Exploring. Writer. Cook. Fun. Nice.

Libby smiled. She liked the order of it. "Exploring new places is one of my favorite things."

"Can you cook?"

Her freezer full of microwave dinners sprung to mind. "I don't cook very often but I can follow a recipe." She'd have to go out and buy a recipe book. "What are *your* requirements for Kate's nanny?"

Adrian seemed surprised by the question. "She needs to be responsible. Trustworthy. Have Kate's best interests at heart. And most importantly, Kate has to like her." He paused. "I think you fit the bill."

"Are you asking me to be Kate's nanny?"

"If you still want to be."

"Yes. Yes, I do." A little thrum of excitement started up in her veins. They wanted her.

"I'll get George to come around with the paperwork in the morning and you can move into the nanny's room down the hall. I have no commitments tomorrow so you won't need to start until Monday night." Adrian was all business.

The excitement died down. Of course. She was only needed when Adrian wasn't working. Libby pushed aside the disappointment. It would give her a couple of days to work on her story.

"All right. I'll see you then." She picked up her bag and waited as he just stood there. Should she shake his hand, kiss his cheek or something?

No, it felt too weird. She waved. "Good night."

"Night, Libby." He didn't move.

Libby hurried out of the room feeling like a fool.

Chapter 5

When Kate got up the next morning, Adrian gave her the good news. "Libby has agreed to be your nanny."

Kate's mouth dropped open and she stared for a second before she jumped up and punched the air. "Yes! Thank you, Uncle Ade." She flung her arms around him and squeezed him tight.

Adrian hugged her back. "It's my pleasure, kiddo." He really hoped he wasn't making a mistake. He had spoken with George about it last night and George had agreed Libby would make an excellent nanny. George had spelled out the two other options: a hired nanny who would be a complete stranger, or sending Kate back to Texas to summer camp. There wasn't much of a decision to make, but he couldn't help worrying. "You need to get ready, because I've got our adventure planned and we're leaving soon."

"Where are we going?"

"It's a surprise, but make sure you dress warm and grab your rain jacket."

Kate didn't move, as if deciding whether to push for more information.

"Hurry up. George is coming with us and you know what he'll say if you're not ready."

Kate grinned and turned, racing into her room to get

changed.

Adrian packed his raincoat and a big umbrella, checking through the rucksack he'd prepared to make sure he remembered everything; Food, drink, sun cream, hat.

Someone knocked on the door.

"I'm ready," Kate yelled.

Adrian peered into her room on his way past and saw she was struggling with her shoes. "I'll stall him."

Kate grunted in response.

Adrian opened the door and his smile stopped on its way across his face. "Emily."

Emily tucked her long blonde hair behind her ears and had the grace to look bashful. "Adrian." She paused. "I behaved badly the other night and wanted to apologize. It was selfish of me to quit and leave Kate without anyone to look after her."

Adrian didn't move. Without a doubt it was selfish and childish of her, but he knew now it was better this way. "She always has me."

Emily's eyes widened. "Of course." She crossed her arms. "I'm sorry for, er, coming on to you. I know it will be difficult for you to find another nanny here, so I'd like to offer to come back to work."

Somewhere down the hallway the elevator dinged, but Adrian barely registered it. Emily wanted to come back after the way she'd behaved? After the way she'd left without the slightest consideration for Kate? Even if he hadn't hired Libby, he sure as heck wouldn't be taking Emily back. "Thank you for the offer, but I've already found someone to care for Kate."

Emily's mouth dropped open but she recovered quickly, closing it with a snap. "Oh. Well then." She paused. "Was it the woman who came yesterday?"

A chill went down Adrian's spine. Was she spying on them? He didn't like the idea. "That's no longer your concern."

"Morning, Adrian." George sauntered up to them. He nodded to Emily. "Miss Smith. Are you here to say goodbye to Kate? Your flight leaves this afternoon doesn't it?"

Emily glared at him before smiling. "Yes, I would like to say goodbye to Kate, if that's all right."

Adrian wasn't sure, but before he could decide, Kate yelled,

"I'm ready, George. I'm no slowpoke." She pushed past Adrian out into the hall and saw Emily. She stopped and her smile disappeared. Looking back at Adrian, she asked, "What's Emily doing here?"

"She's heading back to the US today and she's come to say goodbye."

"Oh." Kate turned to her ex-nanny. "Goodbye. I hope you have a nice flight."

Emily's face looked like she'd sucked on a lemon. "Goodbye, Kate. I hope your new nanny is nice."

Kate's face broke into a grin. "She is. Libby's wonderful."

Adrian practically saw the cogs turning in Emily's mind. He put a hand on Kate's shoulder and gently pulled her closer to him. "We need to finish getting ready. If you'll excuse us, Emily." He didn't wait for a reply. When George and Kate were inside he shut the door in Emily's face.

"Are we going now, Uncle Ade?"

"Yep. Don't forget your bag and a book to read. It's a bit of a drive."

"Okay." She raced back to her room.

"Do you think Emily's likely to cause trouble?" Adrian asked his friend. He clenched his hands. Emily knew too much about them. This was another reason he didn't let people get close. He couldn't trust them.

George shrugged. "I don't know. She's signed the confidentiality agreement, but it might not mean much to her at the moment." He scowled. "We'll have to wait and see."

Adrian rolled his shoulders to relax the tension there. "We'll take it as it comes. Let me get our stuff and we'll go."

***

Twenty minutes later they were in a car driving south toward Phillip Island. Adrian had searched the internet for a day trip Kate would like and discovered there was plenty to do on the island, only ninety minutes from the city. George drove and Kate already had her nose stuck in a book.

"Libby signed the contract this morning," George said.

"She have any problems with the confidentiality agreement?" Adrian asked.

"None. I've changed the hotel bookings and arranged the airline tickets. She's moving rooms today and will be ready to fly next week."

"Good." Adrian was glad there were no issues. "Did she have plans for today?"

"She'd already started working on her book."

The guilt he hadn't realized he'd been feeling disappeared. Of course she needed to write her story. She was probably pleased she had enough time to work while he had Kate.

It suited them both.

George cleared his throat. "She asked for an advance."

Adrian's eyebrows lifted. "Why?" Was she going to take the money and run?

"She's broke. Her car needed repairs and she spent the last of her savings fixing it. She's still waiting to be paid by her publisher for the book tour." George paused. "She seemed embarrassed."

Had Libby just taken the job because she needed the money? Had he made another mistake in hiring her? He pushed his head back against the headrest. "Did you give it to her?"

"I gave her a couple of hundred to see her through. You don't need to worry, Ade. If I hadn't agreed with your choice, I would have said so."

It helped for George to tell him that, but in the end it was his choice and he would have to face the consequences if it had been the wrong one.

Damn it.

He'd keep a close eye on Libby for the next few days.

***

It had been a long day. They'd stopped at a koala park on the way down to Phillip Island and then at a chocolate factory, where Kate had convinced him to buy her more chocolates than were good for her. He'd have to keep control of the stash and dish them out slowly otherwise she'd make herself sick. Then they'd gone on to do a bush tucker tour, which about traditional Aboriginal food, before watching the parade of penguins returning home to their colony on the shores of a beach as the day ended.

Kate was quiet in the back of the car and Adrian turned to see she'd fallen asleep. They'd bought some fast food for dinner on the way back and he promised himself he would make sure Kate ate healthy food for the rest of the week. He'd have to talk to Libby about that and give her some money for groceries. Maybe he'd get Kate to write up a list of her favorite meals so Libby knew where to start.

"Libby knows she has to cook for Kate, doesn't she?" Adrian asked George.

George regarded him for a second and then turned back to the road. "Yes. I gave her the same terms as Emily had."

"And she was happy with that?"

"Didn't bat an eyelid. What's bothering you?"

Adrian checked to make sure Kate was asleep. "We barely know her."

"We know her better than anyone else we could have hired. Kate likes her and I think she'll do a great job." George paused. "You're relaxed around her too."

Adrian scowled and drummed his fingertips against the armrest of the car. He didn't want to think about that.

They arrived back at the hotel and Kate woke up. She yawned and stretched.

"Are we back already?"

"Sure are, kiddo."

Adrian helped Kate out of the car and George handed the keys to the valet. Walking to the elevators, Adrian noticed a woman standing there.

"Libby!" Kate called.

Libby turned, smiled and waved back at the girl. "How was your day?"

Adrian didn't hear Kate's response. He was too busy taking in Libby's appearance. She was wearing a black leather jacket and green top that made her eyes more emerald, but it was the skinny-leg jeans and high heels that attracted his attention. Where the heck had those legs come from? They went on and on and the jeans clung to them like a second skin.

His mouth went dry. What would it be like to peel off those jeans and – Christ, he couldn't have those kinds of thoughts about Kate's nanny.

Kate tugged on his hand. "Can't she, Uncle Ade?"

He realized Kate has said something to him. "What?"

"I said Libby can have a double choc, whipped cream, marshmallow delight with the chocolate we got from the chocolate factory, can't she?"

He swallowed to get some moisture back in his mouth. Everyone was waiting for his answer. "Sure, but not tonight. You need to go to bed."

"Aw."

Adrian smiled at the way she drew out the sound. "No. You can teach Libby how to make it tomorrow night while I'm at the concert."

The elevator dinged, signaling its arrival, and they got in.

Distracted, Kate spoke a mile a minute about what she and Libby were going to do tomorrow night. Libby threw in some suggestions of her own and Adrian began to wish he was able to stay and hang out with them instead of going to work.

He needed help.

George gave him a meaningful look. No hiding his reaction from his best friend. Of course George wouldn't approve – Adrian didn't approve either. He would have to make sure he spent as little time as possible with Libby, but it shouldn't be too hard. He'd managed it with Emily.

The elevator dinged and they all got out. Libby interrupted Kate mid-sentence. "My room's the other way. We'll talk more tomorrow."

"Definitely." Kate turned to Adrian. "We have to walk her to her door."

Adrian bit back a curse. He had promised Kate he would but hadn't thought he'd ever have to. "Of course."

"Oh, you don't have to do that." Libby put up a hand as if to stop them.

"I did promise," Adrian answered. He said goodbye to George and followed Libby and Kate down the deserted corridor, trying to ignore the swing of Libby's hips and the shape of her bottom in her jeans.

Christ. He was doing it again.

Libby stopped and fumbled in her purse for her room card. She slipped it into the gap and the door clicked open. Holding it ajar, she turned back to them. "Thank you for walking me to my room."

"No prob," Kate said.

"My pleasure, ma'am." It wasn't every day he walked a pretty lady to her door.

Libby reddened. "I'll see you tomorrow evening," she said to Kate.

"I'll get Uncle Ade to write down the chocolate recipe for you," Kate said.

Libby smiled at Adrian and it hit him in the chest like an arrow. That smile was something. So open and friendly. "Goodnight."

"Night."

She closed the door and he let out the breath he'd been holding. Kate took his hand and they walked down the corridor to their room.

"Libby's so nice," Kate said. "I'm so glad she's going to be my nanny. We're going to have a great time."

Listening to Kate and Libby chat, Adrian was sure they would have fun. They had clicked and there was nothing forced or faked with Libby.

He was the one having issues.

He needed to get the image of Libby's butt in those jeans out of his head.

Then everything would be fine.

He hoped.

***

Libby double-checked she had everything she needed for an evening with Kate, and then checked everything again.

This was ridiculous. She was prepared and ready to go. Why was she procrastinating?

It was Adrian. The way he'd looked at her last night, the cheetah look that said he wanted to devour her, had her blood hot even now. How was she supposed to behave? No one, not even Clint, had ever looked at her that way.

She was an adult and she'd behave as one. Kate was her main focus and anything else was inappropriate. She would go over, listen to Adrian's instructions and then he would leave and she and Kate would have an adventure.

The hotel had returned all her washing, so she was dressed in regular jeans, T-shirt and jacket. On her feet she had flats. Nothing inappropriate there.

She retrieved her hotel card from its place and walked the short distance down the hallway to Adrian's suite. She let out a deep breath and knocked.

Kate opened the door almost instantly, as if she'd been waiting for her. "Come in, come in."

Libby followed her through to the living area. Kate's laptop was already set up and humming.

"Don't think Libby arriving is going to get you out of drying up."

Libby turned to Adrian at the sink of the kitchenette, his hands in the soapy water washing dishes. A lovely homely image. She hadn't ever seen her father washing up. It had been her job to stack the dishwasher and wash any remaining dishes. She wasn't sure why Adrian would be doing the dishes when the hotel staff would do anything he left on the sink.

"No, Uncle Ade." Kate wandered over as Adrian dried his hands on the tea towel and handed it to her.

"We may have left the lunch dishes for a while." He was sheepish.

"I always do," Libby admitted, ignoring the warm flush she felt at Adrian's cute confession.

Adrian took a purse from the table and handed it to her. "This is your cookie jar money," he said. "It's for groceries and any activities you do with Kate. I'll top it up each week, but tell me if you need any more."

"Do you want me to keep receipts of my purchases?"

He hesitated. "Yes, please."

Libby mentally reviewed the list of questions she'd written down. "Is there anything Kate's not allowed to do?"

"Not particularly. If you go to the movies, choose movies suitable for her age."

"Finished." Kate threw the tea towel on the bench and walked over.

Adrian raised an eyebrow at her and she went to hang the tea towel up with a sigh. Libby smothered a smile.

"You'll need to get some more groceries and snack foods, because we're running low. You might like to talk to Kate about what you both want to eat."

Adrian's cell rang. "Be right there." He turned to Kate. "That's my ride, kiddo."

Kate giggled. "Have fun, Uncle Ade. I'll see you in the morning." She gave him a kiss.

Adrian lifted his gear bag. "Behave yourself." He turned to Libby. "You've still got George's number?"

Libby nodded.

"Good. I'll see you later."

Libby smiled at him as he walked out of the room. When he was gone she let out a sigh of relief.

"You ready to start writing?" Kate asked.

Libby opened the purse she held, checked inside and gasped. More money than she earned in a week. She wasn't going to run out anytime soon. "How about we work out dinner first?"

"Let's get room service again!"

Libby laughed. "Your uncle has given me orders to cook you healthy meals. I'll be in trouble if I ignore him on the first day." She walked over to the small fridge. "Let's see what we've got to work with."

Inside there was half a carton of milk, a couple of eggs and some jam. Not a whole lot. She opened the cupboards until she found a box of cereal, half a loaf of bread and some Cup-A-Soup packets. "I think we need to go shopping."

Kate glowered. "Emily always took me shopping. I don't like it."

"We need to get some food so we can eat, but that doesn't mean we can't make an adventure of it. What's your favorite food?"

"Spaghetti."

Libby was relieved. She cooked so rarely, but she could manage spaghetti. "Have you ever made spaghetti before?'"

"Nope."

"Then I think we need to head to a bookshop first, get a couple of recipe books and decide what we want to cook for the next few days and get our supplies." Libby paused. "We'll need writing rations as well."

"Writing rations?"

"The types of food you can prepare quick smart when you don't want to stop writing but need to eat."

"I get it. We need to get lots of those." Kate said.

"Get your jacket then and let's go."

***

Libby had already found the nearest supermarket and bookshop, so they headed into town, stopping at the bookshop first.

Kate browsed the cookbooks, oohing and aahing over the food until she settled on an Italian cookbook and a basic cookbook. Then she chose the meals she wanted to make and wrote down the ingredients in her notebook.

On the way to the supermarket they passed a Vietnamese restaurant. The rich coriander scents wafting out smelled delicious.

"Mmm, we should have got a Vietnamese cookbook," Kate said.

Libby agreed. It did smell fabulous. She would have to take Kate out for Vietnamese at some stage on the tour.

At the supermarket Kate insisted on pushing the trolley and going up and down every aisle, choosing the ingredients and writing rations they needed. Libby had to stop her when the trolley began to fill.

"We don't want to buy too much, because we have to be able to carry it back to the hotel," she explained, taking a couple of items out. "And we need to make sure we stick to budget."

"Why? Uncle Ade will always give us more money if we need it."

"Just because he's got a lot of money doesn't mean we should spend it. He's given us a very generous amount and to go over would be inconsiderate."

"When I'm older, I'm going to be a writer and be rich."

Libby laughed. "Most writers are lucky if they earn enough to live on, Kate. There are only a few who make a lot of money. If you want to be rich, you should choose a different profession."

Kate frowned. "Don't you make lots of money?"

Libby shook her head. "I work part time as well as writing."

And even then, her budget was tight. She'd learned how to be frugal after leaving home at eighteen. She'd been determined not to ask her parents for any help and they hadn't offered any. Her father had even refused to pay for her arts degree at university because it was a waste of money.

"I'll tell Uncle Ade to pay you more so you don't have to work two jobs." Kate dusted her hands together as if that solved everything.

Alarmed, Libby put a hand on Kate's shoulder. "No, Kate. Your uncle is paying me well. I don't want you to say anything to him. Promise me?"

Kate thought about it a moment and then said, "Okay."

Relieved, Libby led the way to the check-out and paid. She tucked the receipt in the purse to give to Adrian.

"So how much money have we got left?" Kate asked as they walked back to the hotel carrying the shopping bags.

"Enough to have some fun later," Libby told her.

They arrived back at the room and unpacked their shopping, leaving out what they would need to make spaghetti.

It was time to get to work.

***

Several hours later the food had been cooked and eaten, the kitchenette had been cleaned and they'd spent some time writing. Kate now claimed she loved cooking and if writing didn't work out she'd be a chef. Libby had put her to bed, then done some house hunting and applied for a couple of places online. Now she was working on her manuscript, with the ending hurtling toward her and her fingers frantically trying to keep up with her brain.

A knock on the door tore her out of her story. She checked the clock. It was late. She got up and went to the entrance, checking through the peephole to see who it was. A tall, blond woman stood there waiting. She looked slightly familiar.

Cautious, Libby opened the door and smiled at the woman. "Can I help you?"

The woman seemed surprised and stepped back. "Oh, I'm sorry. I must have the wrong room number." Her American accent was low, and somehow strained, as if she was trying to disguise it. The woman looked down at the piece of paper in her hand and then back at Libby. "Room 1010?"

"No. This is room 1001."

"Sorry for disturbing you." The blonde paused mid turn and squinted at Libby. "Are you Libby Myles?"

It was said ever so casually but something about her demeanor had Libby on alert.

"Yes, I am."

"I recognize you from the talk show the other night. My niece is a big fan. She'll be so excited when I tell her I met you." The woman was all smiles.

Libby didn't believe her for a second. Where had she seen her – in the hotel lobby perhaps? "I'm glad she enjoys my books. If you'll excuse me, I need to go."

"Wait. You were on the show with Kent Downer. What's he really like?"

Libby debated her answer. "He was nice," she said, using the blandest adjective she could think of. "Good night."

"Sorry for the mix-up."

Libby shut the door and then peered through the peephole. The woman smiled as if satisfied and walked down the hall.

There was something about the whole episode that felt wrong. Could she have been a groupie of Kent's?

She'd have to ask Adrian.

Suddenly Libby heard a noise from Kate's bedroom. She walked down the hall and listened.

A groan, followed by the sound of a body tossing and turning in bed.

"Mama. No. Mama, talk to me." Kate's voice was full of panic and pain.

Libby rushed into the room. Kate was still asleep but tangled in the sheets, her hair drenched in sweat. Libby hurried over and turned on the star lamp for some light. She put her hands on Kate's arms. The girl's skin was burning hot. "Wake up, Kate." She shook her gently.

Kate stirred but didn't wake. She moaned again.

"Kate, wake up." Libby said it louder and squeezed Kate's arms.

Kate's eyes popped open, wide with fear, and she sat straight up in bed.

"It's Libby. You were having a bad dream."

Kate's faced crumpled and tears flooded from her eyes. Libby sat down next to her and pulled her close. "It's all right. It was just a dream."

Kate pushed her away. "No it wasn't. It really happened. They're really dead." She sobbed harder.

Libby didn't know what to say. She stroked Kate's arm and made soothing hushing noises. Kate flung her arms around Libby and held her tight. Kate's nightdress was soaked in sweat, her little body overheated. Libby's heart broke for the little girl as she hugged Kate back.

When finally the sobs faded and the shuddering died down, Libby reached for the tissue box next to the bed and handed it to Kate. "Do you want to talk about it?"

Kate sat up and took a tissue, blowing her nose hard. She hiccupped.

Libby handed her the glass of water from the bedside table. Kate took a sip.

"It was the same dream as always."

"How often do you get them?" Libby asked.

Kate shrugged. "Not so much now. Maybe once a month."

"Do you want to tell me about the dream?" Libby wouldn't push. She didn't want to make it worse for the girl.

"It's best if you know. You're my nanny now." Kate said it in such an adult manner, as if she'd heard someone else say the same thing.

Kate took a deep breath. "Mama and Dad died in a car accident. I dream about the accident. I wake up in the car, trapped by the front seat – it's pushed against my legs. I can't see Dad properly, just his head in the seat in front, but I can see Mama." Kate paused, closed her eyes and then flashed them open as if she didn't like what she saw when they were closed. "She's bleeding and not moving. She won't answer me and the steering wheel is crushed against her stomach." Kate's voice hitched and she took a shuddery breath.

Libby clasped Kate's hand and rubbed it.

Kate gave a half smile and then stared up at the stars on the ceiling. "Then everything gets blurry but I can hear voices trying to get us out. They're taking too long. They need to be faster but I can't tell them. I can't say anything. And then I wake up." She turned to face Libby. "Mama and Dad died before they got us out of the car."

There was nothing Libby could say. The horror of watching your parents die, or knowing they were dead while you were trapped, unable to help, was unimaginable. No wonder Kate had nightmares. "I'm so sorry, Kate." Libby hugged her tightly.

Kate clung back. "At least I have Uncle Adrian. He takes care of me."

It must have been difficult for Adrian as well. Losing his brother and sister-in-law and then caring for a niece who had been through such trauma.

"How about you get up and take a shower to freshen up?" Libby suggested. "I'll make a hot chocolate for you."

"All right." Kate slipped out of bed. She opened a dresser drawer and took out a fresh nightie before walking down the hall toward the bathroom and disappearing inside.

Libby put a hand to her eyes to stem the tears that threatened to fall and swallowed the lump in her throat. It was her job to be the strong one. To make sure Kate was safe and secure and comforted. She could cry later. She hurried out to the kitchenette and prepared the hot chocolate.

Ten minutes later Kate came out of the bathroom, freshly scrubbed. Libby sat with the hot chocolate and Kate's teddy bear in the living area. Kate wandered over and sat down, clutching the teddy bear to her chest. She tucked her feet up under her and reached for the hot drink.

"How are you feeling?"

"Better," Kate said and took a sip.

"Good."

They sat in silence drinking their hot chocolate. Libby didn't want to make conversation for the sake of it. Kate would talk when she was ready.

As they were finishing their drinks Adrian returned.

"Uncle Adrian's back." Kate put down her mug and raced to the entrance.

Libby stood and turned as Adrian said, "What are you doing up, kiddo?"

"Bad dream."

Libby moved toward the hall as Adrian knelt and held his arms open for his niece. Kate dove into them and he wrapped her in a tight hug. "I'm sorry, Katie."

He glanced up and met Libby's gaze. He was still wearing Kent's make-up but Libby saw past it. There was deep sorrow in his eyes.

It made her heart ache. Libby gave him what she hoped was a compassionate smile and moved away to give them some privacy. She collected the mugs and headed to the kitchenette to clean up.

After a minute she heard Kate say, "It's okay. I had a shower and Libby made me hot chocolate."

"And I see you've got Sebastien Bear to protect you," Adrian said.

Libby smiled. She finished drying the mugs and turned her attention to packing up her laptop.

"Do you want to stay up a bit longer?" Adrian asked Kate. "We could watch a movie."

"Yes, please, Uncle Ade."

Libby turned as they walked into the room.

"Libby, could you stay while I shower?" Adrian asked when he noticed she was packing up.

"Of course."

Adrian turned to Kate. "Will you be all right for a few minutes while I take off Kent?"

Kate nodded and let go of his hand.

"Why don't you get the quilt from your bed and drag it out here?" Adrian suggested.

Kate brightened but then peered toward her semi-dark bedroom in concern.

"Let me help," Libby said. "This sounds like fun." Hoping she wasn't intruding, she walked over and took Kate's hand, leading her into the bedroom. She glanced back at Adrian and he mouthed 'thanks' before heading for his room.

Libby flicked the switch, flooding the room with light, and together they stripped the quilt off the bed. Dragging it into the living area, they arranged it on the couch and then Kate hunted through her DVD collection until she found the cartoon she wanted.

"Do you think your uncle would like a drink?" Libby asked.

Kate paused, tongue between her teeth. "He'd probably like a hot chocolate and something to eat." She headed for the kitchenette.

For the next ten minutes they prepared a small meal and a hot drink for Adrian. By the time Adrian reappeared it was ready and presented nicely on the coffee table.

"We made you something to eat," Kate announced, slipping her hand into Adrian's and leading him to the meal.

Adrian whistled softly. "That looks great. Thanks, kiddo."

Libby went to the table and picked up her laptop bag. "I'd better be going." George had warned her Adrian liked his privacy and she shouldn't hang around longer than necessary. "I'll see you both tomorrow."

"Bye, Libby." Kate didn't let go of her uncle's hand.

Adrian watched her, unspoken words in his eyes. He nodded his thanks.

Libby smiled and let herself out.

She walked the short distance down the corridor to her room and waited until she was inside before she let out a deep breath and let the tears fall.

Chapter 6

Libby woke early the next morning and prepared for her morning walk. Kate's nightmare the night before kept swirling around in her head. The absolute devastation and distress on Kate's face, the vulnerability and despair.

What a thing for anyone to go through.

Libby rubbed her eyes, tucked her cell phone into her rain jacket pocket and opened the door of her room. She gasped as she came face to face with Adrian, who had his hand raised to knock.

He didn't look like he'd slept well. His short dark hair was mussed, his eyes were red and his T-shirt and jeans looked as if they'd been picked up off the floor.

He lowered his hand and took a step back. "I wasn't sure you'd be up yet."

Libby stopped, one hand on the door, and put her other hand over her rapidly beating heart. "I was heading out for a walk. Is there something wrong?"

He shifted his stance. "If you've got time, I wanted to talk to you about Kate's nightmare. George is with her at the moment."

Of course she had time. "Come in."

Adrian entered and she followed him the short distance to the main room. It was a mess. She groaned inwardly. She'd been planning to clean it up when she returned from her walk. Her bedsheets were half on the floor and her pink flannelette pajamas had been dumped in the center of the bed. Libby cringed and moved past Adrian, quickly snatching up her pajamas and tossing them into her suitcase. She shut the lid with a snap and finally threw the sheets back on the bed.

Face aflame, she indicated the armchairs near the window. "Why don't you have a seat? I can offer you an instant coffee or a tea."

Adrian's mouth twitched slightly upward. "Coffee would be great. Black, no sugar." He sat down on the chair facing away from the window.

Libby filled the little hotel kettle and turned it on, before getting out the cups and the tiny long-life capsules full of what was supposed to be milk. Adrian didn't speak, but she was acutely aware of his presence. Why did he have such an effect on her?

The bubble of the kettle boiling broke through her musing and she poured the two drinks. Carrying them over to the little coffee table, she set one in front of Adrian and sat on the chair opposite him.

Adrian reached forward to clasp the cup but didn't drink. "Will you tell me about Kate's nightmare?" He kept his gaze on the cup in front of him.

"Of course." Libby took a sip of her tea. Briefly she spoke about what had happened and how she had reacted.

Adrian sighed and traced a finger around the rim of the cup. "They're getting less frequent but I keep hoping she'll stop having them."

Libby understood. She'd only seen the one and she didn't want Kate to go through it again. "It's a lot for anyone to deal with, let alone a ten-year-old."

"I wasn't there for her." There was guilt in his voice as he looked down at the coffee table. "When the accident happened I was on tour, and it took a day for me to get back."

Libby was surprised he was being so open with her. "Do you mean Kate was alone? Didn't she have any other family to turn to? Your parents?"

The scowl was as fleeting as it was vicious. "Her mother's

family were too caught up in their own grief to really pay any attention to Kate. They left her alone overnight in the hospital." He still couldn't believe it. "She'd just watched her parents die and no one stayed the night with her. When I arrived home she wouldn't let me out of her sight for three days." He looked up. "She was afraid I would leave her too."

He hadn't mentioned his own family. "That must have been difficult for you." Libby flinched inwardly at her inadequate words. She tried to explain. "You needed time to grieve as well."

Adrian met her gaze. "Kate needed me more."

Libby lost her breath with the intensity of his gaze. How strong he must be, to have put his niece's needs before his own grief. She reached out and grasped his hand. "Kate's lucky to have you."

Adrian jerked his hand away and folded his arms over his chest. "Others don't think so."

Libby sat back, sure her face must be the color of beetroot. Adrian obviously didn't like to be touched. She took in his closed body language before deciding what the heck and asked, "Who doesn't think so?"

Adrian shrugged, but then said, "Kate's Aunt Susan wasn't happy I was taking Kate on tour. She thought Kate would be better off in summer camp like her own children."

Libby's mouth dropped open. "But Kate's parents died so recently. It would be cruel to send her away with a bunch of strangers. Doesn't Susan know about Kate's nightmares?"

Adrian unfolded his arms and took a sip of his coffee. "She does, but she didn't think the tour life would be suitable. She believes I spend my nights partying and doesn't think my music is appropriate."

Libby snorted. "She needs to come and see for herself. It's obvious you've got Kate's best interests at heart." She stopped to take a breath, insulted on Adrian's behalf. "She needs family around her, not a bunch of strangers."

A hint of a smile crossed Adrian's face.

"Honestly, you spend every possible moment with Kate and that's more than a lot of parents do, especially if they have to work." She knew all about it.

Adrian chuckled, low and smoky. "I'll tell Susan to speak to you next time she calls."

Libby didn't comment, feeling flustered. She picked up her mug and took a sip, then changed the subject. "What have you and Kate got planned for the day?"

"We're going to explore Melbourne and see what we can find."

"Sounds like fun."

Adrian checked his watch. "I'd better get going. Kate will be impatient to start." He stood but seemed reluctant to leave.

Libby put her cup down and rose, motioning for Adrian to go first. She followed him the short distance to the entrance.

"What are your plans today?"

It took Libby a second to realize Adrian was talking to her. "Oh, I'll be writing. I'm hoping to finish the story today."

"Then do you send it to your publisher?"

Libby grinned. If only. "No, then the polishing starts." At Adrian's confusion she said, "It's a first draft. I'll need to re-read and edit it before it's ready to go."

"How long does that take?"

"Depends on how much work it needs, but generally a couple of months when I'm working full time."

They stood in the doorway now. There was an awkward pause.

Libby cast around for something to say. "Have fun today."

Adrian nodded, his mind seemingly elsewhere. "You too." He turned and walked down the corridor.

Libby gazed after him and then realized she was staring, so hurriedly shut the door before he turned around.

She let out a deep breath and then straightened. She was being ridiculous, mooning after him like some starstruck teenager. There was no way he'd ever be interested in her anyway. No man ever was.

She sighed. Adrian had snatched his hand away pretty quickly when she'd tried to comfort him.

If her past relationship had taught her anything, it was that she wasn't interesting enough to hold anyone's attention – let alone a rock star who had women throwing themselves at him.

She refused to be one of those women.

Remembering she'd been about to go out for a walk, she

checked she had everything she needed and left her room.

The fresh air would clear her mind.

She hoped.

***

Adrian walked down the corridor, refusing to glance back at Libby. He let out a sigh of relief when the door closed. What was wrong with him? Libby was his employee, she was there for Kate. He shouldn't be feeling this way about her. Yes, she'd said all the right things, allaying his doubts about whether he was doing the right thing by Kate, but that didn't mean anything. She was just kind – there was nothing more to it. She'd even reached out to comfort him when he needed it. He'd reacted with an instinct born from his childhood, drawing away rather than allowing himself the comfort he craved. It was a luxury he'd never been able to afford.

No, he didn't need any complications and he sure as heck didn't need to jeopardize Kate's happiness by scaring off her nanny. The less he saw of Libby Myles, the better for all concerned.

He entered his suite and walked through to the living area, expecting to see George and Kate playing a game or watching television. Instead they were both tapping away at the keyboards of their respective laptops.

"Weren't you going to play a game?" he asked.

Kate didn't acknowledge him, but George stopped typing and said, "Kate wanted to get some words written before we head out today."

Adrian pursed his lips. He wasn't sure what to make of Kate's sudden desire to write a book. It was a wonderful goal but Kate had no idea how much effort it required.

"So are we heading out today, Kate?" he asked.

She grunted. "Let me finish this scene."

Adrian exchanged a look with George, who shrugged. Neither of them knew how long that would take.

Adrian filled the rucksack full of snacks and drinks, as well as a fold-up umbrella. It was an overcast and wet day in Melbourne.

Adrian's cell rang and he crossed the room to pick it up. He checked the number and rolled his eyes. "It's your aunt," he told Kate as he answered it. "Hi, Susan. How are you?"

Susan was Kate's aunt on her mother's side and thankfully no relation to Adrian. When Penny had been alive, Susan had been decent company, often laughing with Penny, and they'd had some pleasant dinners together, but since her sister had died she'd become another woman. She was withdrawn, far more conservative and worried about people's opinions. She thought Kate needed a mother in her life, not a rock star uncle, and had been devastated to learn Daniel and Penny had made him guardian of Kate.

"I'm fine, but it's not me I'm worried about. You've been in Australia for almost a week now and I haven't heard from you. You promised to call me each time you moved cities so I knew where you were." Her voice was prim.

He had promised, despite the fact that Susan had a copy of the tour itinerary so she knew exactly where they were at any time. "The first few days were a little hectic and with the time difference, I didn't want to wake you." It wasn't an apology, nor would she get one. She wasn't his mother or Kate's and he didn't owe her anything.

"Well, I'm awake now and you have the day off. What are you doing?"

Adrian bit back his impatience and the urge to say, "Cruising for drugs and hookers." He sighed. "We haven't decided yet. Would you like to speak with Kate?"

Kate made frantic just-a-minute motions and pointed to her screen before continuing to type with her tongue stuck out between her teeth.

"Of course."

"Ah, hang on a minute, she's finishing something. Tell me, how are your kids?"

"They're both having a wonderful time at summer camp. I'm sure Kate would have really enjoyed spending time with her cousins."

Adrian strode away from the table toward the window and looked down at the city below. "I don't believe she's ready for camp." They'd had this discussion before.

"Being away with children her own age could only be

therapeutic, especially with no parents around to remind her of what she's lost." Susan was clearly parroting something she'd read in a self-help book.

"We'll have to agree to disagree." Kate tugged on his arm. "I'll put Kate on." He handed her the phone.

"Hi, Aunt Susan," Kate chirped as she wandered away from the window and around the room.

Adrian smiled, amused at the way his niece never sat still when talking on the phone.

"I'm having a great time. We went to an island the other day and saw koalas and went to a chocolate factory." There was a pause as Susan said something. "We bought tons but Uncle Ade only lets me have a bit at a time."

Adrian and George exchanged looks.

"I'm writing a book." Pause. "No, it's not too hard. I've got Libby to help me."

Adrian cursed under his breath. He should have mentioned Libby to Susan. She was going to hate the fact he'd hired another nanny, one she had not recommended herself.

"Libby's my new nanny."

Adrian held out a hand for the phone and said, "Let me speak to her."

"Libby's wonderful. She's so much better than Emily was. Hang on, Uncle Ade wants to say something." She handed over the phone.

"What is this about a new nanny? Why didn't you tell me? What happened to Emily?"

Adrian held the phone away from his ear as he walked into his bedroom and shut the door behind him. Kate didn't need to hear them arguing. "Emily quit."

"Why? What did you do?"

"She didn't have Kate's best interest at heart," he said.

"What do you mean? Emily came highly recommended by one of my friends. They couldn't stop raving about her."

There was something about Susan that always made him defensive and short-tempered. "She tried to come on to me, and suggested that we leave Kate alone in the hotel room. When I rejected her advances, she quit." He kept his voice low, not wanting Kate to hear him yelling.

Susan was silent for a moment as she regrouped. "What about this new nanny? Who is she? What does she do? What do you know about her?" The rapid-fire questions were like facing a firing squad.

"Libby has been wonderful with Kate. They get on well and are having fun together." He wasn't going to mention Libby's career – she deserved some privacy as well. "Both George and I spent time with Libby and Kate before we agreed she was suitable." Mentioning George was his trump card. Susan had decided since George wore a suit and was his manager, he was more responsible than Adrian. She believed he wouldn't let Adrian make any mistakes with women that would jeopardize his career.

Susan harrumphed. "What's her surname? I'll look her up."

He'd had enough. "No."

Susan gasped.

"I have hired Libby and she is suitable for Kate. I am Kate's guardian, not you. You don't get a say." Even as he said it, he regretted it.

"My concern is always for my niece's welfare." Her tone was high and Adrian pictured her with ramrod straight spine and pinched lips. "You can't stop me from caring. If I don't believe she is being cared for properly, I will do something about it."

Before Adrian asked what she meant, she'd hung up.

He swore and pressed the end call button. He hadn't wanted to anger Susan but sometimes she irritated him to the point where he didn't care what she thought of him.

He was doing the best he could for Kate, but Susan made him constantly doubt himself.

He sank down on the bed and breathed out. Susan's parting words had sounded like a threat.

Daniel and Penny had made him guardian of Kate in their wills. The court had acknowledged it. He didn't think there was any way for Susan to get custody.

But he'd do some research to make sure.

He returned to the living area and both Kate and George looked up.

"Is Aunt Susan mad?" Kate asked.

"She's a little put out I didn't tell her about Emily quitting."

"She's not going to make Libby quit, is she?"

"Of course not." There was no way he'd let that happen. He walked over and slung an arm around Kate's shoulder. "Have you finished your scene?"

"Yep. Saved and backed up as well." She pointed to a memory stick on the table.

"Great. Let's get going then."

"Yippee!" Kate ran to get her raincoat.

Her enthusiasm soothed Adrian, as usual. It reminded him of what George and his sisters had been like when Adrian had first met them. He'd never experienced that carefree excitement and it had taken some getting used to. Now he was older he understood what he'd missed out on in his childhood. He wanted Kate to have all the love, security and stability he'd never had.

Adrian had to believe he could give that to Kate, but Susan had a way of bringing out his insecurities and it made him angry. He was thankful Susan didn't know much about his past. Daniel and Penny had been careful not to talk about it with her.

Adrian turned to George and said quietly, "We need to talk later."

George scowled. "She at it again?"

Adrian nodded as Kate raced back over.

"Come on, slowpokes. Let's go."

Adrian pushed Susan to the back of his mind. Kate deserved his full attention and he wouldn't let Susan spoil the day.

***

Libby stretched and grinned. She was finished! The heady elation that came with writing the final word swirled around her. She breathed deeply in satisfaction and rolled her stiff shoulders.

She checked the clock on her screen. Five o'clock. No wonder she was stiff. She'd been writing almost nonstop since she returned from her walk. Her stomach grumbled a complaint at the lack of food as she re-read the last page she'd written.

It still needed some polishing but it was good. The story was complete, with an ending to satisfy her readers, but there was a hint of what was to come in the next book.

She saved the document, backing it up to her thumb drive

and uploading a copy to her cloud share folder.

She had to find somewhere she could print out a copy and she needed to eat. Shutting down her computer, Libby stood and stretched again and then did a little jig. The hard part was done. Now she would enjoy re-reading, editing and polishing her words until they shone.

A peek out of the window showed her it was raining relentlessly, so she put on her rain jacket, checked her umbrella was in her bag and headed downstairs. In the lobby, she stopped at the reception desk to enquire about the cost of printing her manuscript. She coughed in surprise at the answer, smiled politely and decided to hit the street. There had to be an office supplies store somewhere in the CBD that would print her manuscript cheaper.

Libby walked toward the main shopping precinct, and asked someone walking by if they knew of a print shop. Within minutes she was inside one, listening to the whirr of the printer, waiting for her novel to be printed.

The saleswoman handed over the document and Libby carefully tucked it into the folder she'd brought before putting it in her bag. She thanked the woman and left, her bag significantly heavier than it had been.

Now she had to find something to eat. Her stomach grumbles had turned into roars.

She bounced down the footpath, her spirit high at her achievement, but there was no one to share it with. Checking her watch she noticed it was too early to call her best friend Piper in Houston and her other friends closer to home would still be at work. She whipped off a couple of text messages, standing under the shelter of one of the buildings so she didn't get wet.

It would be nice to talk to someone about it, share her excitement, but she'd have to wait. Now, she really did need to eat.

On her way to the print shop, she'd passed the Vietnamese restaurant she and Kate had spotted earlier in the week. Libby made her way back to it and went inside to be greeted by the hum of diners and the smells of coriander and noodles. Landscape paintings covered the walls, lush pictures of country

Vietnam. The tables were square and covered in white tablecloths, and about two-thirds of the restaurant was full. Her stomach grumbled and she put a hand to it to settle it.

"Can I help you?" the waitress asked.

"Table for one, please." It didn't bother her to dine alone. She'd use the time to study her fellow diners and make notes about their body language and quirks. Something might even give her a story idea.

"This way." The waitress weaved through the tables toward the back and Libby followed.

"Libby! Hey, Libby, over here." A voice yelled over the din somewhere to her right.

Libby scanned the restaurant to see Kate waving frantically and both George and Adrian watching her.

Adrian's gaze was direct – not quite the cheetah of pre-performance, but there was an intensity to it.

Her heart thudded hard.

It wasn't because she was glad to see Adrian. No, it was from surprise.

That was her story and she was sticking to it.

Chapter 7

Libby didn't want to interrupt but she couldn't ignore them. Changing direction, she made her way to their table and smiled at Kate. "Hi. Did you have a good day?"

"It was the best. We went to Luna Park and went on the dodgem cars and the Ferris wheel and the railway and the ghost train." Kate paused to take a breath.

"Sounds like great fun."

"It was."

The waitress came up beside Libby, obviously impatient to seat her so she could serve her other customers.

"I'd better take my seat. You can tell me all about it tomorrow."

"Who are you eating with?" Kate asked, craning her neck to see past Libby.

A flush crept unwelcome onto Libby's face. "No one. I've finished the first draft so I'm treating myself to dinner."

"You should join us."

To Libby's surprise it was Adrian who offered the invitation, not Kate. He seemed a little startled himself.

"I don't want to interrupt."

Adrian shrugged. "You can celebrate with us. We've only just ordered and it's way more than we can eat."

"Go on, Libby. You can tell me about the book." Kate

grinned.

Libby narrowed her eyes. "I'm on to you. You want to find out what happens before anyone else does." She smiled.

"Yep." Kate smiled back.

"Then I'd love to join you."

The waitress next to her sniffed and left the table. Libby ignored her and took the spare seat next to George. As she placed her bag at her feet, she bumped Adrian's knee. He jerked away.

"Sorry." She fought a battle with her embarrassment and lost. "My bag's heavy."

"Women and their bags," George said. "They have everything but the kitchen sink in them."

"In my case it's my manuscript," Libby said.

"So can I read it?" Kate leaned forward.

Libby grinned. "Nope. There's a bit more work to be done on it before it's truly finished." She paused. "Besides, it's not the next one in the series. You'd need to read the one that is at the publisher now."

"It's still worth celebrating," Adrian said.

He was right. Libby beamed at him. There were days when writing was a slog, and to finally be able to write "The End" was fantastic.

"How long has it taken to get to this point?" he asked.

"Six months." Her smile died a little. She'd have to write the next one a lot faster if she was going to meet her new deadline, but she was getting quicker. If she did the edits in a month, she'd be close to her target. If only she could afford to write full time.

The waitress arrived with drinks and Libby ordered a glass of white wine. Adrian sat back sharply. Unsure what she'd done to cause such a reaction she looked around and noticed everyone was drinking soft drinks.

Suddenly she remembered the clause in her contract. She wasn't allowed to drink alcohol when she was looking after Kate. She'd never drink while she was working so she'd not paid much attention to it. Maybe she wasn't supposed to drink around Kate at all.

Adrian let out a deep breath as if forcing himself to relax and asked, "Didn't you say you now have to write a new book every six months?"

"That's right," she said.

"That's going to be a bit of a struggle, isn't it?" George asked with a slight hint of doubt in his tone.

It was, but she didn't need him reminding her. "I don't think this manuscript will need too many edits, which means I can start the next novel early." She shrugged. "Besides, sleep is overrated, isn't it?" She winked at Kate.

Adrian chuckled. "I remember quite a lot of sleepless nights when I was trying to break through," he said. "You can't have forgotten them, George."

George groaned. "I've tried to block them out of my memory," he said and smiled Libby an apology. "I'm sure you'll manage somehow."

"How long did it take you to break through?" Libby asked Adrian, curious to know some more about this private man.

"Seven years." Adrian didn't hesitate. It was obviously something close to his heart.

"Seven long years and some real dives," George reminisced. They shared a grin.

"What do you mean by dives?" Kate asked.

"Dark, smoky and a little run-down," Adrian said.

Kate tilted her head to the side. "Why did you go to them if they weren't nice?"

Adrian paused, obviously figuring out some way to explain. "I wanted to practice performing in front of people, and when you're not well known, it's difficult to get a gig in the nicer places. I needed to let word of mouth grow so more people knew about me."

"Why didn't you use the internet?"

"That wouldn't help me learn how to perform in front of real people," Adrian said.

"How many get-ups do you think we tried?" George asked.

Adrian flashed a glance at Libby. "At least a dozen." He shifted in his seat.

What was he uncomfortable about?

The waitress arrived with four different appetizers. Libby gaped at the amount of food they put down on the table. Adrian wasn't kidding when he said they'd over ordered.

Kate waited until the waitress had gone and then picked up the little tongs next to the rice paper rolls. "Who wants a roll?"

George lifted his plate toward her. "I do."

Kate dished out the rolls and then dunked her own into the dipping sauce, taking a bite with relish. "Yum."

Conversation abated while they each tried the appetizers. Libby waited to see if the others ate using their fingers before she did. She'd been out with people who used cutlery for finger food and thought her downright uncouth for using her fingers. She didn't want to make a bad impression.

The food was delicious and Libby had to stop herself from scoffing it down, she was so hungry. Sometime during the day she'd run out of snacks and hadn't wanted to stop writing to get more.

Curious to find out about how Adrian had created Kent, she asked, "Did you always perform as Kent?"

"No." He took a bite of a little parcel of something.

Was he going to elaborate? She waited.

Adrian swallowed. He sighed. "I tried a few different looks before Kent. The crowd absolutely loved him so there was no real doubt about using him. We signed a record deal less than three months after the first performance."

"Did you sing the same kind of music the whole time?"

"Yeah, it was always rock."

Libby pressed her lips together, thinking. Did a singer's appearance really change how an audience reacted that much? Or did Adrian behave differently on stage when he was Kent? She suspected it was the latter.

"You should see some of the pictures of Uncle Ade before Kent." Kate laughed.

"I'd love to."

"Trust me, you don't want to see them," Adrian said, grimacing. He smiled a little at her, his eyes dancing, his lips turned up just a touch at the sides.

Libby's heart stuttered and she stared at him until a waitress reached in front of her to clear the table and broke her line of sight. Had anyone noticed her reaction? Kate was playing with her fork, and George was handing one of the plates to the waitress. She was safe.

What was it about Adrian that made her react this way? She took a sip of her drink to lubricate her dry mouth. She needed to change the subject. "Tomorrow's our last day in Melbourne, isn't it?"

"That's right. On to Sydney the day after," George said.

"How long does it take to pack up the stage?"

"The crew will do it straight after the show tomorrow night and it will be in Sydney by morning. They'll have a couple of days off before we have access to the center to set it up."

"We're going to climb the Sydney Harbour Bridge and go on a boat cruise and other things too, aren't we, Uncle Ade?"

"Sure will, kiddo."

It sounded like a lot of fun, but Libby reminded herself she wasn't required for the first couple of days while they were in Sydney. Besides, she had her novel to edit. Hopefully she'd get a good portion of it done before she started looking after Kate. But maybe she'd find an activity for the two of them to do. She would see what was suitable for a ten-year-old in Sydney.

The main meals came out and Kate kept chatting about all the things she wanted to do. They were going to be there for just over a week so she should have time to do most of it.

When they finished they decided against dessert and coffee and instead headed back to the hotel. Libby got her purse out but Adrian put a hand on hers to stop her getting money out. A pleasant zing went up her arm and she shivered.

"We invited you to join us. I'll pay."

There was no arguing with him so Libby put her purse away.

It had stopped raining but was dark and cold when they stepped outside the restaurant. Libby shivered, glad she had someone to walk with back to her hotel. In the lobby, Kate chattered about which game she wanted to play when they got back to the suite. She finally decided on a card game.

At their floor they went their separate ways. Libby ignored the twinge of disappointment she felt when Kate didn't invite her to join them. George had told her Adrian liked his space when he wasn't working and Libby had to respect that. She was the nanny, not part of the family.

She'd run herself a bath and read the book she'd brought

with her. Then she'd have an early night, so she could start on her edits first thing in the morning. It would be great. She hadn't had a bath in ages, as her rental shack didn't have one. She'd add some bubbles, have a long soak and pamper herself.

Libby opened the door and walked into the dark, empty hotel room.

She wasn't lonely.

She was perfectly content by herself.

She'd learned she had to be.

Chapter 8

The next night Libby knocked on the door to Kate's suite. To her surprise, instead of Kate's smiling face popping out from behind the door, it was Adrian who opened it. He gave her a small smile. "Come in."

There was something wrong.

Libby stepped into the room. In a quiet voice Adrian said, "Kate's been in a mood for the last couple of hours but she won't tell me what's wrong. Maybe you'll have better luck." Raising his voice as he moved into the room, he called, "Kate, Libby's here."

There was no response.

"She's in her room." He sighed, worry lines creasing his forehead.

"I'll talk to her," Libby said. What had happened for Kate not to be her cheerful self?

He hesitated for a moment and then said, "I haven't had a chance to pack yet, so if you could I'd appreciate it." He didn't look at her while he spoke, as if he was embarrassed. "There's a cooler in the cupboard for the food and Kate generally packs her own suitcase, but you need to gather up all the games and DVDs." He gazed at Kate's room, clearly worried.

His cell rang and he answered it. "I'll be right down."

Libby smiled what she hoped was an everything-will-be-fine

smile. "If I can cheer her up, I'll send George a text." She reached out and grasped his hand, then realized she'd overstepped the limit. Before she could let go, Adrian squeezed her hand and then dropped it.

He turned and knocked on Kate's door, stuck his head in and said a few words. Kate jumped up and gave him a hug before returning to her bed. He closed the bedroom door behind him and turned to Libby. "I hope you have more luck," he said. With one last look at the closed door, he left.

Libby let out the breath she'd been holding.

Knocking on the bedroom door, she called, "Are you all right, Kate?"

"Go away." The voice was loud despite the closed door.

"Is there anything you want to talk to me about?" Was there something Kate couldn't speak to Adrian about?

"No!"

"Would you like anything in particular for dinner?"

"No. Go away. I don't want to see you." There was a hitch to Kate's voice, part anger, part hurt.

Libby's heart fell. Was it something she had done? There wasn't anything she could think of. She paused, her hand hovering over the doorknob. No, she'd leave Kate a little longer, do the packing, and then maybe Kate would talk.

Checking the cupboard and fridge, she sorted out what they would have for dinner, a smorgasbord of leftovers, and then put all the non-perishable items in the bags Adrian had left out. She went around the room collecting the games and DVDs and stacking them on the dining room table, ready to pack. She double-checked the entire room, making sure nothing was left in drawers, under tables or underneath the couch cushions before she was satisfied she'd collected everything.

Half an hour and there hadn't been a peep out of Kate's room. Time for some action.

Libby knocked on Kate's door again before opening it a crack. Kate was lying face down on her bed, Sebastien Bear clutched under one arm. It must be bad for Sebastien to be out. "Kate, can we talk?"

"No." The word was muffled against Kate's pillow.

"I'd really like to know what I've done wrong."

That got her attention. Kate peered suspiciously out from under her armpit. "What makes you think it's you?"

"You gave your uncle a hug before he left, so it didn't seem like you were angry at him." Libby reviewed the night before. Kate hadn't invited her to play games with them and it was Adrian who'd invited her to join them at dinner. "Didn't you want me to join you at the restaurant?"

Kate clammed up and turned away.

Libby sighed. She walked over to the bed and crouched down next to it. "Kate, I can't help if I don't know what's wrong."

"You don't want to help me!" There was so much hurt in Kate's voice.

Libby flinched. "Of course I do. You're my friend, aren't you?"

Kate sat up suddenly, her face screwed up in anger. "You're not here because of me. You're just like Emily. You're here because you like Uncle Adrian."

Libby's jaw dropped open at the accusation. "That's not true."

"I saw how you looked at him at the restaurant!"

Adrian's smile. Libby hadn't thought anyone had noticed her reaction. How could she explain it to Kate?

"You're blushing! I knew it was true. You don't like me and I hate you!"

"Wait!" Libby held up a hand to stop Kate flinging herself down on the bed again. "Can we talk about this, girl to girl? I'll make us a couple of drinks and tell you the truth."

Kate squinted at her as if working out if Libby was trying to trick her.

"Please," Libby said, not sure what she would do if Kate refused to listen.

"Fine." Kate tucked Sebastien Bear under her arm and jumped off the bed, careful not to touch Libby. She stormed past and went to sit at the dining room table.

Libby took her time making the double choc, whipped cream, marshmallow delights before taking the seat next to Kate. Kate scooted her chair further away and wrapped both hands around the mug, staring down into it.

Libby sipped her drink and began. "I asked to be your nanny for a number of reasons. The very first reason was because I like you. You are a smart, funny, cheerful girl and it's a pleasure to spend time with you."

Kate pouted into her mug.

"The second reason was because I really enjoy teaching you how to write a novel. Your ideas are creative and interesting."

Kate cautiously peered up at her.

"The last reason was because it was a job that would give me time to do my own writing. The tour schedule means I can care for you and work on my novel too, which is a double bonus."

"But what about Uncle Adrian?" Kate squinted at her with suspicion.

Libby gave her a small smile. "He was probably the main reason not to take the job."

Kate's mouth dropped open. "But you like him."

She had to be careful here. "Your uncle is a very interesting man – he's smart, kind, and seems to be doing a pretty good job of looking after you."

"Emily thought he was cute."

"I think he's cute as well," Libby confessed. "My heart does tend to flutter when he smiles." She tapped her chest a couple of times and Kate's lips turned up slightly at the edges. "But that's what makes it hard. It's no fun when you think someone is cute and they don't feel the same way about you. So I try to ignore it, but obviously I'm not doing a very good job if your eagle eyes picked it up." Libby smiled. "But you know what? My first priority is you, so the rest of it doesn't matter at all."

Kate had gone back to pouting into her mug. "I liked a boy once," she said finally. "We were in the same class and I used to sit behind him so I could look at him." Her face went red.

"I did that at school too," Libby admitted.

Kate gave her a brilliant smile.

"So what happened?" Libby asked.

Kate shrugged. "He turned out to be a jerk." She pursed her lips.

"They do sometimes."

"But Uncle Adrian's not a jerk." Kate's tone dared Libby to tell her otherwise.

"No, he's not." Which made it harder.

Kate turned around in her chair to face Libby properly. "So what will you do?"

That was the question. "I'll continue to look after you, if you still want me to. Sometimes when you first meet someone and you think they're cute, that's all you see. Then, when you get to know them, you see past the cuteness and they become friends."

Kate considered it. "So you actually do like me?"

Libby heard the plea behind her nonchalant tone and the I-don't-care-if-you-don't shrug. "Absolutely. I was really looking forward to the adventures we were going to have tonight."

Kate grinned and then frowned. "I have to pack."

"I know." Libby grimaced. "We should probably do it as quickly as possible so we can get to the fun stuff. What do you think?"

Kate sighed. "All right." She stood and walked toward her room, then stopped and turned. "I'm sorry I was mad at you."

"I'm sorry you thought I didn't like you."

Kate faltered. "I don't really hate you." She looked down at her feet.

"People often say things they don't mean when they've been hurt." Libby stood and held out her hand. "Friends?"

Kate clutched her hand and shook it vigorously. "Friends." She walked back to her room.

Libby closed her eyes briefly. She had to be careful. Despite Kate's happy nature, she was fragile. Libby didn't want to do anything that might hurt the young girl.

Quickly she pulled out her phone and sent George a text so Adrian wouldn't worry: *Kate's cheered up, everything fine. Libby.*

She had to squash any feelings she had toward Adrian.

For everyone's sake.

***

Later, after Kate had gone to bed, Libby sat staring at her manuscript, not seeing any of the words in front of her. Adrian was bound to ask what had been wrong with Kate. The issue was she didn't know what to tell him.

Frustrated, she pushed the problem from her mind. She wanted to finish reviewing her novel so she could spend the next three days editing. She picked up her pen and began to work.

Some time later – it could have been minutes, it could have been an hour – and she was still staring at the same page.

Damn it.

Standing up, she put the kettle on and stretched. Perhaps she'd simply say Kate thought Libby was going to be like Emily and leave it at that. If Adrian wanted further explanation, he could go to Kate, and Libby would avoid the embarrassment of admitting that a ten-year-old could see she was attracted to him.

But would it be worse, not knowing what Kate might say to Adrian?

The kettle clicked off, signaling it had boiled and Libby poured her cup of tea. She added milk and then picked up the mug, cradling it in her hands as she leaned back against the kitchen bench. She blew softly into the tea to cool it down.

She should be honest. Kate thought Libby was only caring for her because she had a crush on Adrian. Simple and to the point. Libby didn't have to say Kate had been right.

Libby took a sip of the tea. Adrian wouldn't ask for further details – she was sure of it.

Settling back down at the table, she put her mug within reach and picked up her pen. She had work to do.

***

A couple of hours later the door of the suite opened and closed. Libby put down her pen and rose to put the kettle on. Usually Adrian went straight to the bathroom to take off Kent's make-up and then came through for a hot drink and some food. Turning to the fridge she nearly stepped into Kent. Jerking back she put a hand to her thumping chest. "Geez."

Kent stepped away. "Sorry. I didn't mean to startle you. How was Kate after I left?"

Libby took a deep breath to still her racing heart. Kent always filled the space around her and it made her uncomfortable. "We had a chat and sorted things out. She was happy when she went to bed."

He looked relieved. "What was wrong with her?"

"She was mad at me."

Kent raised an eyebrow in question.

Libby hesitated. "She thought I was like Emily, only looking after her because I fancied you." The blush crept insidiously across her face.

Kent's other eyebrow rose to match the first one – an expression that was more Adrian than Kent – and Libby hurried on. "I explained I had offered because I liked spending time with her and we sorted it out."

He stared at her for a long moment, and then his expression changed to the cocky, confident look of Kent. "You didn't say if Kate was right."

Libby's jaw dropped open. Adrian never would have asked that question. She paused for a second too long before forcing out a laugh. "Go and get rid of Kent and I'll make you a cup of tea." She turned, busying herself with the tea bag and mug, aware he was still standing there.

After what seemed like an eternity, he turned and left the room. Libby let out a quiet groan and placed her hands over her face. She'd messed that up.

She should have denied it immediately.

She was a fool.

The only thing to do was to have her things packed and leave as soon as Adrian came out of the bathroom. She had the next three days free and by the time she saw them again, Adrian would have forgotten all about it.

She hoped.

***

Adrian stared at Kent in the mirror. What the heck had possessed him to ask that question? It was utterly ridiculous, but Libby had looked so cute blushing and avoiding his eyes that he wanted to see more of it.

He was a fool. No good could come of it at all.

But could she actually like him?

He shook his head. It didn't matter. He wasn't going to do anything about it. Especially if it upset Kate. He reached for the make-up remover. It was late and Libby was bound to want to leave.

But perhaps in the morning he'd ask Kate what had made

her think Libby fancied him.

He groaned and turned on the shower. Stooping to ask his ten-year-old niece such a question was pathetic. He should forget it had happened at all. He still had to see Libby when he got out of the shower.

Ten minutes later he was refreshed and ready.

In the main room the table was set with a steaming cup of tea and a plate of leftovers. Libby stood with her bag over her shoulder, ready to leave.

What should he say? He had a ridiculous urge to ask her to stay and chat while he ate dinner. The idea of eating by himself suddenly seemed lonely.

"I've packed up everything except what's in the fridge," Libby said, bringing him out of his thoughts. "Kate is packed, and we left out what she's going to wear tomorrow. We're leaving for the airport at nine, aren't we?"

"That's right," Adrian replied, noting the bags next to the table.

Libby was already walking toward the door. "I'll see you then."

Before Adrian could ask her to stay, she was gone.

He sighed and took his seat at the table.

It really was for the best.

***

The next morning Adrian was woken by Kate's excited chatter as she bounded into his bedroom.

"Come on, sleepyhead. It's time to get up."

Adrian moaned, only half in jest, and rolled over, pulling the quilt over his head. It had taken him hours to get to sleep the night before. His head was full of Libby and the way she'd reacted to his question.

Kate laughed and jumped on the bed to shake him. "It's already 8.30 and I've had breakfast and written like a gazillion words."

That woke him up. He never slept this late. He'd forgotten to set his alarm before going to bed the night before. And he still had to pack.

"I made you breakfast." Kate smiled down at him, obviously

pleased with herself.

He sat up and picked up his T-shirt from next to the bed, pulling it on quickly. "Sounds great. Let's go." He threw back the quilt as Kate bounced off the bed and raced back into the main room.

The table was set with a huge bowl of cereal and a coffee. It reminded him of the meal Libby had left out the night before and the conversation they'd had before she left.

"Thanks, kiddo." He took his seat. "Are you ready to go?"

"Yep. Just packed up my backpack and put everything by the door."

Kate's suitcases and the cooler sat in the hallway. "You're way ahead of me." He crunched into his cereal. "Glad to see you're in a better mood today."

Kate flung herself into a chair and looked at him, clearly deciding what she should say. "Me and Libby had a chat and sorted it all out."

"So you weren't mad at me?"

"Nope."

Should he push it further? He'd like to think Kate could talk to him about anything. "Do you want to tell me about it?"

Kate pursed her lips together and then looked down at her hands. "No. It's kind of a secret."

"Really?" Why would Kate say that? Unless what Libby told him wasn't true. Or unless Kate had been right and she didn't want to spill Libby's secret.

This was ridiculous.

He finished his cereal and Kate carried the bowl to the sink to wash. Adrian stood, drinking the last of his coffee. "I'll just have a shower."

"Uncle Ade?"

There was something in her voice that made Adrian stop mid-stride and turn to his niece. "Yes?"

"Do you like Libby?" Her eyes were wide. She was trying, but not succeeding, to sound casual.

What was she up to? "Of course," he answered. "She's a very nice person and takes good care of you."

"Do you think she's cute?"

Whoa. He wasn't expecting that. His thoughts flashed back

to the night before and he smiled at the memory. Kate studied him with a grin on her face. Heck. "Ah, she's attractive, I guess." Lame, Adrian, very lame.

Kate grinned. "Okay, thanks." She turned back to the dishes.

Not so fast. "Why do you ask?"

"Oh, no reason." She shrugged. "You should get ready or else George is gonna be madder than a cut snake."

Unfortunately she was right. Making a note to grill her more at a later date, he headed to the bathroom. Kate giggled behind him.

She was up to something.

Chapter 9

The drive to the airport was uncomfortable. Libby couldn't avoid Adrian, so she just gave him a brief smile and made sure Kate sat next to him. Luckily Kate was her usual chatty self, excited about going on the plane.

After they checked in, Libby spotted a bookstore and took the opportunity to excuse herself to go and browse. She'd made a real mess of it last night. She should have denied what Kate had said immediately, giving Adrian no chance to think she might like him more than she should.

Libby rolled her shoulders and focused on the books.

All four of her novels were on the shelf and a burst of pride swept through her. She had achieved this. Her hard work and persistence had made this happen.

"Excuse me, you're Libby Myles, aren't you?" The bookseller stood next to her.

Libby blinked in surprise. She was never recognized. She smiled. "Yes."

"I recognized you from the TV show last week. Would you mind signing a few copies of your latest book? Customers love signed copies."

Libby grinned. The thrill of being asked to sign one of her books hadn't dulled, despite all the book signings she'd done. "Sure." She followed the woman across to the counter where a stack of her books waited. The woman handed her a pen and Libby started signing.

"Libby, we're going to grab a coffee."

At Adrian's voice Libby looked up. "Be right there."

The bookseller smiled at Adrian. "I'm sorry. It must be a pain for you, knowing someone famous like Libby. I couldn't let the opportunity slide when I recognized her."

Libby whipped her gaze up to Adrian, who was smiling broadly.

"It sure is, ma'am, but we deal with it the best we can."

Libby almost choked holding in the laughter. She finished signing the books and returned the pen.

"Thank you so much," the woman gushed.

"Anytime," Libby said and followed Adrian, Kate and George out of the shop.

After making sure she was far enough away for the bookseller not to hear, she burst out laughing. The absurdity of the situation tickled her funny bone and she couldn't stop. Tears formed in her eyes as she tried to control the laughter.

"What's so funny, Libby?" Kate asked.

Libby gestured for Adrian to respond. She couldn't form any words.

Adrian chuckled, obviously amused by her reaction. He repeated what the woman in the bookstore had said.

George and Kate laughed. "She sure put you in your place," George said.

"I'll have to remember I'm acquainted with a famous author now." Adrian smiled at Libby and winked.

Libby's laughter subsided as her breath caught in her throat. She had to stop reacting to Adrian this way.

"Come on, I need my caffeine," George said. He turned and headed for the nearest coffee shop. Adrian looked at Libby for a second longer than necessary and then turned and followed his friend.

Libby gave herself a moment to calm her rapidly beating heart.

She was in big trouble.

***

It was her third day in Sydney and Libby was really pleased with the work she had done. This manuscript didn't need as much rewriting as her previous one and she was already halfway through her revisions. She'd also applied for a couple more rental properties and had rung her realtor to see if he could help. He said he'd be in touch, but Libby wasn't holding her breath. Today she needed a break and was glad she had to look after Kate.

She'd not seen Kate or Adrian since they arrived at the hotel on Tuesday. They had all sorts of sightseeing plans and Kate had written her a couple of emails to tell Libby about their adventures. Libby missed spending time with them both, but she was glad of the break. Hopefully Adrian would have forgotten all about the conversation they'd had on their last night in Melbourne.

Checking the time, she gathered up her laptop and room key and headed to Kate's room.

It was still early, but Adrian had a number of radio interviews lined up. He answered the door just after she knocked, decked out in his full Kent outfit. He smiled at her slowly and her insides went wobbly. She pasted an answering smile on her face. "Good morning."

He motioned for her to enter. "Morning, ma'am."

Libby brushed past him into the suite. The room had the same layout as the one in Melbourne but was decorated in shades of blue and gray.

"Where's Kate?" Libby asked.

"She's still asleep. She stayed up late watching movies with me last night. I wanted to let her rest." Kent moved next to her, invading her space.

"Have you had a nice time in Sydney?" Libby asked, grasping for some safe, mundane topic.

"Sure have. The only thing we haven't done is climb the Harbour Bridge. I didn't want to take Kate up when it was raining, but Sunday should be fine, so we'll go up then." He glanced at her. "Have you done it?"

"Not yet." Libby had friends who'd done the climb and loved it. "I'm not great with heights."

"Could be a great way to face your fear," Kent said. "I know all about that." The smile was wide, reaching into his eyes and making them shine. Libby's heart galloped.

"Why don't you come with us on Sunday?" he said. The invitation seemed genuine, not the kind where someone felt obligated.

Libby considered it. If there was no climb involved, she would have said yes in an instant, and wasn't that the problem? He was her employer, and she shouldn't feel this way about him. She also had a book to finish, and no time for distractions. "I'll think about it," she said.

Kent grinned. His phone beeped and he checked the display. "Gotta go," he said as he lifted his bag from the table. "Think about the bridge climb. You might enjoy it." He winked. "I'll see you later."

He left and Libby was able to breathe more easily. She put her bag down next to the table and put the kettle on, then peered in at Kate, who was sleeping soundly. Until she woke, Libby would sit down and read her book. Libby had found a number of activities they could do during the day, but she would leave it up to Kate to decide.

***

Radio interviews were part of the promotional gig and Adrian didn't mind them. The co-hosts were generally friendly and asked all the same questions about touring and how much he was enjoying Australia. It was easy work as long as he went as Kent. The women always got slightly flustered when Kent winked at them, which amused Adrian. He did things as Kent he'd never dare do as himself.

He thought about Libby's reaction this morning. Kent flustered her in a way Adrian never did. It generally didn't bother him that women reacted to Kent so differently, but with Libby it did. Part of him wished he flustered her as much as Kent. It was ridiculous. Why would she be interested in a shy, introverted man when there was Kent? He shook his head. How sad – he was jealous of himself.

"We're in here." George pointed toward some glass sliding doors to his right.

Adrian snapped out of his thoughts and followed George

inside, smiling at the receptionist, who looked as if she'd paid particular attention to her appearance today. She called someone to lead them to the studio. Over the speakers the hosts were wrapping up their segment and telling listeners that Kent was coming up next. They introduced a song and the On Air sign above the studio door went dark.

"This way, Kent."

Adrian followed the woman into the studio and took the headphones he was handed.

"This is Natalie and Phil," his chaperone said.

"Howdy." Adrian shook Phil's hand. Phil smiled and said, "G'day, mate." Then Adrian turned to Natalie. She stared at him long and hard before shaking his hand.

Here was someone who was obviously not going to fall for the Kent charm. Adrian squashed down the nerves rippling in his stomach. Kent could handle anything.

The song reached its end and Adrian put his headphones on and sat down in front of the microphone.

Natalie welcomed the listeners back and then Phil introduced Kent.

"Kent, welcome to the show."

"It's a pleasure," Adrian answered.

"It's your first time in Australia – how do you like it so far?" Phil asked.

"It's been swell. The folk here are real friendly and I'm having a ball." Adrian stopped himself from rolling his eyes. He could predict the next question – it would be something about the show.

"There's been a lot of hype about your show. Why do you think that is?"

Adrian grinned. "Because it's the best damned show there is," he drawled. The interview continued, with Phil asking all the questions and Natalie looking more and more disgruntled. Adrian had no idea what was wrong with her. Finally he got his answer.

"Don't you feel any shame for encouraging children's bad behavior?" Her voice was venomous.

Adrian faltered. There were groups out there who protested against his music, mostly mothers wanting to blame their teenagers' bad behavior on his songs instead of examining what was really wrong, but he hadn't expected criticism from a radio station that played his music.

"The influence you have over these children is appalling," Natalie continued. "They worship the ground you walk on. They would kill themselves for you."

Adrian stared at her, caught off guard. Where the heck had that come from? Phil was also staring at his co-host in amazement. "I'm afraid I don't know what you mean, ma'am," Adrian said.

"Your latest song, 'To Be Hurt', is a blatant call for children to self-harm. You're saying they should harm themselves physically so they can feel love."

Adrian shook his head although none of the listeners would be able to see. "That's not what the song means, ma'am." His song, written during a period of despair, was about seeking to reconnect with the world after a childhood full of abuse. Kate had done a lot to help him in that regard. It was impossible not to love the girl.

"Are you telling me I'm wrong?" Natalie said. "That my ten-year-old nephew attempted to kill himself because he interpreted the lyrics to your song incorrectly?" Her voice rose. She leaned forward and Adrian was sure if the desk wasn't between them she would have been up in his face.

Almost killed himself? Adrian felt as if he'd been slapped. The woman had to be kidding, but her expression showed him she wasn't. Kate was ten. Kate had seen her parents die in front of her and she was coping. What would cause a child so young to attempt suicide? It couldn't have been his music, could it? The lyrics ran through his head, but he didn't see the connection. He had to find out more but this was not the place.

Phil filled the silence. "I think we've run out of time." Natalie started talking again, but her microphone had obviously been turned off, because she pressed several buttons, looking angry. "Thanks, Kent, for coming in," Phil said. "Good luck on your tour. For one lucky listener we have a double pass to the show tonight if you call now. Next is the traffic report." He pressed a button and pulled his headphones off.

Natalie sat with tears streaming down her face.

"Mate, I'm sorry," Phil said. "She's not usually like this."

George came barreling in to the room. "What the heck –"

Adrian held up a hand to stop George yelling and removed his headphones. The woman had been through a traumatic time. It wasn't going to help anyone to yell at her.

A man dressed in a suit came into the studio. "Get out," he said to Natalie. He pointed toward the door, before turning to Adrian. "I'm so sorry. I don't know what's come over her."

"Wait." Adrian stood and turned to the older man, who was obviously in charge. "Natalie is distressed. I'd like to speak with her privately."

The man seemed stunned, then nodded and turned to Phil. "You can handle the end of the show on your own." It was a statement, not a question.

"Of course." Phil checked one of the displays. "There are another couple of ads to go."

"This way." The man led them out of the studio to a small office. All of the fight had left Natalie and she followed meekly behind, tears streaming down her face.

When George went to walk into the room, Adrian stopped him. "Why don't you talk with this gentleman for a while?" George had his someone-is-going-to-pay face on and Natalie was in no state to face that. She was hurting. She stood, hugging herself as if she wished she could curl up into a ball and disappear.

George opened his mouth to disagree, then nodded and turned to the man in charge.

The office was mostly gray. Grey walls, gray corner desk with a gray computer on it, as well as a small, gray meeting table with a couple of gray chairs around it. It was depressing. Adrian indicated one of the chairs. "Why don't you sit down, ma'am?" He spotted a box of tissues and brought them over to the table.

Natalie took one and blew her nose.

Now he had the woman alone, he wasn't sure how to begin. Eventually he said, "Will you tell me what happened?"

She wiped the tears from her eyes. "Do you have any children, Kent?"

He was torn between protecting Kate and telling the truth. Finally he said, "I have a niece who is ten."

"Do you see her much?"

"As much as I can."

Natalie seemed satisfied. "Then you know what they're like at that age. So full of enthusiasm. You are his hero." She plucked another tissue. "My sister found him unconscious on his bed last week. Her little boy. He'd cut his wrist and was rushed to hospital. Your song was on repeat on his stereo." She sniffed. "No one knew anything was wrong."

He saw why she'd make the connection. But surely there had to be something else to cause the boy to harm himself. Not even when Adrian had been beaten and locked in the cellar had he considered suicide. He couldn't say that, though. "For me the song is about hurting emotionally, not physically." He paused. Maybe the boy had bigger issues and no one would listen to him. Adrian knew what that was like. "Could I talk to your nephew?"

Natalie regarded him with suspicion. "Why would you want to?"

"To explain what the song means and to find out why he interpreted it that way." Maybe the boy would tell him things he wouldn't tell his parents.

"I won't let him be part of a media circus."

Adrian swallowed his sigh. "I'd prefer to see him without anyone knowing. They'll sensationalize it." He paused. "I could see him today after sound check."

"Let me check with my sister," Natalie said.

Adrian handed her a card. "If she's happy with it, call my manager and he'll arrange the time."

There was a knock on the door and George stuck his head in. "We've got another interview to get to." He glared at Natalie.

Adrian stood. He wanted to soothe her but he didn't know how. There really wasn't anything else he could say. He could deal with the backlash her comments would create, but she had to live with the fact her nephew had tried to kill himself. "Take care," he said.

Natalie nodded and blew her nose.

He walked out of the room and stopped in front of the man in charge. "She doesn't deserve to be fired. She's suffered a near tragedy and isn't thinking clearly. Don't punish her on my account."

George opened his mouth to protest but Adrian shook his head. Instead George said, "Let's go. We're going to be late."

They left the building and jumped into the car. George was already talking a mile a minute about the statement Adrian had to make.

"I know what to say, George." Adrian saw concern and frustration on George's face. "Don't worry. It will be fine." Adrian was sure it would be. He knew what he had to say, just like he knew the Mothers Against Rock would use this incident for their own gain, to protest against rock singers or to bring child suicide to the public's awareness. He couldn't control any of that, but he could make sure his position was known.

"I've given Natalie your card and asked her to call you if the boy's mother is happy for me to visit him."

George considered him. "Why? The media's going to have a field day. You don't want to get further involved."

"What if the attempt was a cry for help?" Adrian asked. "What if this boy has parents like mine? What if no one else sees what's going on?"

George nodded once. "I'll arrange it."

Adrian breathed out a sigh of relief. It was one thing he appreciated about George. He understood where Adrian had come from.

They pulled up in front of the next radio station to discover reporters and cameras already out in front. Damn, they were quick. He was used to this type of publicity, but he needed to shield Kate from it.

"Kent will give a statement after we've finished our interviews," George said, holding up a hand to ward them off. "If you'll excuse us, we're a little late as it is."

They were ushered into the station and into the studio, where the hosts were doing everything but rubbing their hands in glee to have the first interview.

Adrian rehearsed in his mind what he wanted to say. He needed to stay focused and be honest and hope the honesty and concern came through in his voice. Greeting the hosts, he put on the headphones he was handed and sat down.

It was going to be a long day.

***

After Kate had eaten and dressed they planned their day. First stop was to a science museum that was close to where Adrian was performing.

"Let's surprise Uncle Ade for lunch," Kate said. "We could take him a picnic. He'll be doing sound checks and stuff there."

Libby considered it. Adrian didn't want to be associated with Kate when he was in his Kent gear because he was worried she might be a target for his fans. Still, they would be inside the building and all the roadies knew who she was.

"Come on, it will be fun." Kate had hope in her eyes.

"Let me call George and see what he has to say. If things aren't going smoothly, they won't be breaking for lunch yet."

Kate grinned as Libby plugged George's number into her phone.

"What's wrong with Kate?" George's voice bordered on aggressive. He must have caller ID on his phone.

"Nothing's wrong." Libby rolled her eyes at Kate, who giggled. "We're close by and Kate wants to surprise Adrian with lunch. I thought I'd check if it was all right before we came."

"We've got lunch catered," George said.

Libby refused to get riled. "If you're too busy, you just need to say so, George. Kate and I have plenty to do to keep us occupied."

He sighed. "Seeing Kate might help Adrian. One of the interviews didn't go so well today. Go to the back entrance. I'll tell someone you're coming." He hung up before Libby could ask for more detail.

Libby smiled at Kate. "He said yes."

"Yay!" Kate looked around. "Where do you think we can get a picnic?"

"George said they had lunch catered, so we don't need to bring anything."

Kate pouted.

"But perhaps we can buy Adrian a chocolate bar for dessert." Libby pointed to the little deli nearby.

"Good idea."

They wandered over to the shop and Kate took her time

exclaiming over the different kinds of chocolate before choosing one for Adrian and one for George.

At the back door of the entertainment complex, a staff member and a roadie were waiting for them. The roadie greeted Kate while the staff member checked Libby's ID. When the staff member said they could enter, the roadie led them to Kent's dressing-room. "George said to wait in here. We're almost finished on stage."

The dressing-room was of a similar standard to the one in Melbourne: lots of mirrors, a couple of couches and stark white walls. Kate ran over to one of the couches and bounced down on it. "This is going to be fun."

Libby smiled at her but she was concerned about George's comment. What had happened in the radio interview today?

They waited for ten minutes before Adrian walked in wearing his Kent gear.

"Surprise!" Kate yelled, bouncing off the couch.

Adrian jumped back as if startled, but Libby could tell he'd been forewarned they were there.

"Geez, Kate, you scared the life out of me!"

Kate giggled. "No, I didn't. George told you we were here, didn't he?"

"Yep." He held his arms wide and Kate ran into them. He picked her up and swung her around. "It's good to see you, kiddo." Adrian closed his eyes for a second, squeezing Kate tightly. Libby could see the comfort he took from Kate's presence – he'd clearly had a rough morning.

Adrian opened his eyes and gazed at Libby for a moment, as if he was waiting for something, then put Kate back on the ground.

"I'm starved, Uncle Ade. Can we have lunch now?"

"Starved, eh?" He winked at Libby. "I'll have to have words to your nanny. We can't have you starving." His tone was stern and Kate looked alarmed.

"I was just kidding."

Adrian broke into a smile. "Gotcha."

Kate slapped him playfully on the arm. "That wasn't nice. Come on, let's go."

Libby followed them out of the room.

The food was set up in the area behind the stage. The roadies had already helped themselves to plates of food and were sitting on any available surface. George was talking to someone, gesticulating to make his point.

Kate waved at a couple of the men but didn't leave Adrian's side. At the buffet she took a plate and piled it full of food. She peeked over her shoulder at Libby. "Make sure Libby gets a plate, Kent."

Kent turned and guided Libby in front of him, handing her a plate. "After you, ma'am."

She had to learn to speak with her employer without blushing. "Thank you." She took the plate and perused the offerings, choosing a few things that looked interesting. When she was finished, she looked for a place to sit.

Kate was chatting to a group of roadies who were finishing their lunch. She spotted Libby and then leaned closer to one of the men and said something. He grinned and elbowed the man next to him. They both stood.

"Libby, Kent, you can sit over here," Kate called.

Libby saw Kent was as bemused as she was, but they both walked over to Kate. One of the roadies who'd stood directed Libby to sit. "Take my seat, ma'am."

Kate was still standing, balancing her plate with some difficulty as she tried to eat from it.

"Kate, why don't you have a seat?" Libby offered.

"No, no. I'm fine," Kate said in a hurry. She made sideways gestures with her head to one of the other men.

"Have my seat, Kate," he said and got to his feet.

Kate sat, leaving the two empty spaces next to each other for Kent and Libby.

Libby sat, not looking at Kent. Kent stayed standing.

"You should sit, boss. You've been on your feet all day." The roadie who had stood for Libby motioned for Kent to sit and winked at Kate.

"Yeah, Kent. You need to rest your legs for tonight," Kate added.

What was she up to?

Kent gave his niece a look that asked the same thing and sat next to Libby, the space so small his leg brushed against hers.

Her leg trembled and she shifted slightly but couldn't get further away from him. She concentrated on her food.

"What have you been up to this morning, Kate?" Kent asked, leaning out to look across Libby to where Kate sat.

"You tell him, Libby," Kate said and stuffed her mouth full of potato salad, making a big fuss about not being able to talk.

It was odd. Only a few days ago Kate had been worried Libby was there because she fancied Adrian and now she was pushing them together.

The penny clanked in Libby's head as it dropped.

Kate was trying to get them together. Why the sudden change? Had she spoken with Adrian and found out something?

Adrian was waiting for her to comment. "We've been to the science museum and did some experiments."

"Sounds like fun. You didn't blow anything up, did you?"

Kate shoved some pasta in her mouth and indicated Libby should respond.

Libby couldn't help but chuckle. "Nothing we weren't supposed to."

"And what are your plans for this afternoon?" he asked Libby, obviously giving up on getting an answer from Kate.

"Kate wants to do some more writing." He was too close but she couldn't move away. His shoulder brushed hers and she struggled to focus on what she was saying. "We're going to find somewhere overlooking the harbor to write if the weather stays nice."

"Sounds like fun." His tone said he meant it. How many other people would think spending a day writing would be fun? Not many who weren't writers themselves.

"How's the rehearsal going?" Libby asked. God, their conversation was so mundane.

"Really good. The venue is well organized and the acoustics are good."

Libby finished her food and rested the plate on her knees.

"Let me take that," Kate said, jumping up and taking the plate from Libby.

"Thanks."

"Do you want some dessert? Chocolate cake?" She took Kent's plate as well.

"That'd be great. I'll help you," Libby said.

"No, no. You both stay there and I'll get it. Frank will help me." The roadie next to her got to his feet.

Libby had to smile. Kate had the men wrapped around her little finger.

The other men quickly got to their feet as well. "Dessert sounds great," one of them said and they all left, leaving Kent and Libby alone.

Adrian laughed. "Do you get the feeling we're being set up?"

"Kate seems to have had a change in attitude."

"Mmm," Adrian agreed. "I wonder why."

Libby had to change the subject. "George mentioned you had a bad interview this morning."

The change in Adrian was instant. It was as though a shield went up. His eyes were guarded and his body tensed. She wished she hadn't said anything. "Sorry, I shouldn't have asked." She placed a hand on his thigh without thinking, and though he hesitated, he took hold of it.

The shield went down and some of the tension left him. "I need to talk to you about it. It's to do with Kate."

Concern filled Libby. "Did the interviewers know about her?"

"No." Adrian took a deep breath and let it out in a whoosh. "One of the interviewers thought my latest song was encouraging children to self-harm."

Libby gaped at him. "To Be Hurt?" she asked.

He nodded.

"But it's not. It's about yearning for love."

Adrian met her gaze and she saw all the way into his soul. He squeezed her hand. "Yes, it is."

Libby tried to focus on the conversation. "Then why?"

"The interviewer's nephew almost died last week because he cut himself. My song was on his stereo. He was ten." There was real pain in Adrian's voice. "No one had known anything was wrong."

Libby immediately thought of Kate. What kind of trauma had this boy experienced that would make him want to die? And if he could do it, what about Kate? She'd seen horrific things no one should have to see. Was she at risk? "You should talk with

Kate," she said.

"That's what I was thinking." Adrian hesitated. "Maybe we should do it together. She listens to what you say and it might have more impact if we both talked to her."

"Of course." It meant a lot that he would ask her to help him. "Will you have time before tonight's concert?"

"I'll make time." He checked his watch. "If you can be back at the hotel at three."

"Absolutely." She patted his hand. "I'm sure she's fine."

"But I have to check."

"Kent! You ready to get started?" George called out from the stage.

"Geo-rge, don't interrupt!" Kate complained and Libby realized everyone was watching them and they were still holding hands.

Adrian jumped to his feet, letting go as he did so. "Sure am." He turned back to Libby and gave her a genuine smile. "We'll talk later." The Kent swagger as he walked away was so different from Adrian's walk – he really did seem like another person altogether.

Libby stood and moved over to Kate, near the buffet. "What happened to my chocolate cake?" she asked.

Kate scanned the area. "Um …"

Libby laughed. "Never mind. Go say goodbye to your uncle and give him his chocolate bar and then we'll go."

"Don't you want to come say goodbye too?" Kate asked, her eyes wide.

"Already have," Libby answered.

Scowling, Kate went and said her goodbyes.

Chapter 10

After leaving the entertainment complex, Libby and Kate decided it was too cold to go down to the harbor and instead headed back to the hotel room to do their writing. They had stopped to make a hot chocolate when Adrian returned. Libby put out another mug and prepared the drinks while Adrian cleaned up.

He came out with damp hair, wearing low-slung blue jeans and a red T-shirt. Libby ignored the double thud of her heart as he smiled at her, took the mug of hot chocolate she offered and went to sit on the sofa next to Kate, who was curled up tapping on her laptop.

"Can I interrupt you for a minute, kiddo?" he asked.

Kate didn't answer.

"Libby and I want to talk to you about something."

That got her attention. Kate's head whipped up and she looked at her uncle, then Libby, and grinned. "Sure." She put her laptop on the coffee table and picked up her mug.

Oh, Kate had the wrong idea. Hoping she wouldn't be too disappointed, Libby sat on the sofa on the other side of Kate.

Adrian glanced at Libby and then looked back at his niece and sighed. "We need to talk about something serious." His tone was gentle.

The smile fled Kate's face. "What's happened? Has Aunt

Susan died?"

"No. Oh no, honey, no one's died," Libby said quickly.

Adrian took Kate's hand. "Something came up during one of my interviews today. There's been a lot of media attention and there'll probably be a bit more before it goes away. You need to be prepared for reporters outside the hotel."

"But they don't know who I am." Kate looked from one to the other.

"No, but they may want to ask children about my music."

"Why?" She had that wary look children get when they know they aren't being told the full story.

Adrian glanced at Libby for reassurance. She smiled and nodded.

"There was a boy your age who tried to kill himself," Adrian began.

Kate frowned. "Why would he do that?"

"Some people are saying one of my songs encouraged him to do it."

"But that's silly." Kate looked at Libby for confirmation, then back at her uncle. "Your songs are loud, but they don't say anything about killing."

Adrian grinned at Kate's review of his music. "Remember how we talked about how people interpret others' actions in different ways?"

"Like when Aunt Susan said you didn't care about Mama and Dad dying because you didn't cry at the funeral?"

Libby was shocked. What a thing for anyone to say, let alone in front of a child. Everyone grieved in different ways.

"Exactly like that," Adrian said. He paused. "People can interpret song words differently as well. Some people think my song is about physically hurting yourself. They think the boy listened to the words of the song and then tried to hurt himself."

Kate scoffed. "Well, aren't they dumb as dirt?"

"That's not a nice thing to say, Kate," Libby admonished. "People have different experiences and it makes them see the world in different ways."

"I didn't mean the boy, I meant the people who thought it. No one would kill themselves because of a song. He must have had other problems."

She was so matter-of-fact. Libby didn't think she'd had that level of maturity at Kate's age, but then again she hadn't been orphaned.

"What kind of issues do you think he might have had?" Adrian asked.

Kate shrugged. "Maybe he was bullied at school. Or maybe his mama and dad hit him." She clasped Adrian's hand. "Not everyone has a great family."

Adrian's face clouded briefly. "You're right, kiddo." There was something about the way he said it that made Libby think his family hadn't been loving. He'd avoided talking about them when she'd asked about Kate's parents' death.

"Have you ever been bullied?" Libby asked Kate.

"Nah. People make fun of my hair sometimes, but that's just 'cause they're jealous." She said it with such confidence.

"You know you can talk to me about anything?" Adrian said tentatively. "If you're sad and life doesn't seem fun anymore."

"Huh?" She stared at him as if he levitated where he sat.

"Sometimes when people have sad things happen in their lives, they don't want to go on," Libby said. She hoped she was saying the right thing and not putting ideas into the girl's head.

"Like Mama and Dad dying?"

"Yes," Libby said.

Kate's face clouded. "I still get real sad thinking about it, but I know they'd want me to be happy."

"Would you tell me if you ever changed your mind?" Adrian asked. "I spoke to the boy this afternoon and he said he didn't feel like he could talk to his parents about what was happening at school."

Kate leaned over to put down her mug. "You're worried I might kill myself?" Her tone was incredulous and slightly offended.

"No, I —" He glanced at Libby for help.

"The parents of the boy who tried to kill himself had no idea he was sad," Libby explained.

"Uncle Ade, really," Kate said, patting him on the arm. "I miss Mama and Dad so much, but I don't want to join them in heaven. There's lots of stuff I want to do with my life, like write my book."

"I was worried," Adrian said.

"I know. I love you." Kate hugged him tightly.

"I love you too, Katie."

Libby ached for a hug like that, so full of love and acceptance. Hugs from her parents had been perfunctory at best.

Her eyes welled with tears as Kate pulled away.

"You don't need to worry," the girl told her uncle. "You're stuck with me forever. Someone has to take care of you."

"I'm so glad," Adrian said, holding her tightly next to him.

Libby stood up. She should go. This was their time together and she'd be back in a couple of hours when Adrian had to go to work. "I'll leave you two and come back in time to make dinner."

"Stay." Adrian and Kate spoke simultaneously and then grinned at each other and said, "Jinx!"

Adrian turned to Libby and was more hesitant. "That is, if you don't have any work of your own." His gaze was sincere.

"She doesn't. She's already halfway through her edits," Kate said. "You could play a game with us. Uncle Ade said we could play the dancing game today." She jumped up and snatched the computer game cover. "There are lots of songs to choose from."

Libby debated it, torn between wanting to stay and not wanting to make a complete fool of herself dancing. Adrian also looked uncertain.

"It's fun if you don't take it seriously," he said.

"Yeah, I always beat Uncle Ade. I need some better competition." Kate grinned at them both.

Libby laughed. "I feel like a lamb being led to the slaughter. All right, I'll stay."

"Awesome. I'll set up."

Libby helped Adrian move the coffee table and the couch out of the way to make a bigger dance floor, then Adrian fetched a bag of chips out of the cupboard and poured them into a bowl.

"Chips, dancing and beautiful company. I think we're set for the afternoon," he said.

A warm glow filled Libby. It was going to be a fantastic afternoon.

***

"It's ready! Who's first?" Kate asked, standing up and holding the two controllers.

"I think you'd better show me how it's done," Libby said as she took a handful of chips and sat back on the couch.

Adrian took the controller from his niece as she flicked through the songs. He suddenly remembered how uncoordinated he was at this game, particularly when they first began.

He tightened the strap of the controller around his wrist. He really should have steered her toward playing something else, but he'd wanted to see Libby dance. He hadn't thought about the fact that he would have to dance as well.

Forcing a smile on his face, he saw a relatively easy song come up on the television screen. "How about that one?"

"That's easy, Uncle Ade," Kate complained.

He grinned. "Consider it a warm-up." He took his position next to Kate, fully aware of Libby's presence behind him. This was such a bad idea.

He didn't dance. As a rock star, the most he had to do was strut around the stage or play his guitar. He was comfortable with that.

This, on the other hand, required his hands and feet to do different things at the same time.

The music started and he had no more time to ponder why he was doing this. He had to dance.

He tapped his hand to the beat and stared at the screen waiting for the little figure in the corner to tell him what dance move was coming up. Then it was on.

His hands and feet refused to work together from the start and he was already half a beat behind.

Beside him Kate giggled.

"Watch it, kiddo or I'll make you play SingStar," he growled. Adrian paused and then started again, this time in time to the music. His face was hot with embarrassment. Somehow he made it through to the end of the song and then breathed out a sigh of relief it was over. Kate had thoroughly beaten him. He took the strap off his hand and reluctantly turned to face Libby.

She had taken off her shoes and was sitting cross-legged on the couch. Though her lips were turned up with only a hint of a smile, her eyes were laughing.

He raised an eyebrow. "It's your turn next." He handed her the controller.

Libby took it and rose from the couch as she tightened the strap.

"Let's do this song," Kate said, choosing an upbeat pop song from one of the latest boy bands.

Adrian sat on the couch as they took their positions in front of the television. Libby stood directly in front of him and he used the opportunity to admire her figure-hugging jeans.

The song began and Adrian's jaw dropped. Libby was worse than he was. He covered his mouth with his hand to stop himself from laughing as her feet went one way and her arms went the other.

Libby groaned. "Oh my God, this is harder than it looks!" She giggled as she tried to keep up with the movements on the screen.

Adrian grinned as her arms flailed and her feet crossed – and then, with a shriek, she tripped and landed hard on her butt.

Adrian jumped to his feet as her laughter rang out. Kate checked Libby was fine, shook her head and continued to dance. He held out his hand to help Libby up and she reached for it before dissolving into giggles again. The laughter he'd been holding in burst out.

Libby widened her eyes in mock outrage, her laughter coming in gasps.

She was so indignant and completely adorable. Chuckling, Adrian held out his hand again and she took it. He took a firm hold and hauled her to her feet. She collapsed against him and his arms came around her, holding her tightly. His laughter died as he inhaled her honeysuckle scent and felt her warm, soft skin pressing into his chest.

"I'm sorry, I've got no coordination today." Libby smiled up at him and met his gaze. Her lips parted and she seemed to realize she was pressed against him. She took a step back as

Kate finished the song.

"I think you might have won that one, Kate," Libby said.

Kate looked over and grinned. "You two finished laughing yet? It wasn't that funny."

"You didn't see Libby dance," Adrian commented and earned a glare and playful swipe from Libby. His heart was still beating hard after having her so close to him. He grinned back at her and then held his hand out to Kate. "Pass me the controller. I think I might finally win one." He laughed.

***

The lights went out and Adrian strode off stage, the screams thundering in his ears. Tonight had been one of his best performances ever and he was on a high. He high-fived Frank as he walked by and called out thanks to the other guys, who were already preparing for the next show.

What a night. Everything had clicked and the crowd had been wild. This was why he wanted to sing. This was why he'd spent years trying to break out. The buzz was incredible and singing brought him such joy and freedom.

He caught up with George outside his dressing-room and together they made their way toward the back entrance.

"Hell of a show," George commented.

"Sure was." Adrian bounced up and down, releasing some of the energy flooding his body.

Outside the venue the cool air hit him like a refreshing wave. There were fans already there, screaming his name. Adrian waved and ducked inside the car waiting for him. He didn't want to chat tonight. The concert had been so great he wanted to get back to the hotel and tell Libby all about it.

Libby.

He paused.

How had she entered his thoughts, become part of his life, with barely a ripple?

Their afternoon together had been so much fun. He'd actually won a couple of dances until Libby got the hang of the game and started beating him. He hadn't laughed so much in a long time.

He shouldn't be thinking about her like this. No good could

come of it.

"What's bothering you?" George's voice brought him back to the present.

They had been friends for almost twenty years and George knew him better than anyone else alive. "Libby."

George looked at him briefly, then back at the road. "Didn't you say your conversation with Kate went well?"

"Yeah. Libby was a real help."

"Then what's the problem?"

Adrian hesitated. "I'm looking forward to seeing her tonight."

George was silent a moment. "We're only here another couple of weeks."

"I know."

"You should do what I do," George said. "Make sure she knows it's a temporary thing. Just for while we're in Australia – that way there're no expectations. It's been a while since you've had some fun."

Adrian pondered it while the car pulled into the hotel drive. Would Libby do casual? Her face floated before him and he reached for the door handle.

And what about Kate? Would she be hurt when they went home?

He really didn't know.

But he wanted this for himself. Surely he could find a way to make it work.

Kate was old enough to understand about relationships. But she was fragile as well. He'd have to be careful. He sighed.

Libby might not even be interested and he didn't want to make her feel uncomfortable. If she quit, Kate would be devastated.

He'd have to think about it some more.

There was too much at stake.

***

Libby checked the clock for what had to be the tenth time. She'd given up telling herself it was because she was tired and wanted to go to sleep. The truth was she was looking forward to Adrian returning. Finally the clock showed her what she wanted to see. Adrian would be home soon. She put the kettle on.

It had been a fun afternoon with Kate and Adrian. It reminded her of the afternoons when she'd escaped to her best friend Piper's place and played games with Piper's family. There had been a lot of teasing and laughter then as well. Then Piper had returned to the US and Libby had to face high school alone. Books had become her companion.

This afternoon when Adrian had reluctantly left, she and Kate had cooked dinner and watched a movie.

Now Kate was tucked up in bed asleep and Libby was flitting about the suite in anticipation of her *employer* getting home. She had to get a grip on herself.

In a couple of weeks the tour would end and Adrian and Kate would go back to America. Nothing was going to happen.

The kettle boiled as the door to the suite opened. After it closed, the sound of running water came through as Adrian washed off Kent. Libby poured him a decaffeinated coffee and took the mug over to the coffee table.

It suddenly struck her that she was waiting on Adrian, preparing him food like a good little woman.

Her mood deflated with a hiss.

They weren't in a relationship and she wasn't his wife. Besides, the one time she'd attempted to play the good woman with Clint, he'd ended up going home early with a headache.

This wasn't entirely the same. Preparing Adrian a drink was a nice thing to do and could be considered part of her nanny duties.

Her excuses didn't sound convincing, even to her ears. She sighed. She would leave as soon as Adrian had showered.

***

Ten minutes later Adrian walked into the room, all traces of Kent gone. His smile was genuine, as if he was happy to see her.

"How was your night?" she asked, holding on to the back of one of the dining chairs.

"The crowd was amazing." His tone was one of awe. "They knew the words to all my songs and the noise was incredible."

"It must be fabulous to know you've had an influence on so many people." She should be making a move, not making conversation.

He nodded and then sobered. She knew he was thinking about the attempted suicide. "I made you a drink," she said, gesturing to the dining table, and then, embarrassed by her need to be thanked, she turned to pack up her bag.

"Why don't you join me?" He picked up the book she'd been reading and brought it over to her. "I wanted to thank you for talking to Kate with me today." He held out the book and she took it, shoving it into her bag.

"It's fine. I'm glad she's okay." *Fine. Okay.* Great use of adjectives, Libby. Really creative. He got her so flustered, being so close. She turned to put some distance between them but stopped as he took her hand.

Heat rushed up her arms.

Adrian drew her closer to him.

Her heart slowed and beat heavily in her chest.

"You've helped me a lot in these few short days." He took her other hand so she was facing him directly.

What was he doing? She had to stop this.

"You saved my reputation on the talk show, you've become Kate's nanny at short notice and you helped me broach a difficult subject with her today." His voice was soft and he pulled her ever so slightly closer to him. Libby stared at him like a kangaroo caught in a car's headlights.

He brought his hand up and brushed her cheek. "Thank you."

Libby couldn't answer. Every coherent thought in her head vanished with the sweep of his hand over her cheek. She had to say something, even if it was just a murmur in acknowledgement. She parted her lips to respond and suddenly his mouth was on hers.

His lips were warm and gentle and stole her breath away with their tenderness. Heat curled in her belly and moved outward, suffusing her with longing as she wrapped her arms around Adrian's neck and drew him closer. He groaned, deepening the kiss, taking her further until her whole body felt on fire.

All her doubts and fears vanished in the moment. She couldn't think. Every nerve in her body was concentrated on the sensation as his hands slid around her body, cupping her bottom and pulling her closer still.

She held on, meeting his tongue with hers, pouring her passion into the kiss.

"Uncle Ade?" Kate's voice calling from the bedroom stopped Libby cold, as if someone had thrown a bucket of ice water over her. They sprang apart and turned to the door.

Kate wasn't there but her voice came again. "Uncle Ade, are you home?"

Adrian cleared his throat and stepped further away from Libby, not looking at her. "Sure am, kiddo. I'll be right there."

Libby blinked. What had she been thinking? She'd kissed her boss. She had to get out of there. Gathering up the rest of her things, she avoided Adrian's gaze. "I should go."

Adrian nodded, but didn't say anything. He followed her to the entrance, and when she opened the door, he put his hand over hers.

"Libby, I –" He stopped, his eyes full of confusion, and she waited for him to continue.

"Uncle Ade," Kate called.

He glanced toward Kate's door. "I've got to go."

Libby pulled her hand out from under his. "I'll see you tomorrow." She tried to smile but it felt as though her face was cracking. He regretted what had happened, that much was certain.

Hurrying down the corridor, she didn't look back.

Safe in her own room, she sank down on the bed and put her fingers to her mouth. Her lips were warm and swollen from his kisses. He had instigated the kiss but she hadn't held back.

She'd never felt such a rush of tenderness before. It had flowed through her whole body until she felt she must be glowing and then it had ramped up to sparking.

If Kate hadn't been there …

Libby refused to think of what might have happened.

How was she going to face him tomorrow?

Chapter 11

Adrian hurried to Kate's room, refusing to think about what he had just done. "What's up, kiddo?"

"What took you so long?" She was lying curled up on her side.

"I, ah, was walking Libby to the door."

The light from the living room shone into the room and Kate grinned. "Did you kiss her goodnight?"

Adrian took a step back. He checked over his shoulder to see if Kate could have seen them from her bed. No, he didn't think so. He turned back as Kate grinned triumphantly.

"You did! You did kiss her!" She sat up straight in bed and hugged her knees. "I knew you liked her as much as she likes you."

He started to deny it but then realized what Kate had said. "Libby said she likes me?"

Kate clapped her hand over her mouth.

He sat on the edge of the bed. "Spill it, Kate."

Kate played with a loose thread on her bedspread before she looked up. "The other day when I was mad, it was because I thought Libby was only looking after me because she liked you. We had a talk and she said the reason she almost refused the job was because she thought you were cute." Her eyes were earnest. "'Cause you know it's not nice when you like someone and they don't like you back."

"That's right," Adrian agreed. He didn't know if it was Kent Libby liked or Adrian. Though he'd been himself when he kissed her, so maybe he had a chance. "Is that something you know about?" he asked to turn the conversation back to Kate.

She shrugged. "There was a boy once, but he turned out to be a jerk." She squinted at him. "So are you going to kiss her again?"

Damn, she was tenacious. "That's none of your business," he said. "You need to go back to sleep."

"But if you kiss her again and fall in love, then you'll get married and Libby will be my aunt and she can help me finish my book and live with us forever."

Adrian's chest tightened like he'd slammed on the brakes in his car and been thrown hard against his seatbelt. "Hold on, kiddo. There's a whole long way between kissing someone and getting married."

"But you like each other. And you both like playing board games and cards. And hot chocolate." She was looking at him so hopefully.

This was worse than he'd suspected. Kate had attached herself to Libby and it was going to break her heart when they had to leave in a few weeks' time. "Libby lives in Australia, sweetheart. When we leave, she's going to stay here. I don't want you to get your hopes up. A month isn't long enough for two people to fall in love."

"But Mama and Dad did."

They had. It had been love at first sight for his brother and sister-in-law, but perhaps somehow they'd known they wouldn't have long in this life. "That doesn't happen very often. What your parents had was special."

Kate scowled.

"You need to go back to sleep," he repeated. "It's late." Waiting until Kate snuggled back under the covers, he tucked her in and kissed her forehead. "See you in the morning."

"Good night, Uncle Ade."

He knew from her expression she hadn't given up hope. What the heck was he going to do now?

His mind flew back to the kiss. He didn't know what had

possessed him. He'd been planning to thank Libby for being with him while he spoke to Kate about the boy. It was so comforting to have someone to support him and make sure he didn't go wrong. But then she'd got so flustered and he'd never had anyone get flustered around him – around Kent, yes, but not when he was himself. It was just so appealing, he'd wanted to see what would happen if he'd stepped closer. Then she'd parted her lips slightly and he'd reacted before he considered the consequences.

He refused to dwell on how soft Libby's lips were and how she'd reacted. How for that moment, everything seemed right. If it hadn't been for Kate calling out, he wasn't sure where it would have ended.

And that in itself was a problem. He couldn't allow his hormones to run wild when his niece was in the next room.

Tomorrow when he got back from the concert and Kate was safely asleep, he'd tell Libby it had been a mistake.

He rubbed his chest at the stab of disappointment.

He had to put Kate's welfare before anything else. Could he convince Kate there was nothing between him and Libby? Maybe if they kept their – interactions – to when Kate was asleep, she would never know about it.

He was being ridiculous. The best thing for all concerned was to pretend nothing had happened.

The coffee Libby had made him was still sitting on the table. He picked it up and tipped it down the sink.

He'd lost his desire for it.

***

After the concert the next night, Adrian and George rode in the elevator up to their floor. Adrian couldn't wait to tell Libby about his night. They'd sit down and chat while he drank his coffee.

"What are you so cheerful about?" George asked, breaking through his thoughts.

Adrian turned to his friend and then froze. Déjà vu. Heck. He'd been looking forward to seeing Libby.

"It's Libby, isn't it?" George asked.

The elevator dinged and they got out.

"I don't think I've ever seen you so happy and relaxed," George commented.

That was a surprise. Was George encouraging him?

Adrian shook his head. "It would never work. She's my employee. I said I'd never get involved with one of Kate's nannies."

"As much as I agree with you, I have to say I've never seen you this comfortable around someone you barely know."

"It's no good. Kate's already too attached to Libby and it's going to break her heart when we have to leave Australia." He had to think about this rationally and not let his feelings get in the way.

"Kate's going to miss Libby no matter what your relationship with Libby."

George was right, but there was more to it. "Kate is hoping Libby will become her aunt," Adrian told him.

George raised an eyebrow. "Have you set her straight?"

"Tried to. I'm not sure she listened."

George hummed. "Do you want me to have a word to her, see if she'll listen to me?"

It couldn't hurt. Kate needed to realize Libby was staying behind when they left Australia. "That'd be great." It still didn't mean he was going to take things further with Libby.

"Kate's old enough to understand and you deserve to have a little bit of fun."

Adrian had never been tempted by any of the other nannies. What would Susan say if she found out? "Susan would have a field day."

"What goes on tour, stays on tour," George answered. "Do something for yourself for a change." He grinned at Adrian. "I'm going to bed. 'Night." He walked off in the other direction.

Adrian turned to head to his suite. Was George right? Should he allow himself to explore what he felt for Libby? Assuming she was interested. Maybe Libby regretted what had happened.

He entered the suite and went straight into the bathroom to clean off Kent. He'd left some clothes in there earlier, so he showered and washed off the sweat of the concert.

As he dressed he realized he was stalling. He was nervous

about facing Libby again. It had been fine earlier in the day, before he'd left for the concert, because then Kate had been there as a buffer, but now it would be just the two of them.

Annoyed at himself, he finished dressing and left the bathroom before he thought any further about it.

Libby had her back to him and was fussing with something in her bag. She was wearing fitted blue jeans, a red woolen sweater and sensible sneakers. Her straight brown hair was tied back in a plait. He'd not seen any evidence of the skin-tight, skinny-leg jeans and high heels since that night in Melbourne.

"Good evening, ma'am," he said and enjoyed the way she gave a little start before turning to face him.

Her smile didn't quite reach her eyes and her hands knotted together. Was it perverse that he got such pleasure from knowing she was nervous around him?

"How was the concert?"

"Real good." He couldn't explain it to someone who hadn't experienced it – the atmosphere as he stood on stage and had thousands of people screaming his name. They hung on his every word, they were there to see him, and for that single moment in time they were in the palm of his hand. He was the driver – he took them where he wanted to go. He was in control.

"Did you and Kate have a nice night?" He sat at the table and took a sip of the coffee.

"Yes. She wanted to write, so we did." Libby was still standing, and glanced between him and the door. "I should go."

He couldn't let her leave without clearing the air. "Libby, wait. Sit down." He pulled out the chair next to him and turned so he was facing her.

She hung back.

"We need to talk about last night."

"Okay." She sat. Their knees touched and Libby twitched. Desire curled in his belly. She was adorable, but he had to focus. "I don't get involved with Kate's nannies," he blurted and then cursed his bluntness.

Her shoulders slumped slightly, but she nodded. "It's not good for Kate."

No, it wasn't, but, darn it, he wanted this – he wanted her.

Libby's body language suggested she wanted him as well. There had to be some way they could make it work. "Last night was the first time I've broken the rule." He paused and then took the risk. "I want to break it again."

Libby's eyes widened and he had to stop himself from kissing her right then. He took hold of her hand and rubbed his thumb over the back of it. "I'm not good with strangers." She didn't need to know why. "I enjoy spending time with you and I want to spend more time together." He paused. "But if you don't feel the same way, tell me and I'll leave you alone." He waited for her answer.

Libby was quiet for a moment. "I like spending time with you as well." She smiled. "But what about Kate?"

The question made Adrian like her even more. "We're only here for a couple more weeks. She knows nothing serious can come from this." He glanced at her. "At the end of the tour, you'll stay in Australia and we'll go home." It would be a casual relationship, a holiday romance.

Libby faltered and then nodded, maybe a little too quickly. "Of course."

They didn't know each other well enough for anything else, so why was he disappointed? Had he hoped she'd disagree with him?

Adrian tugged Libby closer, keeping his eyes on hers. "The choice is yours."

Indecision crossed Libby's face and then she smiled, her happiness showing in her eyes like a field full of sunflowers. She leaned forward. "Kiss me again."

He needed no further encouragement, and their lips met. There was an initial spark of lust, then, as they kissed harder and deeper, a feeling of contentment swam through him.

He clasped the back of her head, but the plait stopped him from running his hand through her hair like he wanted to. He stood and drew her into his arms, then kissed her again, using one hand to pull her tight while the other worked at undoing her plait. Finally her hair was free and he ran both hands through it, kissing her deeper again, and then ran a hand over her side and up to her breast.

Libby's soft gasp sent desire shooting through him. He

found the hem of her sweater and traced his hand over her bare skin up to her lacy bra and over the swell of her breast.

She moaned softly and pulled back. "No. We can't. Kate."

She was right but he stole another kiss, hugging her closer and sampling her soft, luscious lips. He wanted to go further, do more, but her words echoed in his head. He released her, trying to clear his head, but his body still throbbed. "You're right." He rested his forehead against hers. "You make me forget everything." He'd never had to worry about a child before.

Her hands came up to his cheeks and she kissed him. She inhaled deeply. "I should go."

He wanted her to stay, but he had to ignore what his body was telling him. He had to think about Kate, but if he was going to be good tonight, he wasn't going to wait a few days to see her again. "Come with us tomorrow. We're climbing the Sydney Harbour Bridge."

"I'd love to." She kissed him again and then reluctantly stepped away, reaching for her bag.

Adrian took it from her and taking hold of her hand, he walked her to the door. Carefully he put the bag back on her shoulder and drew her close. He kissed her chastely. Anything else would make him forget his intentions.

"I'll see you tomorrow."

"I'll look forward to it." With a final glance back, she walked down the corridor. He watched until she was safely inside her room.

He'd definitely started something.

And he was happy.

Happier than he'd ever been before.

Chapter 12

Libby stared up at the enormous arch of the Sydney Harbour Bridge looming above her. She was beginning to doubt the wisdom of agreeing to go on the bridge climb with Kate and Adrian. Not only was she not good with heights, she was also taking another day off from her writing.

Was she letting herself get too attached? Should she have told Adrian no? He'd made it clear they weren't going to have a long relationship, that this wasn't going to last longer than the tour. She closed her eyes briefly. As long as she remembered that, she would be fine. She was allowed to do something frivolous just for herself every now and again. She could have a fling if she wanted to. She was a grown woman.

They would be discreet, and make sure Kate didn't have any unrealistic expectations. Neither of them wanted to upset Kate.

She wouldn't get caught up. Today she'd given herself the day off, but she would spend the next two days writing.

If the relationship wasn't going to last, she shouldn't spend her valuable writing time with them.

Her gaze followed the arch up and up to the summit, which suddenly appeared to be half a mile high. Squinting, she saw little ants climbing up the arch – human ants. Damn, it was high.

"Come on, let's go." Kate was bouncing up and down with

excitement and tugging Adrian's hand.

"Settle down, kiddo. If you get too excited, they might not let you climb," Adrian joked.

Kate immediately stopped bouncing but tapped her hand against her thigh instead.

Happy to be distracted, Libby followed Adrian, Kate and George to the check-in point. They were greeted by a very passionate host, who took their details, made sure Kate met the minimum height requirement and set them up with all the safety gear.

Libby put on the special bridge suit and tied her hair back with the supplied scrunchie. Kate jabbered away to their tour guide, asking a million questions, but all Libby focused on was the swirling, sickly feeling in her stomach.

"I need you to all sign the declaration form and we'll be ready to go," their guide John said.

Libby read through the document. Could she say she wasn't fit enough to participate in the climb?

"Libby, are you almost ready?"

At John's voice, Libby realized the others were waiting for her.

"Ah, yes," she said, but she still wavered about signing the form.

"Libby's not good with heights." Adrian's southern drawl interrupted her thoughts.

"Don't worry, Libby," the guide told her. "We've taken loads of people up the bridge who've been afraid of heights. We'll take it really slow for you."

"Think of it as an adventure, Libby. I'll be right ahead of you," Kate said.

"I'll be right behind you to help," Adrian said. "Like you helped me." His smile soothed her nerves.

She could do this. Libby scrawled her signature at the bottom of the form and Kate jumped up and down in excitement.

"Fabulous. Now it's time for the safety briefing." John led them into a room where he took them through all the necessary safety information. Afterward Libby was a little more confident. The guides were definitely ready for anything and took safety seriously. She wasn't even allowed to take her camera in case she dropped it.

Libby followed them out of the check-in center to the start of the bridge climb and allowed herself to be clipped to the safety harness. George was directly behind the tour guide, followed by Kate, and then Libby, with Adrian behind her. The roar of traffic heading over the bridge was dulled by the headphones they wore to listen to John's commentary.

There was metal everywhere. Hard, strong, cold steel below and to each side. Libby ran her hands along it to reassure herself. Someone touched her shoulder and Libby turned to Adrian, who gave her the thumbs up sign.

The climb began, rung after rung, and for a while all Libby did was focus on putting hand after hand, foot after foot, and keeping her breath even. She had never climbed so many steps.

John told them about the history of the bridge and Libby focused on his voice and the climb, not looking down.

They soon reached a platform, where they stopped and rested for a moment. Kate's face was flushed with the exercise but she gave Libby two thumbs up. Libby smiled, breathing deeply, and looked out over the harbor. It was a beautiful, sunny winter's day, still cool, and not a cloud in the sky. There was a light breeze, and in the shade of the huge iron structure it was quite cold. Libby was grateful for the fleece John had given them to wear under the climbing suit.

"How are you going, Libby?" John asked.

"Fine," Libby called. She wasn't going to look down at all. If she kept her gaze in front of her and focused on the horizon, she could pretend she wasn't high above the ground.

"Are we ready to keep moving?" John asked the rest of the group. With shouts of agreement, they all followed him.

It was a long climb. John kept up the commentary, supplying interesting facts about the bridge and pointing out highlights along the way. Libby's stomach finally began to calm and her grip on the rails wasn't as tight.

As they walked along one of the many catwalks, Kate suddenly stopped in front of her and pointed to something below. Without thinking, Libby followed Kate's finger and felt the bottom drop out of her stomach. Her eyes brushed past the kookaburra Kate was pointing at and continued down, down to where the cars were rushing along below.

Her legs turned to jelly, and as they buckled under her, she reached for the railings. Before she hit the catwalk, strong arms seized her from behind and supported her weight. Libby frantically tried to get her legs to function but they wouldn't. Her eyes were glued on the tiny cars below her.

Adrian lowered her to the ground. "Libby, relax. Look at me." His breath was on her neck and she could just hear him over the roar of her fear, but she couldn't obey him.

"Look at me, Libby." He took her chin in his hand and slowly turned her head so she was gazing into his dark brown eyes. "Focus on me. It's all right. You're safe here. You're still connected to the guide rail. Take a deep breath for me."

Libby stared at him as if he were a lifeline. She panted – quick, painful breaths of air.

"Slow breaths, Libby."

She took a shuddering breath in, trying to mimic the deep breath Adrian took.

"Breathe out."

The air exploded out of her.

"Take another slow breath in."

Slowly but surely Libby matched her breathing to Adrian's. It wasn't until she had it under control that she realized he was rubbing her arms, slowly but rhythmically, in time with her breaths. She blinked.

"Do you think you can stand up?" Adrian asked.

Libby focused on her legs. They were weak but she had to stand. Holding on to Adrian's shoulders, she got to her feet, wobbling for a second before her muscles took hold and supported her. His arms surrounded her, both comfort and protection. She was safe.

"Keep your eyes on the metal girders we're following," Adrian said, and pointed.

Libby turned slowly, following his directions, and realized everyone was staring at her. Kate had clasped George's hand and looked worried, but George's expression was more contemplative.

"Sorry," she mumbled.

"Nothing to be sorry about," John said. "It happens to a lot of people. Do you think you can continue?"

Kate was still watching her with wide eyes, her concern obvious. Libby forced a smile. "Yes."

Adrian's hand was resting on her waist, warm and reassuring, and she focused on it. If he faced his fear of the dark every single night at his concerts, she could do this. With a renewed sense of determination she gave Kate the thumbs up and continued the climb.

It took an hour to reach the top of the bridge. Libby found if she kept her eyes moving around it was much easier to cope. She could see all the way to the Blue Mountains in the west. The harbor itself was immense, spreading out through Sydney and beyond. Libby hadn't realized it was so big. Boats of various types were out on the water making the most of the beautiful winter's day.

"Look, Uncle Ade. It's a whale!" Kate pointed and jumped up and down with excitement.

Libby put a hand out to stop Kate jumping, fear gripping her again, and then she looked where Kate was pointing out on the harbor.

Sure enough, there were a couple of whales breaching. Several big whale-watching boats were close by, each about 100 yards from the animals. From up on high, Libby saw the dark shapes under the water and the splash they made when they breached.

"Wow. Can we go whale watching, Uncle Ade?" Kate turned to look at her uncle.

"I'll see if we can get a spot on one of the cruises," he said.

Below them a mother and her calf frolicked in the water. Libby was aware of Adrian right there behind her, his comforting presence close enough so that if she leaned back she would touch his chest. As if knowing her thoughts, he pulled her closer and she allowed herself to nestle next to him. Today she wasn't going to ask any questions about their relationship. Today she was just going to enjoy.

"Over here, folks," John called and snapped a photo when they turned. He motioned to Kate and George to join them and took a few more photos.

"Okay, guys, it's time to start the journey back," he said.

Reluctantly they followed him across the bridge to the other side for their descent.

By the time they reached the bottom, Libby's calves were aching. She stepped inside the check-in point and a wave of giddiness flooded her. She'd done it. She'd climbed the Sydney Harbour Bridge and beaten her fear. She grinned.

"We've got to buy the photos, Uncle Ade," Kate said, striding over to the counter. Libby agreed. She wanted proof she'd done the climb. She was glad George was paying her weekly so she could now afford the pictures.

When they came out Libby stared at the image of herself and Adrian. They looked cozy together, like a couple. She wanted a copy, so while Adrian and Kate were discussing which photos they would buy, she ordered a group shot and the one of her and Adrian. It was silly, but when the tour was over she wanted something to help her remember it, to remind her it had really happened.

When the photos had been printed, they wandered down to Circular Quay and on to the Sydney Opera House.

"Look, Uncle Ade, there's a whale-watching boat coming back in." Kate pointed to the large vessel slowly coming into a jetty.

"Let's go down and see what tours they have," Adrian said, and they all walked along to where the boat docked and waited for the passengers to disembark.

"Wait here and I'll go and ask," George said, leaving Adrian, Kate and Libby on the main dock while he questioned the crew about departure times.

As they waited, Libby scanned the area. The quay was bustling, and there were tourists everywhere, taking photos. Some distance away Libby noticed a blonde woman pointing her camera at them. Libby checked behind to see what she was taking a picture of, but there was nothing there. When she turned back, the woman was gone.

Libby frowned. The woman had seemed familiar. Before Libby could place her, Adrian touched her hand and said, "How are you feeling?"

"I'm all right now."

"I'm sorry, Libby," Kate said, her eyes full of concern.

"It wasn't your fault," Libby said, squeezing Kate's hand. "I was unprepared. I'm glad your uncle has quick reflexes."

Kate and Adrian both grinned.

George returned. "They've got a cruise starting in fifteen minutes and there are places left. Are you up for it?" he asked Libby.

"Sure." She'd given herself this day and she was going to make the most of it.

"Adrian?"

"Please, Uncle Ade. Can we go now?" Kate said.

"All right."

"I'll book." George headed over to the booking office.

"We should get something to eat," Libby said. She'd spotted a takeaway shop nearby.

"Good idea," Adrian said. "I'll get George his usual."

They hurried over, bought the food and got back as the boat was beginning to board. They joined the line and went into one of the cabins below deck, so they could eat while the rest of the passengers were boarding.

Kate scoffed her food with the gusto of someone who had a better place to be. "Can I go up on deck now?" she asked when she'd finished.

"You need to wait until one of us has finished," Adrian told her.

She pouted and checked how much everyone else had to eat. She zeroed in on Libby, who hadn't ordered as much as the men.

Libby laughed and finished off her burger.

"Come on, Libby." Kate grabbed her hand.

"Where are your manners, kiddo?" Adrian asked. "Libby might not be finished."

Kate looked at the empty wrappers in front of Libby, gave her uncle a look that said *duh* and asked Libby, "Will you come out on the deck with me, please?"

"Sure." Libby retrieved her bag from the floor and stood up. "Excuse us, gentlemen."

There were three decks, and of course Kate had to go to the top one. The boat pulled away from the dock as Libby followed

Kate, weaving around the other passengers before climbing the steps to the top. Kate raced to the rail and looked out toward the Harbour Bridge, where they'd seen the whale. She put a foot on the lower rail to climb up and Libby put a hand on her arm.

"No you don't. Can you imagine how much trouble I'd be in if you fell?" she asked, smiling to take the heat out of the scolding.

"All right." Kate lowered herself to the deck but stood on her tiptoes. After five minutes of not seeing anything, she turned away from the railing. "Let's go see if Uncle Ade and George have finished eating yet." Without waiting for Libby's response, she moved down the steps.

As Libby followed she felt someone looking at her and met Adrian's eyes from across on the second deck. He smiled at her and she almost missed her step. Catching herself before she fell, she continued down. Kate hadn't seen him, she was so sure they were in the cabin, and was about to head down the next flight of steps.

"Kate!"

Kate turned and Libby pointed to Adrian and George. Kate changed direction and moved to where the two men were lounging against the railing, talking. Libby paused, admiring the way Adrian stood, leaning back against the railing, his feet crossed. He was relaxed and comfortable.

As she approached she noticed that the teenager standing next to Adrian was wearing a Kent Downer T-shirt. When she got closer, she heard the boy talking about how awesome the concert had been and how he'd love to meet Kent.

Adrian was listening to the teenager, a smile across his face. It must be great to hear the praise and still have your anonymity. The best of both worlds.

Libby joined them and Adrian shifted a little so she could be part of the circle.

"Ladies and gentlemen, if you look to the port side of the boat, you'll see a whale. For those of you non-nautical people, that's the left side of the boat," a voice announced over the loudspeaker.

There was a stampede to the left as passengers rushed to see the whale.

Kate was one of the first, and surprisingly George was right behind her. Libby wasn't sure whether he was concerned for Kate's safety or just as eager as she was. From the grin on his face as he turned to see where they were, she suspected it was the latter.

By this time there was no room left at the railing. She turned to Adrian. "Don't you want to see them?"

"I'd prefer to spend the time with you." He tugged her closer so they were standing facing each other. He brushed a stray bit of hair out of her face. "Have you recovered from your scare?"

Libby nodded, her mouth dry. How could one person affect her so much?

Adrian brushed his lips against hers, a soft whisper of a touch. "Do you want to see the whales?" he asked.

"I've seen whales before," she answered.

He seemed intrigued. "You've been whale watching before?"

"I used to go out fishing as a kid. Sometimes we'd see whales or dolphins."

"With your family?"

"No, with my friend Piper's family on their boat."

"Your parents didn't fish?"

Libby laughed. "Fishing is not the fashionable thing to do."

Adrian checked to make sure George was still with Kate and then pointed to the empty seats on the right side of the boat. "Let's get a seat while we can."

They sat next to each other, their thighs touching. Libby took a breath of the fresh harbor air and sighed. "I'd forgotten how much I like to be out on the water."

"Did you used to go out a lot?"

"Almost every weekend in summer, until Piper moved back to Texas when I was twelve."

Adrian's forehead crinkled. "Didn't your parents miss you?"

Libby laughed, but it was a cynical laugh. "They were always working or off having lunch with their friends, so I don't think they even realized I wasn't at home."

"What about your brothers and sisters? Have you got any?"

"Older brother and sister. They're both quite a bit older than I am. I was the mistake." She said it lightly, but it still hurt to know the truth. She'd messed up their nice, neat nuclear family, and though no one said it in as many words, it had been obvious she was an accidental afterthought. There was a ten-year gap between Libby and her brother. Not wanting to dwell on her own family, she asked, "What about your family? Any regular weekend outings?"

She'd never seen someone shut down so fast. One moment Adrian was smiling at her and the next his face was wiped of all emotion. "No." He glanced away. "We really should get a look at the whales. Come on." He stood and offered her his hand.

Libby wondered whether she should push the issue. No, now wasn't the right time. It wasn't something he wanted to confide in her. She ignored the stab of hurt. They had agreed theirs was to be a casual relationship. She forced a smile and let him help her up. "Sure."

His hand trembled in hers, his whole body tense. She rubbed her thumb over the back of his hand as they walked across the deck. He glanced at her and she put all the openness and support she could into her smile. Some of the tightness released and his eyes lost their shuttered look.

Still, he wasn't going to open up here.

***

Both Kate and George had their cameras out, snapping shots of the whales as they breached the surface of the water close by. Some of the people who had rushed over at the initial sighting had moved away to get something to eat, or to seize the opportunity to secure one of the empty seats.

Adrian kept hold of Libby's hand as he leaned over to Kate and said, "What do you think, kiddo?"

She turned to him, her eyes shining with delight. "They're awesome, Uncle Ade."

His heart swelled and he relaxed further. It amazed him how much joy Kate brought into his life, just by being a kid. She made every moment exciting, made you see it from her perspective, and included him in a childhood he'd never had.

He straightened and watched the two whales leaping out of the water. He'd been stupid not to expect Libby to ask about his family when he'd been prying into hers. He'd wanted to know more about her, but when she turned the questions onto him he'd instinctively shut down.

She seemed to understand. She was still holding his hand, anchoring him to the now so he didn't flash back to those terrible days as a child. Those days when he would rather go hungry than risk upsetting his father with his presence. He wanted to explain to Libby, wanted to tell her all the sordid details, and it scared him. He'd never told any woman, never trusted one enough.

But it might horrify her. She might think less of him, worry he could turn into a monster like his father. He'd always worried it was a possibility. Adrian shared his father's genes. Would she want the extra baggage he brought with him?

He closed his eyes. It didn't matter. This was a fling. In a couple of weeks they would go their separate ways. There was no need to tell her.

As if she knew he was thinking about her, she stroked his hand and when he met her eyes they were kind.

Realizing he was clenching her hand tightly, he relaxed it and tried to smile. There was no reason to confide in her. She didn't need to know.

But part of him wanted her to know.

Chapter 13

Libby was exhausted, but it was a good exhaustion. The type of exhaustion that said, 'I've had an awesome day doing awesome things.'

Even Kate was quiet during the elevator ride up to their floor. She held Adrian's hand and leaned against him as if she didn't quite have the energy to stand straight.

"How about we get room service and watch movies tonight?" Adrian suggested.

"Sounds good, Uncle Ade." Kate stifled a yawn.

Libby grinned. Kate must be tired if she wasn't getting excited over room service.

Adrian turned to her. "Would you like to join us?"

Libby had editing she should do, but right now her brain felt like mush. She might as well give herself the whole day off. She was too tired to work. "I'd love to."

The elevator dinged.

"George?"

George looked at Adrian and Libby, then said, "No, thanks. I've got to check on a few things."

Adrian got out of the elevator and turned toward his room.

"I'll meet you there," Libby said. "I need to have a shower." The harbor spray clung to her skin and she wanted to wash it off.

"George, you can walk me to the door while Uncle Ade walks Libby." Kate removed her hand from Adrian's and took George's instead.

Adrian and George shared a look and George nodded.

"Shall we, ma'am?" Adrian held out his arm in an old-fashioned gesture and Libby grinned.

"Why thank you, kind sir." She placed her arm in his and they walked the short distance to her room.

"Thank you for a lovely day." She leaned forward and kissed him on the lips.

"You're most welcome, ma'am." He drew her into his arms and kissed her again, long and deep, drawing all her feelings to the surface in one sweet kiss.

She checked the corridor to make sure Kate had gone inside and suddenly remembered the blonde she'd seen at the docks. Then Libby realized why she'd seemed familiar. She was the woman who'd got the wrong room in Melbourne.

Libby pulled away and put her hand to her forehead. "I meant to tell you about something. There was a woman who came to the room in Melbourne."

Adrian stepped back. "You never said anything."

"It was the night Kate had her nightmare and I forgot all about it. She said she'd got the wrong room number, but she recognized me. She must have seen the talk show." Libby paused. "I thought I saw her today on the docks taking photos."

"What did she look like?"

"Tall, about your height, and slim, with blond hair and an American accent."

"Kate's ex-nanny was blond. But she was supposed to go back to America a week ago." Concern radiated from him. "I'll show you a photo of Emily tonight and you can tell me if it was her. Or it might have been a fan who'd somehow managed to find out where I was staying. There was an issue with a fan at one of the Melbourne concerts."

"I'm sorry." Libby wished she'd remembered to tell him earlier. If it was a fan, it was stalker-like behavior, and it made Libby nervous. She hugged him and he brought his arms around her.

When she stepped back to look up at him, he brushed his

lips in a feather-like touch over hers. It was gentle and made her feel loved. She wanted to stay here like this forever.

Forever? That was crazy. She'd known Adrian less than two weeks. This was her no-strings tour fling. There was no forever. Adrian had made it clear. He wasn't looking for a relationship.

He squeezed her hand. "You all right?"

"Sure." She gazed down the empty corridor. "George will probably want to get to work."

"You're right. You tend to distract me." He grinned and pulled her close for another kiss. "Don't be too long."

"I won't." Libby slipped inside her room. She leaned back against the door and shut her eyes. Where the hell had forever come from? She couldn't possibly be thinking straight. In another two weeks Adrian would go back to America and she would move into the cheap apartment she'd found and that would be the end. It was a tour romance Adrian might think fondly about from time to time if she was lucky.

She stood hugging herself by the door.

Libby swore softly. She wasn't in love with Adrian. She couldn't possibly be. Sighing, she relaxed her hold. She needed a shower. The water would wash away her foolish thoughts and she'd be able to think straight.

***

The shower helped. Libby had realized she was being silly. What she'd felt was just the early stages of a crush. The stage of dating when everything was so right and so rosy.

She'd got carried away because Clint had never given her this sensation of belonging, this feeling of family.

Clint had never given her much of anything.

After dressing she was heading out the door when her cell phone rang. Checking the display, she almost didn't answer it, but she knew her mother would keep ringing if she didn't.

"Hi, Mum."

"Elizabeth, I thought you would have called when you got home from your tour."

"I'm still over east, Mum," Libby said. What did her mother want? She never called just to say hello.

"Didn't you finish last week?"

"I've got a temp job over here."

"Oh. When will you be back?" There wasn't any interest in what the job was, thank God – just annoyance, as if Libby had messed up her mother's plans.

"Not for another couple of weeks."

"That won't do at all. There's a function next Saturday and as your father and I leave for Fiji tonight, I promised you will be there. Some of my friends are big fans."

Her mother's tone made it clear she was surprised at her friends' taste.

Libby rolled her eyes and suppressed a sigh. Another one of her mother's charitable fundraisers, where Libby would be expected to bid on some extravagant thing she couldn't afford. Thank goodness she had a valid excuse. "You'll have to tell them I'm working."

"Surely you could fly back for the weekend."

Her mother had no idea how little she earned from writing, nor was Libby going to point it out to her. But that was beside the point. She was working on Saturday.

"I'm sorry, Mum. You'll have to give my apologies."

Her mother huffed in displeasure. "I'm disappointed in you, Elizabeth. I don't ask for much."

That was because she didn't care to remember she had a younger daughter until it suited her.

"Next time you'll have to ask me if I'm available first." She wasn't going to feel guilty about this. Her mother would keep at her until she gave in, so she said, "I've got to go. I'm meeting friends and I'm going to be late. Give my love to Dad." She hung up before her mother responded.

She quickly turned her phone off in case her mother called back. Tension drained out of her body and she was suddenly lighter and happier. It was the first time she'd refused her mother.

Most of the time it was Libby who was being refused. Whenever she suggested going out to dinner with her parents, it wasn't convenient. They either had something on, or were expecting something better to come along. She'd learned not to ask anymore.

Right now Libby had someone who wanted to spend time

with her and she wasn't going to let her mother ruin her mood.

She retrieved her key and headed to Kate and Adrian's room.

***

Kate answered the door in her pajamas, her hair damp. "Come in. Uncle Ade's in the shower. I'm deciding what I want for dinner."

The image of a naked and wet Adrian popped into Libby's mind and she paused, her mouth going dry.

"What do you think you'll have?" Kate's voice interrupted Libby's thoughts and Libby blocked the image from her mind. She couldn't have those kinds of thoughts with Kate around. She followed Kate to the table, where the room service menu was open. "What looks good?"

"I'm getting fish and chips." Kate moved the menu so Libby could see.

Libby paged back to the start and then realized Kate was grinning at her. "What is it?"

"You and Uncle Ade were holding hands today," she said with a triumphant smile.

Libby hesitated. "Yes, we were. Are you okay with that?"

"Yes! I knew he fancied you like you fancied him. He was never this friendly with Emily. Generally he's not comfortable around strangers. Dad used to say it was because he was shy. He's not shy with you, though." The shower had revived some of Kate's energy.

Libby wanted to know more about what Kate's dad used to say, but she stopped herself from asking. Adrian would tell her about his background when he was ready.

Adrian came out of the bathroom and Libby quickly turned her attention to the menu.

"We're deciding on dinner," Kate told him.

"Great idea."

Libby turned to face Adrian, trying to seem casual. He wore his usual jeans and T-shirt, blue today, and his hair was disheveled from drying it. He looked refreshed and relaxed. Libby's heart thudded.

"What's the plan of action for tonight?" she asked.

"Order dinner first and then see what movies are available," Kate answered.

Adrian and Libby chose their meals, and while Kate deliberated over which movie to watch, Adrian showed Libby a photo of Emily.

"That's her," Libby said, staring at the photo.

"Darn it," Adrian swore. "Let me tell George she didn't go home." He picked up his cell phone.

"What's wrong?" Kate asked.

Libby checked with Adrian and then said, "I thought I saw Emily today at the docks. Adrian is telling George."

"She went home last week," Kate said and turned back to her movie selection.

"That's what we thought, but maybe she decided she wanted to see some of Australia while she was here." Libby didn't believe for a moment it was a coincidence that Emily happened to be on the docks at the same time as them.

Adrian hung up. "George is going to check whether she was on the flight." He turned to Kate. "If you see Emily, I want you to tell one of us straight away."

"Sure." Kate didn't look up.

"You're not to go anywhere with her if she asks," Adrian continued.

"Why would I? She's no fun."

He smiled and relaxed a fraction. "Swell. What movie did you pick for us?"

Kate handed him a comedy. Libby sat on the couch with Adrian and Kate either side of her. She was concerned about Emily and wondered why she had quit. If Emily and Kate hadn't got on, would she want to hurt the child?

Libby would have to be more alert.

There was no way she would let anyone hurt Kate.

After dinner, they sat down to watch the movie. Halfway through, Kate snorted and Libby turned to see her fast asleep.

"Adrian," she said softly and pointed to Kate.

His face softened and he smiled, the love he had for Kate showing clearly in his expression. "I'll take her to bed."

He lifted Kate up and she barely stirred. Libby stood and went with him to draw back the covers of Kate's bed so he could lay her straight in. Adrian kissed Kate on the forehead and tucked her in. Libby's heart swelled.

She rubbed her hands over her face. This wasn't infatuation.

Libby followed Adrian out of the room.

She was in big trouble.

This was love.

***

Adrian left Kate's door open and moved back to the couch. He was aware of how cozy the situation seemed. He'd seen Daniel and Penny do the same thing with Kate when she had been younger. But he shouldn't be thinking about Libby as a mother. She was Kate's nanny and that was it. He'd made it clear.

These strange feelings must be because it was the first time he'd spent so much time with a woman and Kate.

He settled down on the couch with no interest in watching the rest of the movie. He reached for the remote. "Do you want to watch the end?"

"Not really."

He turned off the television and then stood to put some background music on. "Would you like a cup of tea?"

"You don't have any wine?" Libby asked.

"No." He was surprised she should ask now.

"Then yes, please." She hesitated and then asked, "Adrian, I've been meaning to ask, don't you drink?"

He paused before turning the kettle on. He should have known she would question it eventually. This could be the opportunity to tell her. He turned to face her and leaned back against the kitchen bench. "No. I never acquired the taste." Never *let* himself acquire it.

"I wasn't sure whether it was just in front of Kate. I was going to ask you after we went to the Vietnamese restaurant. I shouldn't have ordered the glass of wine."

He shook his head. "You weren't responsible for Kate that night."

"Oh, good. I was worried." Libby paused. "I've always seen alcohol as a social thing. It seems a little sad to drink by myself, so I only drink if I'm out with friends."

In his experience it was definitely sad and dangerous. The

number of times he'd watch his father drink himself into a stupor, hoping he would drink enough to pass out and not just enough to get angry. He clenched the benchtop tightly and then relaxed his grip.

Libby gave him a concerned look. "Is something wrong?"

The kettle boiled and he turned to make the drinks, taking his time. Should he tell her the truth? It was the perfect opportunity, but was there any point?

Their relationship was short-term, but he acknowledged the part of him that *wanted* her to know. He'd never had that desire before and he could trust Libby with his secret.

It scared him how much he trusted her.

He was uncertain, because he wasn't sure how she would react. Would she think less of him or judge him because of his father? He hoped not.

There was only one way to find out.

When he finished making the tea, he turned to find her sitting patiently watching him. He handed her a mug and sat on the chair opposite her, needing the distance. "My father is an alcoholic." He said it fast, as if it would make it easier, like ripping off a bandaid.

Libby paused with the mug to her lips and then took a sip. "It must be difficult. How long has it been?" Her tone masked the sympathy he didn't want.

Adrian took a sip of his tea, allowing the warm, mellow drink to soothe him. "Since my mother walked out when I was two." Since he could remember.

Libby's eyes didn't leave his as she asked, "Did he drink every day?"

He was unable to look at her. He could still play it down, gloss over the details, and she would never know. But he needed to be truthful for himself.

"He'd have a couple of shots of bourbon before he went to work and then he'd start again the moment he got home. He'd stop when he passed out." He forced himself to see her reaction.

Libby's mouth dropped open. "Who took care of you?"

"My brother Daniel. He was four years older than me. In the early days we'd wait until Dad passed out and then take money from his wallet and stock the freezer full of microwave dinners. Dad never noticed the money was missing."

"What about other family – your mother, aunts, uncles – surely someone noticed what was happening?"

Adrian shrugged. "Mum walked out and didn't look back." He took a breath to calm himself. "Dad blamed me for it. He'd tell me I was so worthless even my own mother hadn't stuck around." He still couldn't understand how she could have walked away so callously. Kate wasn't even his own child, but he would never leave her with someone like his father. "I don't know anything about Mum's family and Dad had been disowned by his. There wasn't anyone to care." When he'd finally got free he hadn't bothered trying to track down his mother. She'd never cared for him.

Libby's eyes were moist.

If she was upset about this much, he wasn't going to tell her the rest.

She pressed her hands to her eyes shut to stop the tears. "What happened later?"

The instinctive defensiveness shot up. "What do you mean?"

"You said, 'in the early days'. That implies something changed."

He clenched his jaw tight. Trust her to notice his slip.

Daniel had told Penny the truth and their relationship had grown stronger.

But he and Libby didn't have the same relationship. Nor were they likely to.

The twinge of regret surprised him.

"Sometimes Dad would get angry before he passed out."

"Did he hit you?"

"When I wasn't fast enough." His heart rate increased as he remembered those nights when he raced around the sofa, trying to stay out of his father's reach. He had to keep Dad's attention on him so he didn't lash out at Daniel.

"How bad was it?"

His father had made it an art to only hit where the bruises wouldn't show. To hit hard enough to hurt but not hard enough to require a hospital trip. "I survived."

Libby placed her half-full mug on the table.

"And your brother?"

"He did his best to keep Dad calm and to keep him away from us. Some days Dad would lock me in the basement as punishment rather than hit me." He had never decided which punishment was worse. The pain of a beating or the terror of the dark and the noises of the rats slinking around him.

"I don't suppose the basement had been converted into a nice, cozy den?" Libby asked, trying to make him smile.

The slightly hopeful look in her eyes lightened his mood. "It might have been cozy for the rats."

Libby stood and pulled him to his feet, wrapping her arms around him in a hug. He rested his cheek on her head and allowed himself to draw comfort from her. She wasn't judging him. She still wanted to be near him.

When she pulled away, she led him to the sofa and pulled him down so they sat side by side.

"How did you escape?"

"It was Daniel. When I was twelve and he was sixteen, he dropped out of school and got an apprenticeship with a builder. Got Dad to sign a consent form one night when he was drunk." Adrian smiled at the memory. They had feared their father might not be drunk enough and would realize what he was signing, but their fear soon turned to jubilation when the form had been signed. "It was George's father who owned the business. They had a flat above the garage they rented to Daniel. We packed up while Dad was at work one day." He'd been terrified his father was going to come home and catch them packing, so he hadn't done much more than throw his clothes in a suitcase. He didn't have much more than that anyway. "They didn't discover I was living with Daniel for several months." Daniel had bought him several textbooks and he'd spent his days doing schoolwork. He hadn't dared go to school in case his father found him there.

"What did they do?"

"They were going to call social services, until Daniel told them everything." It had been a tense few days worrying about whether they were going to be split up. Fearful he would be sent back to his father.

"George's dad, Hank, went to visit Dad and I don't know

what happened, but from then on we were made part of the family. I swapped schools and would go to their house when I got home and do my homework with George. When Daniel finished work we'd have dinner with the family and then go back to the flat above the garage."

"How did George react?"

Adrian chuckled. "Nothing fazes George. He has three sisters, so he was relieved to have some male company." It had been a huge adjustment for both him and Daniel to be part of a normal family. A family who may have teased, argued and shouted at each other on occasion but who always loved each other. He'd been constantly tense, waiting for the laughter to turn to anger and for the beating to follow. But eventually he'd realized it wasn't going to happen.

George had thought Adrian weird at first but he soon understood Adrian hadn't had the same kind of experiences as he had. It was George who had taught him how to swim, how to ride a bike and how to climb a tree.

As a child he'd worshipped George and Daniel for saving him.

Libby rested her hand on his thigh. "No wonder you and George are so close."

"He's my other brother." He closed his eyes at the familiar chest pain he got when he thought about Daniel's death. If it hadn't been for Daniel there was no telling where he would have ended up.

"Do you ever see your father now?"

Adrian pursed his lips. "No." Was she going to judge him?

Libby seemed pleased. "Does Kate know about him?"

"Daniel told her he wasn't sure where her grandmother was and that her grandfather was ill." It really was amazing that his father was still alive. George kept tabs on him, in case he realized who Kent really was and caused them trouble, but so far his father remained oblivious.

"You're amazing." Libby turned his head and kissed him on the lips. "To have survived and come out on top takes a great deal of strength."

She didn't get it. "It was all Daniel and George. They kept pushing me. I would have given up without them. I couldn't stand on stage without crippling panic attacks when I first started. I kept expecting someone to tell me I was a fraud."

"Why did you want to sing?"

Adrian shrugged. "It was the only thing I was good at." It was the only thing that freed him from his life and allowed him to pretend, for a few minutes, he was someone else.

He shifted on the sofa. He was uncomfortable with the way Libby was gazing at him, as if he was some kind of superhero. He wasn't. He was a product of having a brother and best friend who cared for him. He could have just as easily turned out to be like his father.

That was the main reason he didn't touch alcohol. What if one sip undid all the work Daniel and George had done? What if once he started he couldn't stop? What would happen to Kate? He couldn't risk it.

He stood and took both mugs off the coffee table. "Do you want another drink?" He walked over to the kitchenette, giving himself the distance he needed.

"No."

He filled the kettle anyway and put it on, just to have something to do. He'd never told anyone about his past and didn't know what to do now.

The silence stretched out as he made another cup of tea.

Finally Libby spoke. "Adrian, do you really believe you have nothing to do with your success?"

Why wouldn't she let it go? He knew he could sing, but so could thousands of other people. It was George's drive as his manager that had got him where he was. She wouldn't accept it, though. "I don't want to talk about it." His tone was gruffer than he'd meant it to be.

She jerked back as if he'd slammed a door in her face.

He couldn't deal with this now. He was too drained and too raw after reliving his childhood. He sighed and ran a hand through his hair. "I'm tired. Can we talk about this later?" He hadn't meant for it to be an invitation to leave, but Libby stood and collected her things.

"Of course."

He wanted to ask her to stay but there was no point. He'd offended her.

"I'll see you tomorrow evening." She kissed his cheek, ran a hand down his arm and left the suite.

Adrian sunk down on a chair and put his head in his hands.

Had she used his tone as an excuse to leave?

Was she horrified by his background?

Had he driven her away?

Chapter 14

Libby had spent the night tossing and turning after Adrian had told her about his childhood. Her heart ached for the young boy he had been and for the man who still felt so much pain.

It meant so much to her that he'd trusted her with the truth. When he'd shut down, it had stung, until she realized she had to give him space. His defensiveness was a coping mechanism. She couldn't blame him.

She wanted to show him he wasn't defined by his past, that he'd achieved so much and he was nothing like the father he'd described – but first he needed time.

The next morning she sent a quick email to Kate wishing her and Adrian a good day. Libby was going to work on her manuscript while they went to the movies. Libby would head to their room in the afternoon to be with them.

While she was online, she did a search on her name. She liked to keep track of what was being said about her and her books. Reviewing the results, she noticed a link to a popular gossip magazine. That was unusual. She clicked on the link and waited the few seconds for the site to load.

Her stomach plummeted. She shook her head as if she could deny what she was seeing.

On the screen was a picture of her holding hands with Adrian on the docks. The caption read, "Bookish Author

Hooks Rock Star." The story below identified the man in the photo as Kent Downer. Further down was a second photo, with the four of them: George, Kate, Libby and Adrian. Adrian had an arm around Kate. The article questioned who Kate was and whether she was Kent's daughter or Libby's.

Nausea swirled around Libby's stomach. This couldn't be happening. Not only was Adrian's privacy blown but so was Kate's. Adrian had been extremely careful Kate wasn't associated with him because of the potential danger. He'd mentioned his fans could get pretty wild. The only positive was they hadn't mentioned Adrian's real name.

Libby snatched up the hotel phone and called the suite, hoping they would still be there. It rang and rang before finally she hung up. She picked up her cell and called George, annoyed she didn't have Adrian's number. George answered on the second ring.

"Have you seen the article about Adrian online?" Libby asked.

George laughed. "Which one? The one where he's spent the night clubbing in King's Cross or the one that puts him at a meditation retreat?"

"The one of Adrian out of costume which also has a photo of Kate."

George swore.

"I'll send you the link." Libby copied the address and emailed it to George.

"Give me a second." There was silence while George read through the article and then he swore some more.

"I can't get hold of Adrian to tell him," Libby said. "They've already left for the day."

"I'll call you back." George hung up.

***

Adrian hadn't slept well. He couldn't stop thinking about Libby and whether he'd ruined their relationship.

The last thing he wanted to do was go out for breakfast and a movie, but he'd promised Kate.

"Come on, Uncle Ade. I'm starved." Kate bounced around the room with exuberance.

Adrian took a couple of deep breaths to find his enthusiasm. "You got everything you need?"

"Yep."

"Let's go." Adrian followed her out of the suite, his gaze drawn toward Libby's room, but she didn't appear. By the time he reached the elevator, Kate had already pushed the button.

"We're going to the pancake place first, aren't we?" Kate asked as they rode down.

"Of course." Not even Kate's eagerness was working today. He just wanted to crawl back into bed and sleep.

When they reached the lobby, Adrian noticed a number of reporters waiting outside the hotel. It was unusual for them to be there so early, so he assumed some other celebrity was arriving.

"I wonder who they're waiting for," Kate said.

Adrian didn't care as long as he and Kate got through without being recognized. He'd relaxed somewhat over the years but it didn't mean that a reporter wouldn't realize who he was this time around. He headed for one of the side doors, away from the main entrance, and they stepped out into the fresh Sydney morning air and set off down the street.

"There he is!" a voice yelled.

Adrian kept moving, hoping it was just coincidence that the celebrity had arrived as he stepped out of the hotel.

"Kent! What's your relationship with Libby Myles?"

Adrian froze mid-step and shot his gaze toward the reporters. They stormed forward en masse.

Kate grabbed his hand and moved close.

His heart thudded hard. How the hell had they recognized him?

Before he could react, the reporters reached him, each shoving their microphones into his face.

"Why the elaborate costume?"

"Is the girl your daughter?"

Reporters jostled for position, pushing him and Kate toward the building. Camera flashes went off with regular precision, blinding him. Adrian was so stunned he didn't know how to respond.

Kate tripped and landed on the ground with a scream.

Startled into action, Adrian quickly bent over her, shielding her from the cameras. "Kate, are you all right?"

She cradled her wrist, tears streaming down her face. "I think it's broken."

Rage filled Adrian as he swept her into his arms. He had to protect Kate. "I'll take care of you," he said.

The reporters were relentless. "Are you dating Libby Myles?"

"Who's the girl?"

"What do you want to say to your fans about the way you've betrayed them, pretending to be someone you're not?"

He couldn't answer these questions now. He had to get Kate away from them. She couldn't be associated with him.

Even as he thought it, he knew it was too late.

Adrian drew in a breath. "Out of my way. She's broken her wrist because of you morons."

There was a moment of stillness and Adrian used it to push his way back to the hotel and inside. Striding to the reception desk, he demanded, "Where's the nearest doctor?"

The lady behind the desk gawked at him as he put Kate gently on to the counter. "Sit there for a moment, sweetheart. I need to call George."

Kate's tears had abated and she swallowed. "Yes, Uncle Ade."

Adrian's cell rang as he drew it out of his pocket. It was George.

"Get down here with the car. Kate needs to go to the hospital."

"Adrian, your cover has been blown," George said.

"Yeah, I noticed. Hurry up." He hung up.

Kate stared at him with wide eyes, holding her wrist behind her back. "I'm fine. I don't need to go to the hospital. It's not broken. I made a mistake."

Adrian recognized the signs of panic. She was breathing rapidly and starting to shake. It took him a second to realize the cause. The last time she'd been in hospital was when she'd been in the car crash. When Susan had left her alone overnight.

"I'll see if I can find a doctor for you, Katie." He kept his voice low and soothing.

The receptionist had finally got over her shock and was

printing off directions.

"No. No, I'm not going to hospital." Kate jumped off the counter, flinching as she bent her wrist.

"I'm sure the lady has included a doctor in her list," Adrian said and looked at the woman, his eyes telling her to agree.

"Of course," she said and she printed another page.

Adrian first had to get her into a car and then he'd worry about the rest.

"Promise?" Kate asked him. "No hospitals?"

George came striding out of the elevator. Adrian swung Kate back up into his arms to distract her and carried her toward the parking area.

He wasn't going to make promises he couldn't keep.

***

Libby stood and paced the room. Adrian was going to be devastated. Would he blame Libby for attracting attention to him?

It had never occurred to her she would be photographed. So few people recognized her when she was out, and she wasn't newsworthy enough to have her picture regularly in the paper. But even if someone had recognized her, how had they recognized Adrian? The bookseller in the airport hadn't and she'd been right next to him. There was nothing that linked Adrian and Libby except the talk show.

Libby stopped pacing.

Emily.

It had to be. She must have taken the photo and then sent it in, telling the magazine who Adrian was. If you compared a picture of Adrian with Kent, you'd see the similarity.

Could Emily really be so indignant at Adrian that she'd want to hurt Kate as well? It didn't make sense. Emily was the one who'd quit. But then again, Libby only had Adrian's word that Emily had quit.

Libby's cell phone rang and she answered it.

"They're in the lobby. Kate's been hurt and needs to go to hospital," George said.

Libby's heart raced. "How badly?"

"I don't know. I'll call when I have more news. In the

meantime, try and find out what else has been printed about Adrian." George hung up.

Libby started pacing again. She wanted to run downstairs and see what was wrong with Kate, but she didn't dare. She might make matters worse, especially if there were reporters downstairs.

Damn it! She wanted to be with them, not kept in her room like she'd done something wrong.

She stopped pacing. What if Adrian blamed her for this? That would explain why she was being kept away.

If she'd remembered to tell him about Emily sooner, this might not have happened.

Was it her fault?

She sat back down at her computer, all thought of writing already out of her head. She needed to discover the extent of the problem. What was being said about the three of them? If she could put together a list, she could plan how to address it.

And it might distract her from worrying about Kate.

***

One of the hotel staff had taken them down to the valet parking car park so they could avoid the media. Adrian scanned the list the receptionist had given him. The best option was the Sydney Children's Hospital. He gave the directions to George and climbed in the back seat with Kate.

"What happened?" George asked as they drove out of the parking area.

"The reporters were waiting outside for us but I don't know how they recognized us."

"It's on the internet. A photo of you and Libby and the four of us on the docks from yesterday."

Yesterday. No one could have known they were going to be there. It had been a spur of the moment decision. It was if someone had been following them.

"Emily." He said it as a swear word.

"She signed a confidentiality agreement," George growled. "If she has anything to do with this, I'll sue her for everything she's got."

"The damage is done." Adrian's voice was quiet and flat. It

didn't matter if he did sue her. There was no way he could go back to being one of the crowd. People knew who he was now and they knew about Kate. Kate would always be easily identifiable with her long, curly, red hair.

He turned his attention to Kate. "How's your wrist?"

"It's really not too bad, Uncle Ade. I think I made a mistake about it being broken."

He didn't believe her for an instant. "Let me have a look." Gently he took her wrist, noting the swelling, and she gasped in pain before he could even try to move it.

She looked at him with fearful eyes.

"We'll get it checked out, just in case," he said.

"Please, Uncle Ade. Don't make me go to the hospital." Her eyes were wide and watery, beseeching him.

It cut him to the core.

"The hospital is the best place to fix you. We'll get them to put a fancy cast on your wrist and then go back to the hotel." He hoped that was all that was required. "I won't leave you."

George pulled up into the emergency department.

Kate flattened herself against the back seat as if trying to disappear. "No, no, no, no, no."

Adrian's heart wept. "Kiddo, I know you're scared. You need to be brave for me." He couldn't use his example of being scared of the dark because she didn't know he was. "Remember how scared Libby was yesterday on the bridge?"

Kate nodded, but he wasn't sure she was really listening.

"She still got up and finished the climb. You can be as brave as she was." Adrian saw George had fetched an orderly with a wheelchair. "You can even have a ride in a wheelchair." He pointed.

Kate looked outside, but Adrian knew he hadn't convinced her. "Let's take it one step at a time." He got out, walking around to the other side and opening the door for her.

She sat there watching him.

What else could he say to convince her? He smiled for the first time since this all began. "What would Lilly Lionheart do?"

Kate's seemed to focus at the mention of her superhero character from her book. She swallowed. "She'd get out of the car."

Adrian waited as Kate slowly stood up and then sat in the wheelchair that was waiting for her. The orderly pushed her toward the doors.

"Uncle Ade," Kate cried.

Adrian strode next to her and took her good hand. "We'll take it slowly," he said. The look he gave the orderly dared him to disagree. The orderly nodded.

As the doors to the emergency department slid open, the scent of antiseptic, vomit and hospital hit him. He hated hospitals.

Kate took a deep breath and tensed, her hand squeezing Adrian's tightly. "No. No, I can't. Not here. I won't stay here. Get me out of here." Her voice rose to a screech as she tried to get out of the chair.

"Katie, be brave for me." Adrian moved in front of the chair, stopping her from getting out.

Her eyes were filled with panic. He knew she couldn't hear him. Adrian heard George calling for someone to get a sedative. Adrian didn't want that, but he had to make sure Kate was all right.

"Kate, talk to me about Lilly Lionheart. If she was scared, what would she do?"

His words didn't penetrate. She pushed against him with her good hand and kicked at him.

"Get out of my way."

"Adrian, hold her down for a minute." George was next to him with a nurse holding a syringe.

God, they were going to sedate her. He took hold of her forearms and held her while Kate screamed and the nurse injected the sedative. A minute later Kate was calm, staring at him with accusatory eyes.

His heart crumbled and he forced himself to look away.

He had failed Kate. Failed to protect her and betrayed her trust.

"Bring her through here," the nurse said.

Adrian followed the orderly and George through to the wards.

"We need to X-ray the wrist. We're not too busy this morning, so it shouldn't take long. Someone will be along shortly to take her details."

The nurse placed an icepack on Kate's wrist, gave Adrian a reassuring smile and left.

He couldn't bear to look at Kate sitting lifelessly in the chair. Instead he looked at George.

"She's going to be fine," George said.

Adrian knew that rationally, but that wasn't the point. The point was he'd put Kate's life in danger. It was his fault she'd been injured. If he'd listened to his instincts, or reacted faster, the reporters wouldn't have got near her.

He'd promised Susan Kate would be protected from the media and he hadn't been able to keep his promise.

Maybe he should send Kate back home after she came out of hospital. Maybe Susan was right – life on the road was no good for her. Maybe he was just a complete failure as a guardian.

Kate's eyes had been so accusing.

"It's not your fault." George had an uncanny way of knowing what he was thinking.

"It is. I put her in harm's way."

"No, Emily did that by revealing your identity."

That made Adrian stop. He had forgotten about the article George had mentioned. "Show me."

George took out his cell, found the article and handed it to Adrian. Adrian scrolled through it, making note of the pictures and what was written.

He handed the phone back to George as the nurse arrived to take down Kate's details and then they wheeled her into the X-ray room.

"You can stay here," the nurse said in the hall outside the room.

"No. I'm staying with Kate." Adrian was going to keep this promise. "Give me one of those lead-lined vests. I'm not leaving her."

The nurse sighed and handed over a vest before getting Kate set up. Adrian held Kate's good hand while the X-rays were being taken and then wheeled her out of the room.

"We'll have the results in a minute and a doctor will come and see her," the nurse said, and showed him the way back to where George was waiting.

George was scowling at his cell.

Adrian almost didn't want to ask. "What now?"

George hesitated and Adrian tensed. George never hesitated.

"I've been thinking about the Emily thing."

"Go on."

George checked Kate, who was still sitting sedately in the chair. "We only have Libby's word that it was Emily on the docks."

Adrian drew in a breath, but George continued.

"Libby said a woman came to the room, she said a woman was taking photos, and then when you showed her the photo, she said it was Emily. We have to consider that maybe it was Libby who tipped the press. Whoever it was would have been paid a lot for the story."

Adrian had forgotten that Libby had been broke. But she couldn't have possibly done this. Adrian refused to believe it. "She couldn't have taken the photo. She was *in* the photo."

"She could have got someone else to."

The pain in Adrian's chest was surprising. It was sharp and ripped through him.

"Where is she now?" he asked George.

"I told her to wait in the hotel." George's phone rang. "Speak of the devil."

Adrian could hear Libby's voice on the other end of the phone, asking how Kate was.

George raised an eyebrow at Adrian. Adrian nodded his permission to tell her.

"We're waiting for X-ray results. She may have broken her wrist," he said. Adrian heard Libby's voice again, but couldn't hear what she was saying. "Adrian's fine," George said. "I'll call you in a couple of hours when we get out of here." He hung up.

"How did she sound?" Adrian asked.

"Concerned." George sighed. "I like her too, but I have to think of every option."

"I'll talk to her when we get back."

George seemed surprised.

He had to talk to her. It would eat him up inside if he kept thinking Libby could have betrayed him like this. He was sure she was innocent, but he needed to be certain.

A doctor approached them. "Good news. It's only a sprain. I'll wrap it up and give you some painkillers. Then it's just following the RICE principle – rest, ice, compression and elevation."

"She doesn't need a cast?"

"No. She'll be out of here in an hour." The doctor glanced at Adrian. "The sedative will be close to wearing off then."

"Thank you." Adrian was sure trips to the emergency department weren't usually this quick.

"Can I ask where her fear comes from?" the doctor asked as he wrapped the bandage around Kate's wrist.

"Car accident a year ago." Adrian wasn't going to say any more.

"I suggest you see she gets some therapy for it. Next time it could be a matter of life or death," the doctor said.

"I will." The thought of having to go through that again was not something he wanted to contemplate.

After finishing the bandaging, the doctor handed Adrian a pamphlet on sprain care and some tablets.

"She'll be groggy for the rest of the day from the sedative, so just keep her quiet. If you have any concerns, phone this helpline, which will put you in touch with a nurse." He gave Adrian a card.

"Thank you."

"I'll sort out the bill." George walked out.

Kate groaned. Adrian watched her eyes flutter. He needed to get her out of here. "Is there anything else?" he asked the doctor.

"No, you're fine to go."

Adrian took hold of the wheelchair and pushed Kate toward the entrance. The car was still parked where they had left it and Adrian lifted Kate in, doing up her seatbelt.

"Uncle Ade?" Kate's voice was quiet and sleepy.

"Just rest, Katie. I'm taking you back to the hotel."

"All right."

George came out and hopped into the driver's side.

By the time they arrived back at the hotel, Kate was asleep.

***

Libby couldn't concentrate on her writing. After she had found all the articles about her and Adrian and phoned George to see how Kate was, she'd tried to get back to her editing, but she found herself staring off into space.

She'd already had Donna on the phone asking her about the article and Libby had forwarded all the emails from media outlets to her. Donna said she'd review them and then advise Libby how to respond.

At the moment the publicity was the least of her concerns. She wanted to be with Kate, to see for herself the girl was all right, and she wanted to hold Adrian's hand and help him through this, because he would be frantic.

The phone rang. Libby lunged for it.

"We're back. Do you want to come over?" It was Adrian's voice, sounding exhausted.

"I'll be right there."

She hung up and dashed down the hallway to the room. Adrian answered the door, his face a picture of sadness. Libby ran her hand down his arm and smiled at him. He said nothing, but gave a sad smile back before leading Libby into the living room. Kate was lying on the couch with a quilt over her.

"How are you, Kate?"

Kate didn't respond.

Concerned, Libby glanced at Adrian.

"She had a panic attack at the hospital. They had to sedate her. She's still recovering."

Libby hugged him. "I'm so sorry." No wonder he looked so tired. "Will it wear off soon?"

"Yes." He stepped back.

"Did she break her wrist?"

"No, just a sprain. I'll take you through the details later." He gestured for her to have a seat at the dining table, where George was sitting waiting. "We need to talk."

"Of course." They had to figure out what to do about the media attention. "I sent George all of the links I could find."

"What I want to know is how Emily knew where we would be," George said.

Libby was pleased he'd come to the same conclusion as she had. "She must have followed us."

"Followed, or been tipped off?" George watched her.

Libby frowned and then realized what he was insinuating. Her mouth dropped open. "You think I told Emily about the bridge climb?" She glanced at Adrian, who didn't look at her.

Did he believe it too?

Her chest constricted so tightly it hurt to breathe. "How could you think that?" She addressed her question to George but meant it for Adrian.

"You said you were broke. The money you would have been paid for that photo would help you immensely." George's voice was mild.

He thought she would put Kate in danger for money? "How dare you?" Libby stood. "I would never do anything to hurt Kate. Ever."

Adrian put a hand on hers. She met his gaze and saw he believed her.

"Good," George said.

"I didn't think you would," Adrian said.

Her outrage softened. "You believe me?"

"Of course," Adrian said.

"I had to ask," George told her.

Libby couldn't prevent the doubt creeping into her mind. Had it been Adrian's idea and George was just playing bad cop? They couldn't really trust her if they had to ask the question. Libby tried to see it from their point of view. There weren't many options and she had been one of them. Still, the pain was palpable. Slowly she sat again. "So what do we do now?"

"We deny it," George suggested. "Get Kent to make a statement asking the press to leave the poor guy alone."

Libby shook her head. "It's too late. You just need to put a photo of Kent and Adrian side by side and see the similarities. After this morning there are plenty of shots to compare."

"I can't think about this now," Adrian said. "Not until Kate is back to normal." He glanced over at the couch.

Hearing her name, Kate turned toward them and yawned. "Aren't we going to the movies, Uncle Ade?"

Adrian jumped up and went over to her, sitting on the edge

of the couch. "We had to cancel, kiddo. You hurt yourself."

Kate squinted down at the bandage and flinched when she tried to move her hand. "What happened?"

"There were reporters outside who recognized me. You fell and hurt your wrist."

Kate glared at him. "You took me to hospital." It was an accusation.

"The doctor fixed you. It's just a sprain."

Libby stood and went to stand next to Adrian. "How are you feeling, Kate?"

Distracted, Kate said, "Tired."

"How about you watch a movie here then?"

"Okay. Do you want to stay?" Kate's eyes held her appeal.

"Sure. I'd love to." Libby would worry about her editing later.

Kate needed her more.

Chapter 15

The next day the media were back outside the hotel. Adrian and Kate stayed indoors but Libby didn't join them. They were going to have a movie marathon and Libby needed to edit her novel.

She had to keep reminding herself that the relationship she had with Adrian was temporary. She had to convince herself she wasn't in love with him.

Donna had called, wanting to issue a press release and Libby had directed her to wait. She didn't want to release anything until Adrian and George had decided how they wanted to handle it.

At midday her phone rang.

"Why do I have to read about my best friend dating a rock star in the paper? I would have thought you'd have given me the scoop." Piper's Texan accent was lighthearted and joking but Libby's heart sank.

"Oh no." The story had reached the Houston newspapers.

"What do you mean, 'Oh no'? Is it true?" Piper was instantly serious.

Libby deliberated what to do. She had to talk to someone about what was going on, and she trusted Piper. "Sort of."

"You need to spill everything right now," Piper ordered.

Libby sat on her bed, scooting up so her back was cushioned

by the pillows, and told Piper everything. She explained how she'd met Kent, how she became Kate's nanny and how much fun she'd been having with them. She didn't mention that Kent wasn't his real name. It was a relief to have someone to confide in.

Piper was silent for a moment. "Are you in love with him?" Her tone was gentle.

Libby wanted to deny it but Piper knew her too well. "Yes," she admitted. "I am."

"What are you going to do at the end of the tour?"

"I don't know. We agreed it was a fling. I'm going to enjoy it while it lasts." Her words didn't sound convincing.

"You're not that kind of girl," Piper said. "You were devastated after Clint left – and he didn't even treat you well."

"Which paper is the news in?" Libby asked, trying to steer the conversation in a different direction.

"All of them. Kent is a Houston boy and they jumped right on it. I've even had my boss call me and ask me why I didn't know. All the papers are saying the same thing." Piper was an investigative reporter at one of the big Houston newspapers.

Susan would hear about it for sure. "I need to tell him that the news has made it to the States," Libby said. "I'll talk to you later."

"You make sure you call me whenever you need me, you hear? Take care of yourself."

Libby smiled at Piper's concern. "I will." She hung up and dialed Adrian's room. "The story is in the Houston papers," she told him when he answered.

"I know. Susan's already phoned."

"How'd it go?" She couldn't tell from his tone whether he was angry or sad.

"Not great. She's furious Kate was hurt and blames me. She wants me to send Kate back to Texas. Kate's cousins will be home from summer camp in a few days. I just hope things will settle when we fly to Brisbane tomorrow."

Libby knew he didn't believe that things would settle down. "If you need anything, just call." When he murmured his agreement, she hung up.

Part of her had been hoping he would invite her over, just as part of her knew she would have to refuse. She had to do what was right for herself in the long term – meet her book deadline – and not spend all her time with Adrian and Kate. Still, she wished he had asked. Had he decided he'd made a mistake with Libby?

She shoved the thought away, refusing to worry.

Staring at her humming laptop, for the first time in her life she resented having a book contract.

She was annoyed with herself. Adrian had changed her priorities, but he'd be gone soon.

She had to write.

***

They flew to Brisbane early the next morning, avoiding the paparazzi out the front of the hotel in Sydney by using one of the hotel's back entrances. Libby couldn't believe they were still hanging around. The story wasn't that newsworthy.

In the airport Libby spotted a gossip magazine with a picture of Kent on the front and the headline, "Rock Star Dumps US Nanny for Aussie Lover." There was a small picture of Emily in the corner. Her heartbeat sped up. She bought a copy and flicked to the story.

She frowned. The article was an interview with Emily, who asserted she'd been fired and abandoned in Australia so Libby could take her place. It hinted that Emily had once had a relationship with Adrian but didn't claim it outright. It also hinted that Emily was concerned Kate was being neglected. "Sources" close to Kent refused to comment.

Libby's doubt outweighed her anger at the story. If it was true Emily had been fired, it would explain why she was so upset, but Adrian had said she'd quit.

She scanned the article again for a clue about the truth. No, it had to be a lie. Emily had insinuated Kate was neglected and that certainly wasn't the case. The relief Libby felt at this thought didn't push away all of her doubt. She'd been lied to by someone she'd trusted before.

Libby took the magazine back to the business class lounge, where Adrian and Kate were waiting. Kate was sitting on one of the couches reading while George and Adrian stood talking.

"What have you got?" Adrian asked.

She showed him the story and waited for his reaction.

His expression went fierce and he swore. "George, take a look at this." He held out the magazine and George took it.

"Why did Emily quit?" The question came out before Libby thought about the consequences.

Adrian checked where Kate was before he answered. "She came on to me. When I told her I wasn't interested, she walked out."

"Oh." Libby didn't know what to say.

Adrian took her hand and rubbed his thumb over it. "None of Kate's nannies interested me before you." He studied her, waiting for her reaction.

Libby forced a smile. It might be true, but it didn't mean their relationship was going to last. She needed to distance her heart from him.

As if hearing her thoughts, Adrian tugged her closer. "Have dinner with us tonight. We can talk after Kate goes to bed." His expression was earnest.

Libby's willpower melted away. "All right."

He smiled.

Some of her doubt faded. Libby stepped back as George spoke.

"The only lie is that she was fired. It's the magazine implying things." He frowned. "She doesn't mention that Kate is your niece, so the press are going to keep right on speculating."

"What's going on?" Kate asked, looking up from her book.

"There's a new story, kiddo," Adrian said, showing her the magazine.

Kate read the article, snorting at some of the things written.

"It's all lies. Can't you tell them that?" Kate looked at her uncle.

"I don't think they'll believe me."

"We need to say something," George told him. "This isn't going to go away, especially if Emily gives more interviews."

Adrian ran a hand through his hair. "Why don't you draft something up and we'll go from there?"

George nodded.

Before Libby asked what she could do to help, an airport

attendant came over to tell them it was time to board. As they gathered their things, Libby realized she needed to address the article this time, no matter what Adrian chose to do. Emily was portraying her as some kind of harlot. Libby needed to consider her own statement. Would people read the article and stop buying her books for their children?

She couldn't discuss it with Adrian now. There were already people taking their seats in business class and she didn't want to be overheard. She took her seat next to George. She would talk to them when they got to the hotel.

She might not be able to protect her heart from Adrian but she could protect her career.

***

The flight was uneventful, but as they drove into the hotel, Libby's heartbeat sped up.

"Paparazzi." George swore.

"We have to get Kate straight inside the hotel." Adrian turned to Libby. "Can you manage on your own?"

"Sure," Libby said, her skin tight with nerves. The car pulled in and cameras flashed. George got out of the driver's side and pushed his way around to the back door closest to the hotel entrance, where Kate sat. He opened the door while Adrian got out of the front seat. With George on one side and Adrian on the other, together they hustled Kate into the hotel.

Libby clambered across the seat to follow. The reporters had closed in behind the three of them and Libby was left by herself. As she stepped out of the car, Adrian, Kate and George disappeared into the hotel. The doorman barred the media from following.

They turned, saw Libby and surrounded her.

Cameras snapped wildly and she was jostled back and forth as the reporters jockeyed for space. She was only a couple of yards away from the entrance but she couldn't move.

Voices clamored around her, yelling questions.

Libby took a deep breath and smiled. "Excuse me," she called. "I'd like to get through."

No one moved. Bodies pressed up to her and microphones were shoved in her face.

"Libby, is it true you're dating Kent Downer?" one man yelled.

"Did you force Kent to sack Emily?"

"Who's the little girl with Kent? Is she Kent's daughter?"

Libby put up a hand to ward them off. "No comment. Please, I'd like to get through." She couldn't move and she was being blinded by the flash of the cameras.

Being polite was not going to get her into the hotel.

Fear slowly built as the air seemed to disappear and she struggled to breathe. She had to get inside. Lowering her shoulder, she pushed forward and rammed up hard against one of the reporters who wasn't budging.

"Answer our questions and we'll let you through," he said with a wink and a grin.

Anger bit its way through the fear.

She brought her knee up right into his crotch and got a jolt of pleasure as his eyes widened, his jaw dropped and he crumpled over.

Pushing past him, Libby came face to face with Adrian.

He'd come back for her.

He grasped her hand and pulled her after him as he muscled his way to the door and then gently pushed her through before him.

Libby gasped in relief. She turned back to see the reporters all pressed up against the glass windows, peering in.

"This way." Adrian kept hold of her hand and led her behind the registration desk to where Kate and George were checking in. Adrian exhaled deeply.

Kate gazed at Libby, concern on her face.

Libby smiled at her. "Are you all right, Kate?"

Kate's nod was hesitant, her eyes uncertain. "What about you?"

"Fine. Your uncle rescued me." She smiled her thanks at him.

"You seemed to be handling yourself. Did you knee that reporter in the crotch?" Adrian was bemused.

Libby shrugged. "It was the only way to get past."

"I don't want to think about the headlines tomorrow," George commented, but grinned at her. He turned from the desk with keys in hand. "Let's go."

Libby followed along behind them to the service elevator, feeling calmer and more relaxed with each step she took. This attention was utterly ridiculous.

For the first time in her life she hoped another celebrity would have a major meltdown.

Anything to draw attention away from Adrian and Kate.

**

After Libby had settled her things in her room, she headed to Adrian's suite to spend the afternoon there.

In between getting her butt kicked playing the dancing game, she, George and Adrian put together a couple of statements for the media. Libby planned hers methodically, making sure she answered every question that had been posed. Kate had helped, pouring over the articles and identifying different points that needed to be addressed.

In the end Libby kept her statement brief, avoiding any mention of a relationship with Adrian and instead simply stating that she was working for Adrian. She posted a copy on her website and blog, and forwarded a copy to her publicist.

After Kate had gone to bed and George had left, Libby finally had some time alone with Adrian. She wanted to know more about the Emily situation and how Adrian was coping, but she wasn't sure how to broach the subject.

Adrian shut the door to Kate's room and settled with a groan on the couch beside Libby. "What a day."

"Kate seems to be coping well," Libby said.

"Having to go through the reporters again shook her up, but spending the afternoon doing routine things has settled her," Adrian said.

"Do you think the media will go away now we've made statements?"

"As long as Emily doesn't continue her claims they should."

"She's quite disgruntled, considering she quit."

Adrian heard her unasked question. "I promise you there was nothing between Emily and me." He looked at her intently to see if she believed him. "Susan recommended Emily, and to keep the peace, I agreed.

"It was a few days into the tour before I suspected Emily might want to be more than just the nanny. I wasn't comfortable around her, but she and Kate seemed to get along and I didn't want to upset Kate.

"The night of the talk show, Kate had gone to bed and Emily suggested she could help 'relieve' some of my worries. She thought we could leave Kate alone and go to her room."

Libby gaped at him. "Did she know about Kate's nightmares?"

"She'd seen them herself."

"What did you say?"

"I told her I wasn't interested. She got embarrassed or angry and quit."

It was no wonder Emily was disgruntled. Adrian had rejected her but not Libby. A tiny doubt pried its way in. Emily was far more attractive than she was. Libby couldn't work out why Adrian wouldn't be attracted to Emily. Had Adrian just got bored?

"Hopefully she'll leave it alone now you've made your statement," Libby said.

Adrian murmured an agreement. "I hope this doesn't affect you too much," he said. "Though that reporter today will think twice before getting in your way again." He chuckled.

Libby pushed away her concerns and smiled. "I honestly didn't think about what I was doing. It was a gut reaction to go for the crotch. He's not likely to write anything nice, I'm sure."

Adrian slid closer and put an arm around her. "We'll deal with it together."

A thrill went through Libby as he drew her toward him. He sounded like he meant it.

"You've helped me so much. I won't let you down," he said.

Before Libby could respond, he kissed her. It was a gentle kiss, soft and caring. Libby's heart sighed as she kissed him back. She wouldn't let the experience with Clint make her mistrust every other relationship she had. She would enjoy this while it lasted.

Adrian deepened the kiss and pulled her closer so she was on his lap. One hand twined into her hair while the other one slid up her jumper to her breast.

A tingle of heat ran over Libby as he caressed her, running his thumb over her nipple. She gasped and arched into him for a moment before needing to touch him as well. She ran her hands down his chest before slipping them under his top and running them over his smooth, hard body.

Adrian dragged his mouth away and stopped her hands. He breathed heavily. "We can't do this here." He stood and pulled her to her feet, wrapping his arms around her and kissing her again. He pulled back, swearing softly. "My room?"

He was giving her a chance to change her mind if she wanted it.

Libby didn't need to consider it.

"Yes."

Chapter 16

Adrian lay staring at the ceiling, his arm around Libby, her head on his chest. He focused on controlling his breathing, but all he wanted to say was "Wow."

He ran a hand over Libby's naked back, and for this moment, everything in his life was perfect. Sex had never made him feel this way before. It was generally a fun way to spend a couple of hours. With Libby it was something else. He didn't want to examine it, or pick it to pieces, he wanted to enjoy this comfort and the closeness of Libby lying next to him.

It had been a long time since he'd had sex as himself. Usually he was in his Kent gear.

He kissed her forehead and she tilted her head to look at him and smiled. She stretched up and kissed him, humming her pleasure. "I should go," she said.

She was right, but he didn't want to break this moment. He wanted her to stay here, spend the night with him, wake up with him.

The thought made him freeze. He'd never felt this way about anyone before. He never spent the night. This thing with Libby was supposed to be casual. A no-strings-attached tour romance.

Libby turned her head to look at him. "Are you okay?"

Adrian forced a smile onto his face. "Of course." He kissed her, enjoying her taste, and then sat up. "You're right, you should go." The words came out bluntly and he hated the look of hurt that crossed Libby's face. It was for the best, though. She wasn't expecting anything more than a temporary romance and he couldn't get attached. He retrieved a pair of boxer shorts from the floor while Libby got up and dressed.

He turned as Libby was slipping on her shoes. She didn't look at him as he came around the bed and he felt like jerk. When she was dressed, he pulled her close, unable to let her go thinking that the sex meant nothing to him. She watched him, waiting.

Adrian decided on the truth. "I'm sorry you can't stay," he murmured, kissing her softly. "I'd like you to, but I don't know how Kate will react."

"I understand."

Adrian walked her to the door of the suite and they paused. He wrapped his arms around Libby, reluctant to let her go. "Will you come over tomorrow and help me amuse Kate?"

There was only the tiniest hesitation. "Sure." She kissed him quickly on the lips and opened the door. "I'll see you in the morning."

Adrian watched her walk down the hallway to her room. Had he read her wrong? Perhaps she hadn't been hurt by his bluntness and he'd made her uncomfortable with his intensity.

It was just a fling.

He would do well to remember that.

***

Libby stood in front of the door to Adrian's suite the next day, tapping her hand against her thigh in a nervous beat. She wasn't sure how to behave now or what to say. The sex had been incredible and she'd fallen even more in love with him. But he'd reminded her with his bluntness that it was just a temporary romance and she'd done her best to pretend it meant the same to her.

Finally she got up the nerve to knock. Libby heard Kate's voice and the thud of feet coming to answer. Kate flung open the door. "Hi, Libby!" She beckoned Libby to come in.

"What have we got planned for the day?" Libby asked as she walked through to the living area.

"You need to help me convince Uncle Ade we should go to Sea World," Kate said.

Adrian looked less than impressed by Kate's suggestion but smiled at Libby anyway.

"There are still reporters outside the hotel. I told Kate she can wait until tomorrow, and then hopefully the reporters will have gone away."

"But Uncle Ade, that means we can do only two of the theme parks," Kate complained.

"With your sprained wrist, you won't be able to go on some of the rides anyway. We'll stay in the room today and we can play games."

"I'm tired of playing games and watching movies."

Libby could understand both of their concerns. What could they do that would keep them both happy? "What about working on your novel?" she asked.

Kate pouted. "I'd rather go to Sea World."

Libby smiled at her. "I know. Me too, but waiting an extra day will make it even more exciting."

Kate gave Libby a look which said she didn't believe her and huffed. "I'll set up my laptop." She headed for her bedroom.

Libby turned to Adrian, nerves in her stomach. "Morning."

He smiled at her slowly and walked closer. Checking Kate was still in her room, he took her hand and kissed the back of it. "Morning."

The zing traveled all the way to her toes. Adrian squeezed her hand and dropped it as Kate came back.

Libby had to focus on Kate. She set her laptop up on the table next to Kate's, relieved she would have a chance to get some more writing done, as she was falling behind. She asked Adrian, "What are you going to do today?"

"Since you two are going to be writing I might as well get in on the act." He indicated his guitar. "I've got a few tunes playing in my head."

"Do you write your own songs?" Intrigued, Libby realized she hadn't asked Adrian about his music.

"Mostly, but sometimes I collaborate with others."

"Libby, I don't know what's going to happen next." Kate's voice interrupted their conversation.

Adrian turned away and Libby settled at the table next to Kate. "Where are you up to?"

As Libby and Kate debated options, Adrian settled on the couch and started playing his guitar. Every now and then he'd stop, write something down and then replay it, making adjustments as he went.

Libby listened to him strum while she helped brainstorm ideas with Kate. When Kate had decided what was happening next in her story, Libby left her to write while she checked her emails.

There were dozens, many more than usual, and the subject lines said things like "You should be ashamed," "No longer buying your books," "Bad role model for children."

She clicked on the first email and read it, amazed at the hatred it contained. She clicked on another with a similar tone from a woman whose husband had had an affair. Libby's hand covered her mouth as she read the third.

All of these people believed the lies Emily had told. They all thought Libby had stolen Adrian away from Emily and that she should be ashamed of herself. They all said they would never buy her books and would make sure none of their friends did either.

Libby had never expected this level of response, hadn't expected anyone to believe the rubbish that had been written. She hadn't truly believed Emily's accusations would threaten the dream she'd been working so hard toward for the past eight years.

"Libby, what's wrong?" Adrian's voice brought her back to her surroundings. He watched her from the couch.

"Some emails about Emily's article."

He stood and walked over. Libby clicked on another one so he could read it.

His face was grim. "Do you think they read your statement?"

Libby checked the time the emails were sent. "If they got my email address through my website, they had to have seen it. It's on the homepage."

"What's up?" Kate looked up from her laptop.

Libby forced a smile. "Just a couple of people who believe what Emily said in her article."

"Well, they're dumb as dirt." Kate went back to her writing.

Libby grinned at Kate's assessment. "Do you think I should respond?" she asked Adrian.

He shook his head. "It won't help. They won't believe anything you say."

Libby counted the number of emails. There were twenty. Were there other people who thought the same as these women and would encourage their friends to stop buying her book? She hit the forward button and sent one through to Simone and Donna at her publishers with a question about what to do.

Her stomach was queasy. Libby wanted to give Emily a piece of her mind and tell her how her selfish actions had affected all of them.

"It will blow over soon enough," Adrian said and caressed her shoulder.

"I hope so."

Libby went back to her editing, wondering if this would be the last book she ever wrote.

***

The next day the reporters had disappeared from the hotel and Adrian kept his promise to Kate, taking her to Sea World with George. As much as Libby wanted to join them, she told Adrian she needed to work on her manuscript. The response to Emily's accusations had made Libby remember how important her writing was to her.

Her heart still screamed that she spend every moment with Kate and Adrian while she could. The time was rapidly approaching when she would have to say goodbye and they would head back to America.

But her head scolded her severely. Adrian had made it clear their fling was temporary. Her publisher was giving her the opportunity to fulfil her dream of a being a full-time author, and she couldn't throw it away over a man who wasn't going to be in her life for long.

Her experience with Clint made sure her head won.

***

Adrian was weary. He'd had a great day with Kate and George

at Sea World, but today he wanted nothing more than to rest. He sat at the table and booted up his laptop. He needed to make sure nothing new had surfaced from their Sea World trip.

The knock on the door signaled Libby's arrival.

Part of him wanted to race Kate to the door. He and Kate had had fun yesterday, but something had been missing. Someone.

How had Libby become part of his life so quickly?

She would have loved Sea World, but he understood why she hadn't come. What they had was temporary and Libby had work to do.

Adrian was googling his name as Libby walked in.

As usual she wore jeans and a top, yellow this time, and loafers. There wasn't anything extraordinary about the outfit, but when she smiled it zapped his whole body.

"Howdy," he said.

"Hi. Any latest news?" she asked, nodding toward his laptop.

"I was just checking." Adrian scanned the screen and all the blood rushed out of his head.

No.

It couldn't be. He clicked the link and waited for the page to load.

Please, don't let it be him.

Libby asked what was wrong, but he couldn't answer her. The picture showed an old man, haggard skin, dirty long black hair, wearing clothes that could do with an iron.

Adrian's stomach churned so much he thought he might vomit.

The man had aged a lot in the past twenty years, but Adrian still recognized him.

His father.

The headline read, "Rock Star Abandons Father to Poverty."

"What is it, Uncle Ade?" Kate's voice was right next to him and it brought him back to the real world. He put an arm around her to comfort himself.

"Give me a second to read this, kiddo." His voice sounded strange, dull, to his ears.

Libby's hand was on his shoulder and he met her concerned gaze and then turned back to the screen. Libby and Kate gave him the strength to read on.

The article began with how Adrian's father had struggled to take care of Adrian and his brother after his wife had walked out on them. It said he'd worked as many shifts as he could to provide for the boys, to give Adrian singing lessons, and to take care of them by himself.

Adrian snorted to release some of the anger that was building.

The article continued. The moment Adrian had become successful, it said, he had left without looking back, cutting all ties with the man who'd struggled to bring him up as a single father. He'd even gone as far as to change his name. The boy the man had raised was called Adrian Hart – not Kent Downer.

Adrian swore. His father had destroyed the last bit of anonymity he had. Damn him.

His father went on to say he hadn't spoken out before but when he'd read how Adrian had treated Emily, he knew he needed to say something. The apple hadn't fallen far from the tree. He couldn't allow Adrian to abandon his partner like Adrian's mother had abandoned them.

Adrian stared at the screen in disbelief. Who the hell did his father think he was? Pretending he knew anything about Adrian's life, pretending he cared, pretending he had been a good father.

Adrian didn't want to read on. His stomach was in knots and his head pulsated with tension.

Libby rubbed his shoulders, gently reminding him he wasn't alone.

He could do this. He let out a deep breath.

What else did the bastard have to say?

When asked who Kate was, Adrian's father said he wasn't sure. She could be his granddaughter, but if she was, he'd not met her. His heart was deeply saddened by the fact he didn't know.

There was no way Kate would ever meet her grandfather. Daniel hadn't wanted her anywhere near him and neither did Adrian. She didn't need to be exposed to that.

"Is it true, Uncle Ade?" Kate turned to face him, her eyes concerned.

Adrian sighed. He hadn't realized she had been reading. "No."

"Dad said Grandpa Hart was ill. What's wrong with him?"

It wasn't a conversation Adrian wanted to have now. Not while his head was still spinning at having the bastard thrust into his life again. He didn't want to deal with this, but he had no choice.

What had driven his father to suddenly make a statement? Was it because Adrian's photo had been splashed all over the news, exposing him as Kent? Had his father only just realized who Adrian was?

If so, it was another thing he owed Emily.

The newspapers and magazines would pay his father well for his story, no matter what the truth was. Perhaps that was all it was. A need for more money, for more booze.

"Uncle Adrian?" Kate's voice was quiet, almost fearful.

Adrian rubbed his face with his hands before pushing his chair away from the table so he could turn and face Kate. He took hold of her hands, conscious of Libby standing behind him, a silent support.

"My father is an alcoholic," he said.

Kate gasped.

"When we were young, he didn't take very good care of your dad and me, so we ran away. George's dad and mum cared for us until we grew up."

"What did he do?" Kate asked.

How could he explain the sadness, the neglect, the fear, to someone who had always been surrounded by support and love? "He forgot to feed us when he was drunk," he began.

"Did he hit you?"

Trust Kate to come straight to the point. "Why do you ask?"

"Charlie's dad gets drunk and hits his mum," Kate said, naming a child from her school.

Adrian deliberated for a moment. She needed to know the truth. "Yes, he did hit us."

Kate's expression turned sorrowful. "Then you were lucky Hank and Marla were so nice." She hugged her uncle.

Adrian held on to her tightly. He had been lucky, but it wasn't so simple.

"You need to tell the reporters he's lying. Then they'll go away."

Adrian smiled at her view of the world. The reporters wouldn't go away, they'd swarm around for more information, wanting to drag out every sordid detail about his past.

She didn't need to know. "I don't want to bring Hank and Marla into this." George's parents had saved them but Adrian still didn't know what Hank had said to his father. He wasn't sure if they could get into trouble for not reporting the case to social services. He sighed. Perhaps it was time he found out.

"They won't mind."

She was right. They wouldn't mind confronting the media, exposing Adrian's father. Since he was twelve, Hank and Marla had been his parents and had protected him. But in this, he wanted to protect them.

"I'll talk to George."

"I'll get my notebook and we can make a list of what is right. Then George can write up a statement." Kate strode away into her room.

Adrian watched her go. She was determined to see things right. His heart swelled with love. He would do whatever he could to protect her from the worst people in this world.

It was the one thing Susan and he agreed on. Kate's welfare came first.

Susan.

He swore.

"What's wrong?" Libby's hands tightened on his shoulders.

Adrian turned to her. "Susan knew nothing of my childhood. She'll see what my father says as proof I'm neglectful." He drummed his fingers over the table. "And if I tell the truth she'll question my parenting skills and whether I could succumb to alcohol." Would this be the final straw? Would Susan sue for custody of Kate?

Kate came back into the room before Libby could respond.

"I'll write down all his comments and you can tell me what the truth is," Kate said as she sat down with her notebook and started her list.

He couldn't do this now. He had to talk with George, work out what he was going to say, get past his gut reaction, which was to hide until it all went away. "I'll do it tonight after the concert," he said, checking the time. "Tonight I want you both to stay inside. Neither of you needs to face the press outside. They'll be back after this."

"But Uncle Ade, we were fixin' to go to the movies," Kate protested.

He hated saying no. Hated the fact she hadn't been able to do all the things they'd planned. She deserved better. "Not tonight. Order one of the movies through the hotel."

He'd promised Susan Kate wouldn't be harassed by the media. He didn't want to lose Kate, but maybe he was being selfish. Susan would be able to give her a more stable home environment.

Adrian's phone rang. "That'll be George. Will you be all right?" The concern was clear on his face.

Kate was pouting, but she nodded.

He stood and turned to Libby. She opened her arms and he stepped into them, drawing strength from her calm support.

"We'll work it out," Libby whispered.

Adrian closed his eyes briefly before he stepped back. She knew the right thing to say.

Forcing a smile on his face he looked at Kate and said, "See you later."

"Bye, Uncle Ade."

Libby squeezed his hand.

He needed to go but he wanted to stay here with them.

This was his safe place.

Maybe Libby was right. They would work it out.

Together.

Chapter 17

Adrian walked to the door slowly, his shoulders hunched up defensively. Libby wanted to run after him and tell him everything would be fine, but she couldn't guarantee it.

She wanted to call Adrian's father and tell him what a monster he was, tell him to leave Adrian alone and withdraw his comments.

It wouldn't help, though. What was done was done, and if he retracted his statement there would be speculation as to whether Adrian had paid for his silence. There was nothing she could do for Adrian.

Next to her Kate sniffed.

Libby turned and saw Kate's watery eyes. She pulled Kate into a hug. It would have been a shock to find out her grandfather was an alcoholic who beat his children. "How are you feeling?" Libby asked.

Kate stepped back. "I know Grandpa is lying but I'm angry he's made Uncle Ade so sad. Uncle Ade's nothing like his father says." She sighed.

Libby was sure there was more to it. "Is there anything else worrying you?"

That made Kate look up. She bit her lip. "Aunt Susan won't like it."

It was what Adrian had said as well. Did this woman know

nothing about Adrian? "Does it matter what your aunt thinks, if you know it's not true?"

"Yes," Kate said. "I overheard Uncle Ade talking to George. He thinks she's waiting for a reason to take me from him." Her eyes showed her misery. "I don't want to live with Aunt Susan. I like living with Uncle Ade."

Of course she did. Adrian was a fantastic father figure. Libby gave her a hug. "There are ways of proving that what Emily and your grandpa are saying isn't true. Your Aunt Susan won't have a reason then."

Kate didn't look convinced.

Before she could soothe Kate further, Libby's phone rang. It was Adrian. He'd only just left. Concern skittled over her skin. "What's wrong?"

"Susan phoned. She's read about my father." He was grim.

It wasn't good news. "What did she say?"

"She insisted on talking to Kate immediately so I've given her your cell number. She'll probably ring the second I hang up. Don't let her rile you up."

Libby wanted to swear. She wasn't sure what she should say to this woman. She was expecting an ogre, from what Adrian had told her. "What's she likely to say?"

"She thinks you and I are carrying out debauched acts in front of Kate. She's not being at all rational."

Still listening, Libby sat down on the couch and gave Kate a small smile. Kate hovered next to her, twisting her hands together. Libby patted the couch and Kate sat.

"All right," Libby told Adrian. "I'll do my best not to sound debauched."

Adrian barked out a laugh. "Call me after." He hung up.

Libby turned to Kate. "Aunt Susan is going to call. She's seen the articles about Emily and your grandpa and she's worried about you."

"I don't want to talk to her. She makes me mad when she says stuff about Uncle Ade."

Libby placed a hand on the girl's shoulder. "I know she does. Try to remember she's doing this because she cares."

Libby's cell rang. She checked the display. International number. "Are you ready?"

Kate nodded.

Libby answered her phone. "Hello."

"This is Susan Montgomery, Kate's aunt." The American accent was southern but refined, reminding Libby of old movies set on cotton plantations.

"Adrian told me you might call," Libby said into the silence.

"I'm sure he did. I'm sure he told you what to say." The refined accent couldn't disguise the snide remark.

Libby forced herself not to smile. "No ma'am. He knew I wouldn't let Kate speak to anyone I didn't know, so he rang to tell me you were calling. You wouldn't believe the number of people who've rung believing the rubbish that's been printed about Adrian. First Emily and now Adrian's father. Honestly, you would think people would have more sense than to believe everything they read."

There was silence and Libby pictured all the wind going out of Susan's sails. "Yes, well, those magazines can be very convincing. One assumes they check their facts before going to print."

"You'd hope so, but I guess if one side doesn't comment by the deadline they print it anyway. It's so sad."

"But the way Adrian has treated his father is appalling. The picture of him in the paper showed he was suffering."

Libby tensed. The woman was determined to think the worst of Adrian. Libby's tone was one of controlled anger. "Did your sister never mention her father-in-law to you?"

"No." Susan's tone was full of grief.

"Then perhaps you need to consider why that was and not believe what you've read."

"Don't you dare make assumptions about my sister. You didn't know her." The grief had been replaced by anger.

Libby closed her eyes. She needed to tread carefully. "No, I didn't. I'm sorry."

The silence was full of indignation. Finally Susan said, "May I speak with Kate?"

"She's right here." Libby passed the phone to Kate. She hoped she hadn't made things worse.

"Hi, Aunt Susan."

Susan's voice was going a mile a minute, but Libby couldn't

make out the words. She breathed out slowly to defuse the anger still simmering.

"It makes me mad," Kate said to her aunt. "Those reporters are nasty, but Uncle Ade and Libby have been protecting me. We haven't really left the hotel, but hopefully it will be better when we go to Perth."

More talking and Kate rolled her eyes. "Uncle Ade never drinks."

Libby sighed.

"Are Jemma and Jason back from camp yet?" Kate asked, changing the subject. A pause. "I'm fine, Aunt Susan. I had an awesome time at Sea World. Can I speak to Jemma?" Another pause, then Kate grinned. "Hi Jem, how was camp?" Kate stood and paced around the room as she spoke with her cousin. The energetic ten-year-old who had been missing for the last few days came back with a vengeance as she regaled her cousin with stories of what she'd been doing in Australia and New Zealand.

Shrieks of laughter came from the other end of the phone. It suddenly hit Libby that Kate was probably lonely for company of her own age. Someone to laugh and swap secrets with.

"I'll Skype you tomorrow." Kate hung up and handed the phone back to Libby. "Jem had to go because it's an international phone call."

"Are you close with her?" Libby asked.

"Yeah. She's my best friend. She wanted to come on tour with me but Aunt Susan wouldn't let her."

"That's a shame."

"Totally, we would have had an awesome time." Kate turned and put a hand over her mouth. "Not that *we* haven't had fun," she said quickly.

Libby laughed. "Don't worry, I haven't taken offence. It must be hard being around adults all the time."

"Sometimes I wish Jem was here, but I'll see her in a week when we go back, and I didn't want to go to summer camp."

Another week and they'd be gone. Libby pushed away the sadness. "Feeling better now?"

"Yeah. Let's watch a movie."

Surely after talking with Kate, Susan would see there was nothing wrong. Kate was obviously happy.

Libby hoped Susan realized that.

***

Adrian's patience was rapidly dwindling. The past few days since his father had been interviewed had been a nightmare. The media circus outside the hotel had only intensified as reporters tried to get Adrian to comment on his father. Then Emily was interviewed again and asked about Adrian's father. She'd claimed not to know of Adrian's name change and said Adrian had never mentioned his father.

At least one of those statements was true.

Today his father had hit the US talk shows. He'd been given some time in the make-up chair so he appeared respectable, but Adrian could see through it. He'd started watching one but quickly stopped. There wasn't a sentence of truth that came out of the man's mouth and Adrian couldn't bear to watch it. He left it to George, hoping his father would say something that would trip him up.

Adrian refused to make a statement. Libby arrived one afternoon as he and George were arguing about it.

"You have to say something. Your silence makes you appear guilty."

"No." His voice was flat. "I don't tell people close to me about my father – I'm not dredging up the past for a bunch of strangers." He was not going to let the bastard have any more of him. His father had already had too much influence over him. Adrian was still dealing with the emotional scars from the first twelve years of his life.

"You don't have to give any details." George thrust a piece of paper at Adrian.

It was a brief statement that basically said nothing new. He screwed it up. "The reporters won't stop if it's only a few details. They can smell a story here."

"I want to say something."

Adrian and George both stopped and stared at Kate.

She put her hands on her hips, readying herself for a fight. "I want to tell them the truth so they go away."

No way. There wasn't a chance in hell Adrian was exposing Kate to any more reporters. "This doesn't concern you, Katie."

"It does too!" Kate shouted. "I've been stuck in this room for days now. I'm sick and tired of it. I want to go out. I want to see more of Brisbane. Why won't you tell them to go away?" She finished her speech with a sob.

Adrian's heart bled. He constantly felt like he was failing her. "I know it's hard on you, kiddo. I'm sorry."

"Can I speak to the reporters?" Kate asked, glancing back at Libby with hope.

"No. They'll lose interest soon." Adrian prayed he was right.

"I hate them, I hate them both." Kate stormed into her room and shut the door with a bang.

Adrian swore softly. This whole situation was the hardest on Kate. He hated the fact she couldn't go out, but his first priority had to be her safety.

Libby walked over to him and ran a hand over his arm. "Why don't you let her write a statement? It might make her feel better, even if she never gives it to the press."

Adrian scowled. "I'd rather not encourage her." If he let her write it, she'd want to release it.

"Are you sure?" Libby pushed.

No, he wasn't, and that was the problem. He didn't know what he should do. "Yes, I'm sure," Adrian snapped. "I know what I'm doing." He stood. He had to get away. To George he said, "We should get going." He grabbed his bag and walked out without another word.

He couldn't deal with this now.

He needed time to think.

Time to cope with this out-of-control mess his life had become.

Time.

***

Libby stood where she was, her body frozen in response to Adrian's words. She'd never seen Adrian's temper but there it was lashing out at her.

She felt ill. Not about what he'd said but how he'd reacted. He doubted himself, doubted what he was doing, and she'd questioned him, bringing up his insecurities. She knew it from the tone of his voice, the way he hadn't looked at her when he replied and the slump of his shoulders as he walked out.

She needed to apologize.

The last thing she wanted to do was make him doubt his decisions.

She picked up her cell phone and dialed Adrian's number, hoping he wouldn't be too mad to answer.

It went straight to voicemail.

Libby left a message apologizing and hung up.

Letting out a breath she went to the kitchenette and poured a glass of water before knocking and letting herself into Kate's room.

"You want to talk about it?" Libby asked.

Kate was sitting on her bed, ripped magazine pages scattered around her. "They're both stupid liars. It's Emily's fault I can't leave the room. If she hadn't started this, Grandpa Hart never would have known who Uncle Ade is. Why can't I say something to the media? Why can't I tell them the truth about Grandpa Hart and Emily? It's not fair."

Libby let Kate rant and handed her the glass of water and some tissues. She understood Kate's anger and frustration.

Maybe if Kate talked to Emily she could convince her to stop speaking with the media. Emily had been Kate's nanny, after all. She knew some of what Kate had been through.

"What would you say to the media?"

"Emily's a stupid liar."

Libby suppressed a smile at the vehemence of Kate's words. "How do you think that will make Emily feel?"

"I don't care. She hasn't cared about me."

How could she phrase this so Kate would understand? "I think if you said that it might make her sad and a little angry. If someone made you angry would you stop what you were doing?"

Kate opened her mouth to respond and then paused. "Probably not," she admitted.

"When you were angry with me, what made you change your mind?" Libby asked.

"You understood what was wrong and tried to make me feel better."

Libby smiled at her. "What would make Emily feel better?"

Kate thought about it and then screwed up her nose. "I don't think Uncle Ade will want to kiss her."

Libby chuckled. "No, I think you're right. Didn't you see Emily after she quit?"

"She came to say goodbye."

"And what did you say to her?"

"I said goodbye and wished her a good flight." Kate paused. "She asked about you and I said you were wonderful."

"How do you think she might have felt about that?"

"She might have been jealous." Kate opened her eyes wide. "Do you think it's my fault Emily said all those lies?" Kate asked in a small voice.

"No! Not at all." Alarmed, Libby put an arm around Kate. "You aren't responsible for other people's actions. Emily chose to do what she did for her own reasons. What you need to think about is what you could say that might make her think about how you're feeling."

"Should I lie?" Kate asked.

"No. Of course not. There must have been some things you did with Emily that were fun."

Kate considered her answer. "I did get to read a lot of books when she was my nanny."

It wasn't a lot to work with.

"Do you think if I emailed her and told her that she would stop lying?"

Libby hedged. "You'd better ask your uncle." She'd put her foot in it enough already.

"I'll write something down." Kate got up, snatched her notebook and started writing.

Libby hoped she'd done the right thing.

If only there was a reporter who would actually ask the tough questions and get Emily to admit the truth.

A light bulb went off. Libby examined the idea from all sides and couldn't see how it would fail. Checking the time, she calculated the difference and then dialed.

"Piper, I need a favor."

***

Adrian walked into his hotel room, but instead of heading for the bathroom, he went in search of Libby. She was packing up her laptop at the dining table.

He'd felt like a jerk all evening. He hadn't meant to snap at her, but the house arrest was getting to him. He was second-guessing all his decisions and to have Libby disagree with him made him third-guess them.

He wasn't sure how to get the media to leave them alone.

Libby's voicemail message, which he hadn't got until after the concert, showed she understood, but he felt as though he was walking on eggshells. Any wrong step and he'd crush the lot.

Libby looked up as he walked over and gave a cautious smile. "Hi."

"Howdy." He stopped next to her and saw the concern cross her face. "I'm sorry for snapping at you earlier." He sighed. "This whole situation is getting to me."

Libby took his hand. "It's getting to us both. I'm sorry I made you doubt your decision."

He breathed out in relief. It meant so much that she understood. "How's Kate?"

"We talked about it. She'd like to send Emily an email, but I wasn't sure if you'd want her to."

Adrian frowned, trying not to be defensive. "What did she want to say?"

"She wants to thank Emily for being her nanny and ask her to tell the truth."

That was a surprise. When he'd left, Kate hated Emily. Libby had said something to change her mind. "What did you say to Kate?"

Libby looked down for a moment. "Initially Kate wanted to tell Emily she hated her, but I explained it might make Emily worse. So we decided to try the carrot method instead of the stick." She waited for his reaction.

It was better than Kate talking to the media, but an email could be forwarded on to anyone. "I'll think about it." He'd check what Kate wanted to say tomorrow.

There was still a distance between him and Libby, both literally and figuratively. He wanted to bridge it. Stepping forward he pulled Libby into his arms. "I'm sorry for earlier."

She smiled at him. "I know. It's all right."

It wasn't. He'd lashed out at her, not with fists but with words. In his experience they could be equally damaging. The bruises his father gave him had faded but the words – the accusations that he was useless and that he was the reason his mother left – stayed with him even now.

Adrian wanted to show Libby how much she meant to him. He wanted to hold her all night. He appreciated her support and was sorry for his actions. "Will you stay tonight?"

"Until the morning?"

He nodded. He hated it when Libby left in the middle of the night, as if they had something to hide. As long as they were up before Kate, it wouldn't be a problem.

Libby smiled at him, wide and open, her whole being radiating her pleasure. "I'd love to."

He relaxed and kissed her softly. "Why don't you get a change of clothes?"

He walked her to the door and waited there until she reached her room. Then he went into the bathroom for a quick shower.

Part of him was nervous about Libby spending the night. He'd never slept the whole night with anyone. He'd always left after sex. No one knew he always slept with a night light. He closed his eyes as he let the water spray over his face.

But Libby knew about his fear of the dark. She knew more about him than any other woman.

He shut off the shower and toweled himself dry.

He'd never expected to open himself up to someone like he had with Libby. He trusted her.

He'd miss her when he went back to America.

The sharp ache in his heart caught him by surprise. He rubbed at his chest. He'd made it clear their relationship was temporary. Anything else was impossible. They lived in different countries.

But Libby's best friend lived in Texas and Libby didn't have a good relationship with her parents ...

The quiet knock on the door stopped his train of thought. He pushed the thought away, slung the towel around his waist and went to answer it.

He'd think about it later.

***

The next day they flew to Perth. Libby's heart lifted as the Swan River came into view just before they landed. This was home.

She was looking forward to taking Kate home with her to get away from the reporters, who were still interested in Adrian's story. Adrian had decided it was the best course of action.

Libby's car had been left in the long-term car park and she went to fetch it while the others waited in a private area of the airport. The reporters jostled around her for a statement as she came out of the terminal.

"Why did you steal Emily's job?"

"Why did Kent abandon his father?"

"How is the little girl related to Kent?"

She wasn't able to push through the mass of bodies, so she held up a hand and waited until they had settled down somewhat. She was tired of all the accusations. Tired of being harassed. Didn't these people have anything better to report on? "The little girl did not have a nanny when I started working for them," she began, answering the first question. She turned to the second reporter. "You'll need to speak to Kent about his father. Now if you'll excuse me, I'd like to fetch my car."

Questions were shouted at her and microphones shoved in her face. She tried to walk around but it didn't work. Frustration bubbled up inside her. They were crowding her and robbing her of the time she had left with Adrian and Kate. She just wanted to go home. As she was close to tears, a burly security guard came up and pushed the reporters away.

"Come on, folks. Let the lady through." He helped her on the bus to the long-term car park.

"Thank you." Libby smiled at the man.

"No worries, love."

As the bus doors closed, Libby let out a sigh of relief. She'd had enough of this nonsense. She wanted to give Emily a piece of her mind, but she had to trust Piper had it under control.

She collected her car, and a few minutes later, Libby pulled up into a section of the airport where Kate and Adrian were waiting.

Adrian frowned when he saw the car. Libby knew it wasn't much to look at and it might be ten years old, but it had just been repaired and was clean. Kate jumped in and George loaded her bags into the boot. Adrian came around to the driver's side window and leaned in.

"If there are reporters at your house, bring Kate to the hotel." He glanced around.

"I'll take care of her, Adrian." Libby placed a hand on his.

"I know you will." He gave her a half-smile.

The fact Adrian trusted her with Kate gave Libby such a thrill. "I'll see you soon," she said. Adrian was going to join them after he'd checked into the hotel and made a media statement.

He nodded.

Libby drove off, avoiding the reporters who were still waiting for Kent to come out of the airport. She breathed a sigh of relief as she turned onto the highway and no one was following her. The road here was familiar and she allowed herself to relax.

"How far away do you live?" Kate asked peering out the window at the industrial sector they were driving through.

"About an hour from here. It's south of Perth, close to the beach."

"Can we go swimming?"

Libby laughed. "It might be a bit cold." Today was a beautiful winter's day with the sun shining, but there was still a nip to the air.

Libby turned on to the freeway and headed south for about an hour before leaving the freeway to head west.

Ten minutes later she was pulling into the carport of an old weatherboard beach shack. There was no drive, just compacted dirt, and the grass was in need of a mow. Despite its age she was going to miss this place when she moved in a couple of weeks.

"Wow, this place is old," Kate said.

Libby laughed. "It's one of the original shacks built in this area. Let's get inside and I'll show you around."

Libby unlocked the front door and carried their bags in, enjoying the creak and groan of the old floorboards as she walked across them.

"Your room is over here." Libby led Kate to her office, which had a single bed in it. The bedspread was pale blue and there was a small chest of drawers in the corner that Libby had salvaged from an op shop and redecorated, as well as her writing desk and a bookshelf.

Kate jumped on the bed and bounced up and down. "This is great."

Libby dumped her case in her room, then called to Kate, "Are you hungry?"

Kate wandered into the hall and followed Libby through to the kitchen at the back. "No. Do you think we could go to the beach? I'd really like to get out."

Libby felt the same way. After so many days not being able to leave the hotel, she was eager to get some fresh air. "Absolutely."

She picked up her house keys and two hats, one of which she gave to Kate, and said, "Let's go."

"Yes!" Kate pumped her arm and raced down the steps toward the car.

Libby locked up and then gestured to Kate. "It's not far. We'll walk."

Surprise lit up Kate's face. She raced over to Libby and they wandered down the street.

"The trees here are real different from back home," Kate commented.

"Most of these are native to Australia," Libby told her and pointed out the few she knew the names of.

They crossed a road and the ground gradually began to rise.

"Wow, some of these houses are huge!"

Libby laughed. "This area is called The Bay. All of this used to be sand dunes, but now they're big blocks. You need a fair bit of money to live here."

"But you live across the road and your house isn't big."

"This is a newer area."

They reached a path that ran parallel to the beach and Libby turned toward the lookout. Together they climbed the steps and gazed out over the sound.

The water was calm today, a dark blue with the occasional ripple as the wind blew over it. The sound curved around in a C shape and on the horizon were some small, rocky islands. To the north Libby saw houses but to the south it was mostly sand dunes. On the beach itself a man walked his dog and a woman jogged up the sand. The rest of the long shoreline was deserted. Libby breathed in a deep breath of the salty air. This was home.

"It's so quiet here," Kate said.

It was. Even in the summer there weren't huge crowds on the clean, sandy beaches.

"Do you want to go down to the water?" Libby asked.

"Yeah."

They turned and made their way down to the beach. Small piles of seaweed had been washed up in sections and Kate spent her time exploring what had washed up. They walked a couple of miles before they turned back.

Kate was more relaxed than she had been in days and the tension in Libby's shoulders melted away. The hush of the waves washing up on the shoreline, the smell of the salt and the seaweed, and the gentle refreshing breeze soothed away all the troubles of the moment. Libby would have to bring Adrian here when he arrived.

Kate found a bit of driftwood that she swore was shaped like a person and decided to take it as a souvenir. "That way I'll remember our walk on the beach after we leave," Kate told Libby.

Libby smiled but didn't answer. She was all too aware she had less than a week left with them. The rest of her editing could wait. She'd do it while Kate slept and would spend as much time as she could with Adrian and Kate before they left.

They walked back down the street, the sand dunes muting the sound of the wash of the waves on the shore. When they turned onto Libby's street, Libby's heart sank. Parked outside the shack were three cars with different television stations logos on the side. The reporters hadn't spotted them yet.

"What do we do?" Kate asked.

Libby retrieved her house keys from her pocket. "We'll go straight up to the house. Hopefully they won't notice us until we get close and we can get inside before they realize we're not already there."

Her heart pounded in her chest. She didn't want any more

pictures of Kate splashed across the television.

They were still a hundred yards from the house when the first reporter spotted them. The cameraman with him turned on his camera and pointed it in Libby's direction.

Libby seized Kate's hand. "Walk faster." She kept her head down, shielding her face with the brim of her hat, and kept her body between Kate and the cameras. The other reporters realized what was going on and moved toward her.

"Who's the girl with you?"

"Kent said your relationship was temporary. Does that mean you're not dating Kent?"

Libby felt like she'd been shot, but she didn't stop walking. She'd look up Adrian's statement when they were safely inside.

"Why did Kent abandon his father?"

Libby ignored the questions and trotted up the steps to her front door. Her hand shook as she fumbled to put the key in the lock, but finally it went in and she opened the door, pushing Kate in front of her.

She slammed the door behind her and let out a deep breath. "Are you all right?"

Kate turned to her, her eyes flashing. "No, I'm not. I'm mad. Those stupid reporters ruin everything. I want to tell them what I think of them."

Libby shepherded Kate away from the entrance where the reporters wouldn't be able to hear the girl's shouts. "I know it's unfair. Let's have something to eat. Maybe they'll go away."

On cue someone knocked on the door. Libby flinched but ignored it.

She put on the kettle and searched through the cupboard for something to feed Kate. Her eyes fell on a box of instant soups and she pulled them out.

Kate paced up and down the kitchen.

"Can you fetch my laptop?" Libby asked. "It's in my carry-on bag in my room." That would give her something to do for a moment and Libby wanted to get online and read what Adrian had said.

Libby pulled out some mugs, tipped the powdery substance in and poured boiling water over it, stirring it vigorously.

It was then she heard Kate talking loudly.

Libby dropped the spoon and raced to the front door, which was wide open. Kate was standing on the porch, her notebook in her hand, talking to the reporters who were standing around her, cameras rolling.

Libby's stomach plummeted. No. She blinked, hoping the vision of Kate in front of the reporters would disappear.

It didn't.

She faltered, unsure what to do.

"Kent is my uncle. He's been taking care of me since my parents died. Emily quit as my nanny and Libby took her place." Kate glanced down at her notepad.

Libby couldn't stop her now, not without causing a scene, which might make matters worse.

"My grandpa is not a nice man and you shouldn't believe what he says. I would appreciate it if you would leave us alone now, because I'm not allowed out and you're ruining my whole holiday. Thank you."

Kate closed her notebook, turned and walked inside with her head held high.

The reporters looked stunned. Libby hesitated and then followed up Kate's words. "As you can see you're upsetting my friend. Please leave now."

She closed the door and went to find Kate.

Kate was face down on her bed sobbing. Libby ignored the nausea she felt and sat down next to Kate and rubbed her back. "I'm sorry, Katie." She couldn't be mad at the girl for what she had done. She'd been cooped up for days and wanting to speak out about it.

Libby closed her eyes briefly. Adrian was going to be furious when he saw the footage. He might even think Libby had encouraged Kate to give the statement.

"They made me so mad. The things they said about you and Uncle Ade. It's not true. You're both good people and I love you both." Her voice was muffled against the pillow.

Libby's heart swelled and her eyes grew moist. "I love you too, kiddo."

Kate sat up then, wiping her hand over her eyes and nose. "Really?"

"Of course."

Kate threw her arms around Libby and hugged her tight. "Will you come back with us? You and Uncle Ade can get married and we can all live together and we won't have to be apart."

Libby's throat closed up. There was nothing she wanted more in this world, but she couldn't lie to Kate and say it would happen. "I don't know, Kate. It's not something your uncle and I have discussed."

"But you love him, don't you?"

If only life was that simple.

Kate was waiting for an answer.

Libby couldn't answer her. "Why don't we talk about this later? Our soup is going cold and I need to ring your uncle and tell him what you did."

Kate bit on her thumbnail. "You're going to tell on me?"

Libby forced a laugh. "No, I'm going to prepare him. You might have your face on television."

"But they wouldn't do that, would they?" Kate looked incredulous.

"They might." Libby was certain they would. It was too good a sound bite. And Adrian was going to be furious. Nerves played table tennis in her stomach.

Kate bit her lip. "They really are stupid heads."

"Yep, they really are."

Libby led the way into the kitchen and handed Kate one of the mugs. Then she set her laptop up on the kitchen table.

Kate sat at one side of the table glumly stirring the soup around.

Libby dialed Adrian's cell but it went through to voicemail. She didn't want to explain what had happened in a voice message, so she said, "It's Libby. We're both fine. Call me when you can."

One of the reporters had implied that Kent had made a statement. She turned to her laptop and after a moment found an article on one of the Perth-based news pages.

Quickly she scanned it. The article said Kent denied all Emily's claims of a relationship. When asked about Libby, he said she was doing some temporary work for him and refused to answer any questions about Kate or his father.

Libby bit the inside of her lip. She picked up her phone and called George.

"What's wrong?"

"Is Adrian with you?"

"Hang on, I'll put you on speaker."

"Is Kate all right?" Adrian's voice came through full of concern.

"Yes, we're both fine. We went for a walk on the beach and when we returned there were reporters waiting at my house."

George swore.

"We got inside without too much trouble."

"Then what happened?" Adrian's voice was quiet but his tone said he knew there was more to come and he wasn't happy.

Libby stood and walked down the hallway to her bedroom. "Kate made a statement to the reporters."

There was silence.

"What did she say?" George asked.

"She said Adrian was her uncle, Emily had quit and her grandpa wasn't to be trusted. She said the reporters were ruining her holiday and told them to go away."

"You let her speak to the reporters when I said she wasn't to?" Adrian didn't give her a chance to respond. "Did they get a picture of her?"

"They had video cameras. I'm pretty sure they were on."

"You'd better bring her back to the hotel." The phone went dead.

Libby hung up in shock. Adrian's voice had been so cold. He thought she'd let Kate talk to the reporters against his wishes. She would have to explain when she got to the hotel.

She pressed her hands to her eyes. It was her fault. She knew Kate was angry and she should have kept a closer eye on her. She should have taken the time to convince Adrian to let Kate speak.

She walked down the hallway to check outside. The reporters had left. Obviously they had got what they'd come for and were returning to edit their pieces for the next news bulletin.

Libby returned to the kitchen, where Kate was still stirring her uneaten soup. "We need to go back to the hotel."

"Is Uncle Ade mad?" Kate asked in a whisper.

"I think he's a little upset," Libby said, forcing a small smile. "Are you going to eat your lunch?"

Kate shook her head.

"Then we'd better get going."

Libby carried Kate's suitcase back out to the car. She debated taking her own luggage and then packed it just in case.

She wasn't sure how welcome she would be.

***

Adrian paced the room, unable to sit down. How could Libby have gone behind his back like that? He'd trusted her, been so sure she'd understood him, understood why he didn't want Kate in front of the media.

Could he have been so wrong?

"It might not be too bad," George said from where he sat at the laptop, trying to find further details.

Adrian grunted. It hardly mattered what Kate had said. The issue was that she'd said anything. Libby had let her and Susan would be furious. The last conversation he'd had with Susan had not gone well. It would only take one more thing before she'd be suing for custody of Kate.

Something like Kate giving a statement to the media.

He huffed and ran his hands through his hair. "Found anything yet?" he asked George.

"Yeah, there're a couple of teasers up on the websites. Turn on the TV." George checked his watch. "I think it will be on the news bulletin."

Adrian did as George asked and then walked over to check the articles. All of them led with the fact that Kate was Kent's niece not his daughter, and that Libby was her nanny, adding stupid comments about women not having to worry, he was still available.

The news update came on, capturing Adrian's attention. He walked closer as someone knocked on the hotel room door. He left George to answer it while he watched the report.

The footage focused on an old weatherboard beach shack that had seen better days. The reporter did her piece to camera, explaining that Libby had brought the mysterious young girl home with her.

The report then cut to footage of the front door opening and Kate standing there with a piece of paper in her hand. Libby was nowhere in sight. The cameraman moved to get a better shot and Libby appeared standing behind Kate in support of her.

The pain was nauseating. Until that moment, he had hoped that maybe it had been a mistake, that maybe it wasn't as he suspected, but pictures didn't lie. Libby was standing behind Kate, obviously complicit in what was happening. Then Libby added her few words further, proving his worst fears.

"I'm sorry, Uncle Ade." Kate's voice was quiet as she came into the room. Adrian turned to face her, not able to even look at the woman he'd put all his trust in.

"It's not your fault, kiddo." No, Libby was to blame for this. He held his arms open. "Come here."

Kate rushed forward and threw herself into his arms. Adrian held her tight, his eyes closed.

When he opened them, he was looking right at Libby.

She didn't flinch.

She wasn't sorry for what she'd done.

God, it cut him to the core.

Adrian broke his hug with Kate and said to her, "I think they'll leave us alone for a while now. What would you like to do for the rest of the day?"

"Libby can show us the city," Kate said, glancing back at Libby.

He could barely look at the woman, let alone spend any time with her. How could he have been so wrong? "I think Libby probably has some editing to do. We can explore the city on our own." His tone was light but there was no compromise to it.

Kate looked back at Libby, her eyes full of apology.

Adrian's cell rang. Relieved at the interruption, he snatched it, but then his heart sunk. Susan.

Surely she hadn't seen this already. It was close to midnight in Houston.

"Susan," he said.

He heard Kate's quiet gasp but focused on what Susan was saying.

"You promised me Kate wouldn't be hounded by the media and yet you let her speak directly to them. What the hell do you think you're doing?"

Adrian had never heard Susan so mad. "It wasn't my intention to let her speak to the media. She did it while she was with her nanny."

"You obviously haven't chosen someone who will care for her properly. I've given you enough chances, Adrian. I can't risk Kate's welfare anymore. I will be suing for custody."

No, this couldn't be happening.

Adrian sunk down on the couch. "I'll fight it." He had to. He loved Kate and he'd promised Daniel he would take care of her.

"You won't win." Susan hung up.

Adrian sat holding the phone, staring at it as if he could make it disappear.

"Adrian?" George's voice.

"She's going for custody of Kate." He lowered his head into his hands as Kate wailed, "No, no. I don't want to live with her."

Adrian didn't want to turn around, didn't want to face Libby, but he had to soothe Kate. He half-turned and motioned to Kate. "Come here."

George was leading Libby toward the entrance. Adrian didn't know what he'd do without George there to help him.

Kate dashed over and Adrian pulled her onto his lap. He'd prepared for this conversation even as he hoped he'd never have to have it.

"You need to think about what you want, kiddo. If you lived with Aunt Susan, you wouldn't have to worry about the media and you'd get to be with Jemma all the time."

"Don't you want me to stay with you?" Her voice was small.

"Of course I do. We have a lot of fun and I love having you here, but I want the best for you. If you want to live with Susan and Jemma, I would understand."

Kate's face got that set, stubborn look, so like her father that Adrian's heart ached. "You can't get rid of me that easily. I want to stay with you. You're so much more fun than Aunt Susan. She never has the time to play games."

The relief washed over him like a wave. If Kate wanted to stay with him, he would fight with everything he had to keep her.

He wouldn't let Susan have her.

And the fight would keep his mind off the pain of Libby's betrayal.

Chapter 18

Libby drove home in a daze.

After Susan had called, George had taken her by the arm and led her to the door, telling her Adrian needed some time to think things through.

She'd wanted to refuse to leave, to explain the situation, but then Adrian had said Susan was suing for custody. Libby knew he wouldn't listen to anything she had to say right then. His mind would be on the bigger issue.

Still, Libby couldn't quite believe Adrian hadn't given her the chance to explain. Had their relationship meant nothing to him? Had he just grasped the opportunity to end it now, rather than in a few days' time?

The doubt threatened to overwhelm her, but she pushed it back.

No, she would see them in a couple of days when Adrian had his first concert in Perth. Then she would have a chance to explain.

She pulled in to her drive and turned off the car. As if on cue her phone rang. She checked the display. "Hi, George." She tried to make her voice sound normal.

"Adrian has asked me to call you and let you know your services will no longer be required for the rest of the tour." His tone was pure business.

Libby's jaw dropped. "What?"

"You won't be needed as Kate's nanny. The rest of your contract will of course be paid out."

Libby could barely believe what she was hearing. "But –"

"I'm sorry, Libby. Adrian can't afford any more stunts like the one today."

"He doesn't want to hear my explanation?" She hated the quiver in her voice.

George paused. "No."

Tears welled in her eyes and she forced them back. The lump in her throat was hard to swallow. "Tell them both I'm sorry and if there's anything I can do to help, they just need to ask."

"I will." George hung up.

Libby sat there trying to stem the tears. She wouldn't cry over this. She'd known it wasn't going to last. She'd told herself she wouldn't cry when it ended. It had just ended before she'd expected it to.

Losing her battle against the tears, she forced open her car door and rushed up the porch. When she finally got her front door open, she stumbled through and slammed it behind her. Then she gave in to the urge, sank to the ground and sobbed.

***

Libby didn't know how long she sat there for, just that the warmth of the day was dissipating, being replaced with a chill. Slowly she got to her feet and went into the bathroom to wash her face.

Staring in the mirror she examined herself critically. Her eyes were red, her cheeks were blotchy and her plain brown hair hung straight and boring to her shoulders. Really, when she looked at herself, it was a surprise that Adrian had wanted to spend any time with her. Maybe all she had been to him was a convenient body.

She pressed her eyes shut.

No, surely she'd learned from Clint. Surely the way Adrian had behaved showed her he cared.

Or was she so desperate to be loved that she had imagined something that hadn't been there?

Again.

Libby splashed water on her face, patting it dry with a handtowel. She had to find something to do. She couldn't spend the rest of the day questioning her relationship or lack thereof with Adrian. She had to keep busy.

Her writing wouldn't help her now. Her concentration was shot.

Instead Libby rang her real estate agent and arranged to go through the unit she'd rented sight unseen.

Half an hour later she was in front of the ten unit complex. It had been built in the seventies with typical brown brick and decorative white metal railings. There was nothing inspiring about it at all, but it was a roof over her head. Libby greeted the estate agent and followed him to the ground floor apartment.

The door opened straight in to the main living room. The orange shag carpet had been flattened from years of use and there were several large brown stains on it. Libby forced a smile as she walked through to the original seventies brown kitchen. The tiny bathroom with shower and basin was also the same brown.

No wonder no one was keen to rent the apartment.

The main bedroom was just big enough to fit her double bed and a single wardrobe, as long as she didn't want to open the doors fully, and the second bedroom would fit her desk.

At least it was relatively clean.

"You can move in whenever you're ready," the agent said.

Libby still had two weeks left at her other rental, but there was little point in delaying the inevitable. Moving would keep her mind off other matters. She blocked the thought of Adrian from her mind as she accompanied the real estate agent back to the office to sign the papers and get the key. On her way home she picked up a stack of packing boxes and then rang a removalist to arrange for her furniture to be moved at the end of the week.

Now all she had to do was pack up her life.

And put her heart back together.

***

The media had calmed down somewhat since Kate gave her

statement, but George kept monitoring the situation. Adrian wasn't interested. The only thing that mattered was that he could lose Kate. The promise he'd made his brother – to always care for Kate if anything happened to him – would be broken and there was little he could do about it.

Thoughts of Libby popped into his head with irritating frequency, but whenever they did he tried to block them. She was to blame for this. If she hadn't let Kate speak to the media, Susan wouldn't have sued for custody.

He wished it didn't hurt so much.

"Ade, you need to watch this." George beckoned him over to the laptop.

Adrian walked over and peered over his shoulder at the news clip playing on the screen. When Emily's face appeared, he tensed. "What's she doing now?"

Emily was sitting across from a female reporter with short, honey blond hair.

The interview began with the reporter asking Emily about her history with Kent. Emily went into detail about working as Kate's nanny and how she had fallen in love with Kent and thought he loved her too. Emily's eyes welled up.

Adrian had seen enough. The reporter wouldn't question her but would show sympathy, and he didn't need that now. He reached for the mouse as the reporter said, "Can you give me more detail?" Her tone was mild, but there was something in it that implied she didn't believe Emily.

When Adrian turned to walk away, George said, "Keep watching."

The question caught Emily off guard. "What do you mean?"

"Can you give an example of what Kent did to make you believe he cared for you?"

Emily paused a moment too long. "Of course." Another pause while she thought of something to say. "He held the door open for me."

The reporter smiled. "How gallant of him. You don't get many gentlemen around these days. Did he hold the door open for Kate as well?"

Emily hesitated and then nodded, her movement jerky.

"Then perhaps Kent was being polite. Can you give another

example?"

"He kissed me," Emily blurted, staring at the reporter as if daring her to contradict what she'd said.

The reporter tilted her head to the side. "If that was true, you would have said it first."

Emily opened her mouth to respond but the reporter didn't give her a chance. "Why don't you tell the truth? Why don't you tell the people watching how you offered yourself to Kent and he rejected you? Why don't you tell the viewers how you wanted to leave an orphaned girl alone in a strange hotel room while you had sex with Kent? A young girl who, I might add, still suffers from nightmares after the tragic death of both her parents less than a year ago." The reporter paused and the camera zoomed in on Emily's face, which was as startled as a rabbit. "You put your own desires before the safety and care of your charge."

Adrian stared at the screen, not quite believing what he was hearing. Where had the reporter got those details from?

Emily was silent for too long.

"You don't deny it. Being Kate's nanny was an easy job, wasn't it? Does she deserve the trouble you've caused her? All she wants is to spend time with her uncle and now that is jeopardized because of your lies."

Under the reporter's stern gaze Emily crumpled. Tears streamed down her face. "I only wanted to get back at Kent. I didn't think of how it would affect Kate."

"Go on," the reporter encouraged. "Why don't you tell the truth?"

Emily sniffed. "It's true. Kent rejected me when I suggested we take our relationship further. Then he hired a new nanny and started seeing her almost straightaway." Her tone was bitter.

"Is Kent a good guardian for Kate?" the reporter asked.

Emily nodded. "He spent every spare minute he had with her. They never invited me to go with them. It was the Kent, Kate and George show. I had to amuse myself."

Despite himself, Adrian felt a surge of sadness for Emily. She sounded lonely. He hadn't ever considered that.

"So to get back at him you started these rumors and revealed his true identity."

Emily looked miserable. "I'm sorry."

"You only thought of yourself." The reporter was showing no sympathy. She turned to the camera. "You've heard it from the source. The accusations about Kent Downer are untrue. I'm Piper Atkinson for *Houston News*."

The video went black.

"How'd you find the interview?" Adrian asked.

"Piper emailed it to me." George hesitated. "She's Libby's friend."

Adrian shut his eyes at the rush of emotions flooding through him. Libby must have given her the information. This was another betrayal. She'd promised to keep his secrets and she'd told her reporter friend.

He really couldn't trust her.

"Ade, this has got to help in our case to keep Kate."

Adrian paused and thought about what Emily had said. George was right, but it still didn't change the fact that Libby had broken her promise. And she'd told the reporter details about Kate that were private. Had she ever cared about either of them?

Kate wandered into the room. "What's going on?"

George pointed at the laptop. "Watch this, kiddo."

Kate screwed up her face. "What's she saying this time?" she asked.

"Watch."

The interview played through and when it ended Kate whooped. "Yes! High five." She and George slapped hands. "This is awesome. We should celebrate." She turned to Adrian. "Aunt Susan has got to see this and know it's all been lies. Then she'll let me stay with you and we'll take care of each other."

Adrian's chest was so tight he wasn't sure he could breathe. He wasn't so confident Susan would give in so easily.

He leaned over and hugged her. "I love you, Katie."

"I love you too, Uncle Ade." She hugged him and then sat back. "I'm starved. What's for lunch?"

Adrian smile at her exaggeration. "Spaghetti." He stood and went to the sink to drain the pasta.

Kate turned around in her chair. "Why do you think the reporter asked different questions?"

George answered her. "The reporter is Libby's friend Piper."

Kate grinned. "I bet Libby asked her to do this."

Adrian paused. "What makes you think that?"

"'Cause Libby always said you've got to fight for what you love and she loves us."

Adrian couldn't answer. The lump in his throat was too large.

She didn't love them.

If she did, she wouldn't have gone behind his back the way she had.

She didn't care about him at all.

***

When Libby didn't arrive before Adrian's first concert in Perth, Kate was furious. "You lied to me, Uncle Adrian. What have you done to Libby?"

Adrian ignored the ache in his heart and stood up from the couch where they had been watching a movie. "She broke her contract when she let you speak with the reporters. She can't look after you anymore." He was still coming to terms with the fact she thought she knew more about Kate's needs than he did. He walked toward the sink to place his mug in it.

"It wasn't her fault. She thought I was getting her laptop when I went outside."

Adrian stopped mid-step. "What did you say?" He must have misheard.

Kate had her hands on her hips. "I went outside by myself. She thought I was going to her room. She had nothing to do with it. I *wanted* to speak to the reporters and *you* wouldn't let me."

Libby hadn't betrayed him? But the footage had showed her supporting Kate.

"I thought if I spoke to them they would leave us alone. I wanted to go out." Kate's voice was soft.

Adrian covered his shock and continued across to the kitchenette. "She should have kept a closer eye on you." Dread curled in his stomach. If what Kate said was true, he'd made a huge mistake. He hadn't let Libby explain, had believed the worst of her, had blocked her out. He'd gone back to his defensiveness.

"But what about you? Don't you miss Libby too?"

Adrian's heart clenched. He missed her more than he'd thought was possible. He'd wake up already looking forward to seeing her and then remember what she'd done. He'd finish sound check thinking ahead to when he'd return to the hotel and then remember she wouldn't be waiting for him. He shouldn't have such strong feelings for someone he'd known for three weeks.

He wasn't going to tell Kate the truth. "First and foremost Libby was your nanny. She failed in her duties to protect you and I can't risk it again."

"But you love her! You can't punish her because of something I did." Kate's anger melted and became wails of anguish.

Adrian paused. Did he love Libby?

No, he couldn't possibly. It was ridiculous to fall in love in so few days. She was just easy to be around.

He turned to face Kate. "We're going home to Texas in a couple of days. Libby's home is here. Do you think it's right to ask her to leave her parents behind?" He hated himself for playing the parent card, but it was the only thing that might stop Kate wanting something she couldn't have.

"She might if you asked her." Kate's voice was quiet but he saw her thinking things through.

"Why don't you get your backpack? George is waiting."

Kate picked up her bag and, subdued, followed Adrian to the door.

He felt like the biggest jerk in the world.

***

Libby threw herself into moving. She packed like she was doing a time trial and had everything arranged within a day. As she reviewed the boxes she realized she didn't have a whole lot to show for her life.

The only person she'd spoken with was her neighbor, who had dropped by to give Libby the mail she'd collected. She'd promised to forward along any more mail that came after Libby left.

By the end of the week Libby had settled into her new apartment.

Saturday came and went without a phone call from Adrian or George. Libby finally gave up. He wasn't going to call.

She threw herself into her final edits to keep herself busy. She'd put the photo from the bridge climb on her desk, but after a day she slipped it into her drawer. She couldn't look at it without tearing up.

Kate emailed her every day, asking her to visit, and she hated the emails' pleading tone. Libby simply told Kate she had to work on her manuscript, because she knew she wouldn't be welcome at the hotel.

When Libby checked a news website on Monday night, she found an article saying Kent had finished his tour and headed home. The tiny part of her that had hoped Adrian would change his mind and realize he loved her died.

She hadn't even been allowed to say goodbye to Kate in person.

Libby allowed herself a night of tears but woke the next morning determined to put it all behind her. She had known from the beginning the relationship was temporary. She had been stupid to fall in love.

It was too late now. She needed to move on.

If only it didn't hurt so much.

In the week before her new job started, she finished her novel, sending it to her editor two months before her deadline. There was none of the usual flush of success she felt when she finished a novel. Adrian had taken that away from her too.

Libby began her next novel, working until late at night. She was determined to meet her shorter deadline and it didn't hurt that when she fell into bed she was too exhausted to dream.

By the time she started work, she'd finished a third of the book.

Amazing what heartbreak did.

***

Adrian finished his concert tour and flew home to Houston with Kate. During the last few days in Perth he'd refused to ask George if he'd spoken to Libby. There was no point. He'd messed things up and Libby hadn't tried to explain. She obviously didn't care for him enough.

Besides, he'd been busy gathering the evidence he needed to prove to a court he was a good guardian for Kate.

They arrived home exhausted from the flight and slept for hours. Kate woke him. "Uncle Ade, can Jemma come over?"

Adrian opened his eyes and stretched, simultaneously feeling the comfort of being home and the strangeness of not being in a hotel room. He checked the time. It was after midday.

"Sure. Why don't you call and invite her? We can pick her up in an hour." He needed a shower to wash some of the jet lag away and his stomach was grumbling for food.

Kate grinned and raced for the phone while Adrian hauled himself into the shower.

When he'd finished and dressed, he headed for the kitchen, where he found Kate rummaging through the cupboards for something to eat.

"We'll stop for some groceries after picking up Jemma," Adrian told her as he reached over her to snag the cereal box.

"Jemma's not allowed to come over," Kate said. "But Aunt Susan said I could go there. Is that all right?"

Adrian forced a smile. "Sure. Let me eat something and I'll take you."

Kate grinned and ran to get organized.

What was Susan playing at? Jemma had always played over here. The girls had spent hours in the pool or holed up in Kate's room working on some secret project or other.

Did she still believe the hype the media was putting out? More likely she was thinking about the court case, and how badly it would look if she let her daughter play at Adrian's house when she was trying to prove he wasn't a fit guardian.

He'd not received any summons or details about a hearing, so maybe she'd changed her mind.

Adrian hoped she had but didn't believe it.

On the drive over, Kate talked a mile a minute, pointing out what had changed in their six weeks away. As they approached Susan's drive, Kate sighed. "I wish I could show Libby all of this. We'd have a great time exploring."

Kate might as well have shot him, for the shock it gave him.

She hadn't mentioned Libby in days. He'd hoped she realized Libby had been part of their life only temporarily.

He'd made such a hash of it.

Adrian pulled into the drive. "Here we are, kiddo."

As he opened the door, Kate's cousin Jemma came running out of the house. Kate scrambled out of the car and they met halfway, stopping to do some greeting ritual with their hands before hugging each other.

Adrian watched their enthusiasm bubble over. He wished Susan had allowed Jemma to go on tour with them. Both girls would have been a handful, but they would have loved it, and Kate wouldn't have had to spend so much time in adult company.

He followed them up the drive to where Susan was standing at the front door. Kate greeted Susan with a quick hug before disappearing inside.

"Hi, Susan," Adrian greeted her, inclining his head.

"Adrian." She crossed her arms and stood in the doorway as if guarding it.

He had to talk to her about the media and the accusations, but this wasn't the right time. Perhaps after she had seen Kate was fine and had no scars from the experience, she would realize their niece was being properly cared for. He'd talk to her when he picked Kate up.

"I'll be back at five," he said.

"That will be fine."

He wasn't going to get anything more from her. He gave a half-smile, turned and went back to his car, pretending nerves weren't playing dodgem in his stomach. He'd buy some groceries on the way home and rest.

***

Adrian didn't get a chance to talk to Susan when he picked Kate up. Kate and Jemma were waiting on the front step of the house. Jemma was wearing a pink dress that was too nice to be wearing around the house. Kate said goodbye to her cousin and jumped in the car. "They're going out tonight and Aunt Susan is still getting ready," she said when he asked about the dress.

He'd speak to Susan later.

"Did you have fun?"

Kate squirmed. "Sort of." She paused. "I didn't know how to tell Aunt Susan I don't want to live with her, especially when she was asking me a lot of weird questions."

Immediately Adrian was alert. "Like what?"

"Like what happened with Emily and if Libby ever stayed overnight."

Adrian clenched the steering wheel tighter. He kept his tone light. "What did you say to her?"

"I told her Emily was no fun and she was more interested in you than me. And I said Libby didn't need to stay overnight because she had her own room."

Adrian smiled, pleased Kate didn't understand what Susan was implying. He was thankful that the one time Libby did stay, they'd been up before Kate. "Did she ask anything else?"

"Only if I spent much time with the crew, but it was only those last few days in Perth, really."

Susan was fishing for information, but to what end? Adrian changed the subject. "How was Jemma?"

"Great! She had fun at summer camp but agreed I had the better holiday. Maybe Aunt Susan will let her come next time." Kate told Adrian all about Jemma's summer camp adventures until they reached the house.

Kate followed Adrian into the kitchen and took a seat at the table while he pulled items out of the fridge for dinner.

"Uncle Ade?"

The tone made Adrian turn. "What is it?"

Kate sat head down, playing with her hands. Finally she looked up. "Aunt Susan asked about Grandpa Hart. She asked if I'd met him and what you and Dad had said about him." She looked down again. "I didn't want to tell her your secrets, so I said he wasn't well." She glanced at him. "Is that all right?"

Adrian's heart clenched at her loyalty. He should have told her what to say if anyone asked her. He pulled out the chair next to her and sat down. "Of course. If Aunt Susan asks again, tell her to talk to me. If she's got any questions, I'll be able to answer them."

"Okay." Kate smiled at him. "Are you going to talk to Grandpa Hart now we're back?"

George had asked him the same question, wanting to know whether he would confront his father after all these years.

His twelve-year-old self still cowered at the thought.

His adult self didn't see the point. His father would say what he wanted and there was nothing Adrian could say that would change his mind.

His father could have tried to contact him when he discovered Adrian was a rock star instead of going to the media. George's contact details were listed on Kent's website, but there had been no attempt.

His father had never cared for Adrian as a child and he sure as hell didn't care for him now.

Adrian still needed to answer Kate, though. "I'll think about it." He stood up. "How about I make you some dinner?"

He didn't wait for her response.

Chapter 19

Libby's new job held no interest for her. She caught the train into the city four days a week to cover the maternity leave of the personal assistant to a big mining company executive.

She attended meetings, took minutes, organized any travel arrangements and nagged the executive to sign things like a mother nagged a child to clean up its room.

In the past she'd enjoyed the human interaction in a job like this, and the organizing, but now her mind constantly drifted to Adrian and Kate, the adventures they'd had or the simple ritual of being there when Adrian got back from a concert.

Then one day the news that Susan was suing for custody of Kate finally hit the newspapers and the circus started again.

Many of her new colleagues wanted to know what had happened or what Kent was really like. Libby was polite but told them firmly she wasn't going to talk about it.

The next day Kent was back in the headlines because his father was facing eviction and Kent wouldn't help him.

Libby's heart went out to Adrian. He'd hate the attention, hate the way his father had thrust himself into his life again.

But there was nothing Libby could do to help.

Later that evening Libby was at home working on her new manuscript. The radio was on low and she was having difficulty concentrating. Her cell rang and she was grateful for the interruption until she saw it was her mother. Libby hadn't spoken to her since she'd refused to attend the fundraising event, though she had emailed to tell her parents she was moving. They hadn't offered to help.

She pressed the answer button on her phone. "Hi, Mum."

"Elizabeth, I've just returned from Fiji to read some nonsense in the paper about you and some rock star."

Libby sighed. "Just ignore it, Mum." There wasn't any point telling her about it. It was all over now.

"But why are they mentioning you?"

"I took care of Kent's niece while I was over east. It's not a big deal." Not anymore at least.

Her mother gave a sigh of relief. "I was sure they must have got it wrong about you having an affair with him." She laughed as if the idea was ridiculous.

Libby sat upright, wounded to her core. She'd had enough. "Is it so unbelievable that someone as attractive as Kent Downer might be interested in me? Am I so unappealing?" Libby couldn't hide the hurt in her tone.

"Well, ah …" Her mother had nothing to say.

And that stung just as much. Weren't mothers supposed to jump to your defense, tell you what you wanted to hear, support you when you were feeling low?

"Just because you can't stand to be around me, it doesn't mean I don't have friends." All the years of pent-up hurt came pouring out. "I know I was a mistake. I know you and Dad didn't want me. But that doesn't make me unlovable." She was trying so hard to believe it, but most days she failed.

"The young girl I looked after loved me. She wanted me to move to America." It was just her uncle who didn't want me, Libby thought.

She paused, giving her mother a chance to speak, to say anything, but there was silence. No denial, no anger, nothing.

Libby swallowed down the tears. "Goodbye, Mother."

She hung up.

The last vestige of hope that her parents did love her evaporated. Libby's heart stung but there was a sense of release as well.

As if on cue, Adrian's song came on the radio. She listened

to his voice, remembered watching him in the television studio that first day, the absolute attention he commanded from everyone in the audience.

But he was wrong.

He shouldn't be yearning to feel, to be hurt. The absence of feeling was so much better than feeling too much. Loving people who didn't love you was the worst pain of all.

Somewhere deep inside anger stirred, just a tiny rumble, but Libby lunged for it. Anger had to be better than this pain.

She was tired of being ignored, tired of trying to make herself into someone her parents would love, tired of letting people treat her as if she was unimportant. If they didn't care for her as she was, they weren't worth the effort.

The anger turned, directing itself at Adrian. Here he was singing about wanting to feel hurt and yet he had shut down every time Libby tried to get close. Instead of giving her the chance to explain, trusting that she wouldn't have let Kate speak to the media on purpose, he'd believed the worst of her.

And what was even more pathetic was the fact that she'd let him believe it, she'd slunk away with her tail between her legs and hadn't fought for herself. Just like she had with Clint.

Well, damn it, it was time she broke the cycle.

Fuelled by her anger, she grabbed her phone and dialed Adrian's number, not caring what time it was in Houston.

It rang once, twice, three times before going to voicemail. Libby took a breath and at the beep she spoke.

"Adrian, you never gave me a chance to explain what happened with Kate and so I'm taking the opportunity now.

"Kate was angry when the reporters found us and she went outside on her own. I should have kept a closer eye on her and for that I'm sorry." Libby took another breath. "I love Kate and I would never do anything to put her in harm's way. I'm sorry things ended the way they did between us, but I guess it's for the best. You're still trapped by your childhood, shutting out those who care for you. I deserve better than that. I deserve someone who is going to trust me, who is going to love me for who I am. I don't need you in my life."

She hung up and her anger evaporated.

Tears streamed down her face, blurring her vision, but she

let them fall. She needed to get this out, needed to finish grieving so she could get on with her life. She sat at her desk sobbing until she was dry. Her eyes were tender, her throat was raw and her head pounded.

In that instant she made a vow.

She wasn't ever going to fall in love again.

**

The next morning Libby rang in sick. She had tossed and turned the whole night and her head still ached from her crying jag. She knew if anyone mentioned Kent to her she would burst into tears and she just couldn't handle that at the moment.

Getting changed into her walking clothes, Libby headed out into the gray, drizzly morning. It suited her mood perfectly and the cool, crisp air cleared the cobwebs in her head.

In a better frame of mind when she got home, Libby booted up her laptop, made breakfast and checked her emails. There was one from Kate.

Kate said she was fit to be tied because the court had assigned someone to supervise her time with both Adrian and Susan and they hung around for at least two hours at a time. She said Uncle Ade was a mess because he hated strangers and kept making mistakes.

Kate apologized again for all the trouble she had caused and for making Libby and Adrian fight. She wanted Libby to call Adrian because he was sad, and she was sure Libby would make him happy again. Kate had finished her story and wondered if Libby still wanted to read it. Aunt Susan was being a pain and wouldn't let Jem stay over, but Kate didn't like staying at Aunt Susan's place because she kept asking stupid questions about Uncle Ade.

Libby heard Kate's voice as she read the email. She pushed back the tears and hit reply, sending her a chatty email about what she'd been up to, telling Kate she missed her and that she would love to read her book. She avoided all mention of Adrian.

Libby read the email twice to make sure there was nothing that could be misconstrued and pressed send.

Some of the strain she'd been carrying around since she'd been fired left her. She might have lost Adrian but she hadn't lost Kate. She loved that girl.

Hearing the familiar noise of the postie's bike outside, Libby wandered out to collect her mail. There was some junk mail and a letter from her publisher.

Libby slipped her finger under the flap of the envelope and tore it open. It was her royalty statement.

In the past she'd earned out the advance on her three previous books but not much more than that. Certainly not enough to survive the six months between payments.

Libby wandered across the lawn as she scanned the cover letter. The sales figures were high. Higher than she expected. She checked the statement and stopped dead in her tracks. Her hands shook.

She forgot to breathe as her mouth dropped open. She counted the zeros again.

Libby gasped in a breath. What if it was a mistake? She had to call her publisher.

She raced inside and phoned the royalties department, her legs shaky.

"I've just received my royalty statement and I wanted to make sure there wasn't a mistake."

The woman on the other end of the phone confirmed Libby's details and brought up her account, quoting the same figure as on the check.

"Are you sure it's right?" Libby didn't dare hope. She couldn't handle another blow so soon.

The woman laughed. "That's what it says here. Congratulations."

Libby thanked the woman and hung up, lowering herself gingerly into a seat.

She pinched herself and it hurt. She wasn't dreaming. The statement was real.

She giggled, the excitement bubbling up inside and overflowing as hysterical laughter poured out her mouth. Tears ran down her face and she swiped them away.

Blotting at her eyes she took a deep, shuddery breath. "Oh my God."

She checked the statement again to make sure she hadn't imagined it. This was really happening. She could write full time.

Libby ran her hands over the paper. It was real. This was real. She'd achieved her dream.

She was a full-time author.

She wanted to dance, to sing, to scream her news from the top of the building. Libby whirled around.

Who could she tell? She had to tell someone her news or she'd burst.

She checked the time. Piper might still be awake.

She snatched her phone up and dialed.

Piper's voice answered but it was her answering machine. Damn it. Libby left a slightly garbled excited message and hung up.

Who else could she tell?

There was only one person who would understand exactly what this meant. One person who up until a few weeks ago would have celebrated with her. One person she really wanted to tell but couldn't.

Adrian.

Her mood deflated with a hiss and she plopped down onto the chair. Her eyes welled with tears and angrily she brushed them away. No, she wasn't going to let him ruin her mood. She deserved this happiness, this thrill of excitement. She'd earned it.

Libby stood up, snatched her bag from the hook it was hanging on and headed out. She was going to buy herself a cake to celebrate.

She didn't need anyone else to help her.

She would celebrate on her own.

***

Adrian walked through the house for the third time, checking to make sure it was clean and tidy, and there was nothing that could say to the caseworker that Kate wasn't being looked after properly. He hovered in the lounge room, wondering whether he should put away the book Kate was reading, and then decided it showed one of her interests.

But could it also say to the social worker that he wasn't paying Kate enough attention? That she had to find her amusement in a book rather than with Adrian?

Hell, he was second-guessing his second guesses.

He hated these visits. The only thing that made them slightly bearable was the knowledge that Susan was getting them as well.

"Uncle Ade, can I go for a swim?" Kate wandered into the lounge room where he was still debating over the book.

Adrian looked up. "Sure – but don't forget the caseworker will be here soon."

Kate screwed up her face. "How many more visits do they have to make?"

Adrian shrugged. "A few more, I guess. They want to make sure they make the right decision."

Kate squeaked in exasperation. "But I told them I want to stay with you. I even made a list of why you were better than Aunt Susan."

Adrian smiled at the memory. As soon as Susan had sued for custody and the supervised visits began, Kate had started preparing. She'd made lists and kept her room tidy, and Adrian suspected she had even started misbehaving when she was with Susan. He wasn't sure where she'd learned this confident, list-making, go get 'em attitude, but he liked it.

Libby's face suddenly sprung up in front of him. He shoved it away.

But it made sense. Making a list was exactly the kind of thing Libby would have done.

Would there be a time when he could think of her without this tearing ache in his heart? He wasn't sure.

He'd picked up the phone a dozen times to call her but had put it down again.

He'd falsely accused her, hadn't even let her explain. She'd never want him back and it was his own fault.

The doorbell rang.

"That will be the caseworker," he told Kate. "You ready?"

"Yep. We're gonna show them we're meant to be together."

Adrian smiled and went to answer the door.

He wished he felt as confident.

***

Libby woke feeling lighter than she had in weeks. She hadn't just bought a cake to celebrate but also a new laptop and printer. Then, feeling guilty about the extravagance, she had done her budget.

If she was sensible, her royalty money would last her for a year, and by then she should know whether her sales would continue to support her full time.

Libby adjusted the lamp on her desk so it was in the right place and turned on her computer to start her day of writing. She'd rung the temp agency the day before and told them they would need to find someone else. As her computer came to life she opened her email. There was a message from Kate.

After Libby read it, she reached for the phone and then stopped herself. She couldn't call Adrian. Not after the way they had parted.

But something had happened, because Kate had to stay with her Aunt Susan until the court case. Kate was devastated and was pleading for Libby to help her.

Checking the time difference, Libby chose to call George. He would know what was going on and she had to find out if there was some way she could help.

Nerves skittered over her skin while the phone rang. She had no idea what reaction she was going to get.

"Hello, Libby." George's voice was polite with maybe a hint of surprise.

"I heard that Kate is staying with her aunt," Libby blurted. "Is there any way I can help?"

"Who told you?" There was definitely surprise there.

Libby hesitated. She didn't want to get Kate into trouble.

George filled the silence. "It had to be Kate."

"She sounds worried. Do you want me to write a statement? I could say how well Adrian cares for her."

"I appreciate the offer, Libby, but I'm not sure that's a good idea. Susan knows you and Adrian were lovers. Anything you say would be disregarded almost immediately."

Libby huffed. He was right, of course. "Is there nothing I can do?"

George was silent. "I'm collecting statements from others. Yours might help when viewed alongside them."

"Fine. When do you need it?"

"We go to court in two days."

"So soon?"

"Susan knows someone in the department," George growled.

"How's Kate holding up?"

George laughed. "She's a real trooper. She's made lists and written her own statement, she's even got her cousins fighting against their mother. We've nicknamed her Lilly Lionheart."

Libby's heart swelled. The name of Kate's superhero in her story. "She'll love that." Libby paused and then asked the question. "How's Adrian?"

The silence was so long Libby didn't think George was going to answer. "He swings between fighting for her and convincing himself Susan can give her a more stable home life."

"That's ridiculous." Kate and Adrian belonged together.

"You and I both know that. The whole situation with his father really set him back."

George was telling her more than he probably should, considering how her relationship with Adrian ended.

Her head swirled with thoughts. She loved Kate and she loved Adrian. He might not reciprocate that love, but she couldn't stand by and watch him lose Kate without doing something. Would a reference be enough?

Her stomach twitched with nerves. "I'll send you the character reference as soon as I can. If you think of anything else I can do, let me know."

"Will do."

Libby hung up. It was probably the last time she'd hear from George.

Chapter 20

Adrian was preparing lunch in the kitchen, though he wasn't hungry. Kate had been living with Susan for a couple of days now, and while he'd been allowed to speak to Kate on the phone, he hadn't been allowed to visit.

He missed her.

The court case was tomorrow and strangers would decide whether he'd get Kate back.

"How do you think it will go?" he asked George.

George's phone beeped, signaling a message. Adrian searched for his own cell and saw it lying on the bench. Picking it up, he noticed it was turned off. The battery must have run out. He'd not checked it in days, as he hadn't been in the mood to talk to anyone. He plugged it in to charge.

"I honestly don't know how it'll go," George said. "We've got statements from everyone who knows you and Kate, Emily's video confession and the supervised visit reports. The only thing we haven't responded to is your father's accusations."

They'd had the discussion multiple times, but Adrian had never worked up the courage to face his father. He kept convincing himself that it wouldn't help.

But what if it did? What if something his father said could make the difference between winning custody of Kate and losing it? Would not knowing eat away at him?

Adrian turned his phone on and noted a missed call. He dialed to listen to the message.

Libby's voice washed over him like someone had thrown a bucket of cold water at him. He was so startled that her words didn't sink in until the last sentence – "I don't need you in my life."

He boosted himself on to the kitchen bench as he replayed the message. The only other time he'd heard Libby use that tone was the day after Kate's nightmare when she'd come to his defense against Susan. It was her somebody-needs-their-head-examined tone and this time it was directed at him. He couldn't prevent the smile that covered his face. He loved that tone, could picture her indignation and the way her eyes flashed fire when she spoke.

He loved her.

Adrian froze. He loved Libby.

How could it have taken him so long to realize it?

"You all right?" George's voice waded through the shock.

Adrian nodded as he listened to the message a third time. Libby was right. He was trapped by his childhood and she did deserve better than that. But the fact that she had called to tell him gave him hope. She had to care for him. Maybe he hadn't completely ruined things with her.

"Do you want to go through our statements again?" George asked.

The question brought him back to the now. He couldn't think of Libby at the moment, he had to focus on winning the court case. There was still one more thing he could do.

Fear shivered unwelcome down his spine. Adrian fisted his hands. It was time he freed himself from this fear. Time he freed himself from his past. Adrian braced himself and then said, "I'm going to visit my father."

George's eyes widened briefly. "Are you sure?"

Adrian nodded, not as certain as he'd like to be.

"Do you want me to come with you?"

"No." He could do this. He had to do this himself.

Before he could change his mind, he stood up and walked out of the house, feeling like he was walking into a minefield.

But the thought of Kate – and Libby – gave him courage.

***

Adrian drove through his old neighborhood, the stress building the further in he drove. He hadn't been back since the day he and Daniel had run away, but it had hardly changed. The school he'd attended was to his left and on the right he drove past the supermarket where he and Daniel had bought their microwave dinners.

Then he turned into his old street and his heart beat heavily in his chest. He pulled into the drive and turned off the engine. He stared at the house, not ready to go in.

The paint was peeling away from the timber cladding and the grass in the front was long and unkempt. The porch sagged and the wood was a silver gray color from neglect.

He gripped the steering wheel and focused on his breathing as the memories tried to overwhelm him.

He could do this. He had to, for Kate and for himself.

He thrust the car door open and climbed out, forcing his feet to keep moving toward the house.

The steps groaned as he climbed onto the porch. The front door was open and through the flyscreen Adrian could see into the house. The hallway was lined with empty bourbon bottles.

The twelve-year-old inside him shuddered. Adrian took a deep breath and knocked, the sound like a gunshot to his ears.

In another room he heard someone getting to their feet and walking toward the door. He fought the urge to run.

"If you're here to sell something, I'm not buying." It was his father's voice, the deep Texan accent slightly slurred as it preceded him into the hallway.

Fear pricked Adrian. Was his father drunk?

The man entered the hallway, walking slowly, and finally looked up. He met Adrian's gaze and his jaw dropped, his expression first shock, then perhaps fear.

"Hello, Pa." Adrian was pleased his voice was steady.

His father closed his mouth and grunted. "Didn't think I'd see you again."

Adrian didn't know what he'd expected his father to say, but it was more than that. Pushing past the surprise, he focused on his purpose. "I want to talk about the lies you've been spreading."

"Those suckers will believe anything," his father said, not the least bit apologetic.

Anger began to dissolve Adrian's fear. "Don't you care how those lies might have affected me?"

"Why should I? You and your no-good brother left and never looked back. I suppose he's got some hifalutin job as well."

The grief hit him. "Daniel's dead."

"How?" There was shock in the old man's eyes and sorrow in his voice.

Adrian was so surprised he answered immediately. "A car crash a year ago. It killed Daniel and his wife. Kate was the only survivor."

His father squinted at him. "Kate's the red-haired girl?"

"Yes," Adrian said. "Your granddaughter."

His father unlatched the flyscreen door and pushed it open. "You want to come in?"

Adrian didn't. The thought of crossing the threshold into the house that was his prison throughout his whole childhood filled him with dread, but there was a vulnerability in his father's eyes that he had never seen before.

Adrian walked in through to the living room.

It hadn't changed in the eighteen years since Adrian had been inside. The brown couch he'd raced around so many times to evade his father, the coffee table that had been chipped when he'd tripped and his father had pushed him into it, the dirty, threadbare beige carpet. The whole room had an odor of stale cigarettes and bourbon.

His father hovered near the doorway, uncertain. "You gonna sit?"

"No." He couldn't. There was no way he could relax in this room.

His father walked over to the sideboard and poured himself a drink.

"Don't." Adrian's tone was sharp.

The old man's hand shook but he put the glass down. "You tryin' to order me around in my own home?"

"Someone needs to." Adrian didn't want to hang around

here. The fear he'd felt for all these years had evaporated and been replaced by pity. The man's life revolved around the bottle.

"I came here to talk to you about Kate."

"My granddaughter?" His father seemed stunned.

Adrian nodded. "Daniel named me guardian of Kate if anything happened to them. Because of what you've been saying, Penny's sister believes I can't care for Kate and is trying to take her from me."

"The bitch." Adrian's father was outraged. "You can't let her do that." He didn't seem to comprehend his part in all of this.

"It would help if you withdrew your accusations about me."

His father's outrage was replaced with calculation. "How much is it worth to you?"

Adrian blinked in surprise. His father had gone from grieving to outraged to calculating in a space of seconds. This was the man Adrian remembered. "Kate is priceless." His voice was cold. "But you won't get a cent out of me. If you have any shred of decency left in that alcohol-pickled brain of yours, you'll do what's right. You'll retract your accusations and tell the truth." Adrian walked toward the door and then stopped. "You never cared for your own children, but this is your chance to do something for your grandchild."

Disgusted, he brushed past his father and headed to the entrance. Once outside he took a deep breath of fresh air.

He was relieved to be out of there. He stalked over to his car and climbed in. Glancing toward the house, he saw the silhouette of his father in the window. The anger dissipated. The man wasn't worth it.

Adrian knew his visit wouldn't make any difference. His father didn't give a damn.

But as he backed out of the drive, the chains that had bound him to this place for so long gave way.

He was no longer fearful of this man.

He was no longer a prisoner of his childhood.

He was free.

***

The next morning dawned sunny and bright. Adrian was up early and spent an hour pounding out his nerves on the treadmill.

Today would decide his and Kate's fate.

After facing his father, he felt more optimistic than he had since the whole saga began. The visit had proven to him that he was nothing like his father.

Afterward he'd called Hank and Marla to see if they had any record of Hank's meeting with Adrian's father. Hank had recorded the whole event meticulously and Adrian read the information with interest. It showed him how easily his father had given them up, which was bound to help the case.

Adrian made breakfast and ate it with gusto. He was going to win this.

As he was struggling to do up his tie, the phone rang. It was Kate.

"Uncle Ade, it's going to be all right, isn't it?" Her voice was small and scared.

Adrian wished he could tell her it would be. "No matter what happens, we'll still see each other." He paused. "I love you, kiddo. Nothing is going to change that."

Kate sniffed and Adrian's heart ached. "I love you too, Uncle Ade," she said.

Adrian checked the time. "I'll see you soon." He hung up.

***

George met him outside the courthouse and they walked in together. Susan and her parents were on one side of the room with Kate. Adrian acknowledged them with a nod of his head as Kate ran over and threw her arms around him.

"I've missed you," she told him.

Adrian squeezed his eyes tightly. "I've missed you too, kiddo. Have you had fun with Jemma?"

Kate checked if anyone was near enough to hear. "Not nearly as much fun as we have at our place."

Kate's grandmother walked over.

"How are you, Virginia?" Adrian asked.

She was stiffly polite. "Well, thank you, Adrian." She turned to Kate. "Katie dear, you need to come with me now."

They had arranged for Kate's grandmother to take care of Kate during the hearing. The judge would talk to Kate at the end.

"I'd rather wait with Uncle Adrian until he goes in, Grandma," Kate replied.

Adrian smothered a smile at the way Virginia pinched her lips.

Before she could argue, a clerk came out, took everyone's details and invited them into the room.

Adrian turned to Kate. "Be good for your grandma, kiddo. I'll see you when we finish." He gave her a hug and she clung to him for a minute longer. Adrian shut his eyes. When he looked up, Virginia was waiting impatiently.

"Come along, Katie."

Adrian watched his niece go and then walked into the courtroom with George and his lawyer by his side. He had to win this.

When the preliminaries were done, Susan stated her case, explaining why she was seeking custody of Kate.

"Kate needs a stable family environment. The recent incidents have shown Adrian cannot provide that for her. She has been assaulted by the media and hasn't been allowed the freedom a child needs to explore." Susan paused. "In addition, she needs siblings and a woman's influence in her life, particularly as she reaches puberty. Her best friend is my daughter, Jemma, and they will be able to grow up together.

"Adrian's behavior on his most recent tour has shown he is irresponsible and cannot possibly give her a safe environment to grow up in."

"Please elaborate further," the judge requested.

Susan went into detail about the Emily incident and showed the footage of Kate in front of the media. "The matter involving Adrian's father have shown that Adrian is irresponsible and turns his back on family when it doesn't suit him. He is likely to decide one day that he no longer wants Kate and will leave her heartbroken."

Adrian's mouth dropped. He hadn't been expecting that. George looked equally surprised.

"Do you have anything to prove these claims?" the judge asked.

"Adrian's father has been on a number of talk shows." One

of the clips was played.

"He's lying," Adrian said calmly.

"You will get your chance to respond, Mr. Hart."

Adrian sat there drumming his fingers on the table while Susan summarized her case. The tour schedule wasn't suitable for a ten-year-old child, she was surrounded by adult men frequently, there were no children for her to play with, her nannies were more interested in her uncle than her and she had been exposed to an unhealthy relationship model.

Adrian simmered with anger. How could Susan portray Libby like that? She knew nothing about her. She hadn't seen Libby helping Kate with her story, playing games with her, teaching her to cook. Libby had given up her writing time to be with Kate when the media had been at their worst. She'd done everything a mother would do for her child.

He froze. He examined the thought carefully, poking it from all sides to see if it held. Yes, Libby had loved Kate.

Adrian was so distracted he didn't realize it was his turn to speak until George elbowed him. Adrian refocused on the scene. The judge was waiting for him. George shoved a notebook at him, outlining all the points he needed to respond to.

Adrian stood up. He wasn't going to let Kate go without a fight. He breathed in to calm his nerves and breathed out again. "Your Honor, I love my niece and I want the best for her. If at any stage I believed I couldn't care for her properly, I would hand her over to her aunt." He paused. "The recent publicity surrounding my tour has been difficult. Emily was Kate's nanny, but she quit when I rejected her advances. She left me without a nanny for Kate and I was fortunate a friend offered to help. A couple of weeks ago Emily admitted this in an interview."

The footage was played and Susan murmured, "How much did you pay the poor woman?"

Adrian breathed deeply to control his anger and continued. "I took Kate on tour with me as I wasn't comfortable with her going to summer camp. She still has nightmares about the crash in which her parents died and I didn't want her facing them alone. I offered to take Kate's cousin Jemma with us, so Kate would have someone her own age to play with, but Susan didn't allow it." He picked up a copy of Libby's contract. "This is the schedule both nannies had. You will note they only looked after Kate when I had work commitments. The schedule was designed to ensure I had time with Kate, and so we could explore the countries we were in. I thought it was a good opportunity for her to expand her horizons and learn about the world." He held up another statement. "This is from one of my road crew. It states that Kate rarely socialized with the crew. I was concerned some of their more colorful language might rub off on her and so I kept her contact with them to a minimum."

The clerk read the statement out.

Susan sniffed but didn't say a word.

"My father's accusations are entirely false." He took a deep breath. "The truth is my brother and I ran away from home many years ago. I was twelve and he was sixteen." The admission was a relief.

Susan gasped but Adrian didn't give her a chance to speak. "My father is an alcoholic and abused us. We had to steal money from his wallet to buy food to survive. When he found out, he would beat me or lock me in the basement for hours." Adrian peeked at Susan to gauge her reaction. Her mouth was open and she looked stunned.

"Do you have any proof?" the judge asked.

"My foster-father documented everything." Adrian handed over Hank's records and waited while the judge reviewed them. Finally the judge nodded for Adrian to continue.

"I know what it is like to be neglected, to have an unstable home life and to fear for your safety. If I ever thought Kate was in danger, or that my lifestyle would disadvantage her in any way, I would allow Susan to be her guardian." He paused. "I truly believe I can care for her." He sat down.

The judge gazed at him for a moment, with a look Adrian could not read, and then glanced down at his notes. "You haven't mentioned this last nanny, Libby," the judge said. "There was a photo which showed the two of you together, and reports that you were a couple."

Adrian still remembered the warmth of Libby in his arms. How she felt so right and filled him with such joy. He paused. "Libby cared for Kate until the publicity around Emily and my father became too intense. After Kate had her say on camera, we parted company."

"Did this Libby make a statement?" the judge asked.

Adrian stood. "No –"

"Yes, your Honor. It's here." George stood, pulling out a bit of paper.

Adrian's heart stopped and he stood rigid. Where the heck had that come from? George hadn't said a word to him about it and he hadn't dared ask Libby for a character reference after the way he'd treated her.

The judge read the statement and passed it to his clerk. He steepled his fingers together. "That's quite a statement, Mr. Hart."

Adrian held his breath as the clerk read out Libby's words.

Chapter 21

"I met Adrian on a television show in Australia. The next day he brought Kate to one of my book signings and we became friends. When I discovered Kate's nanny had quit, I offered to look after her. The tour schedule was such that I had time to do my writing and also be Kate's nanny.

"Kate was a delight to be around, eager, friendly and kind. She has such an optimistic way of looking at the world and I loved the time I spent with her."

Adrian heard Libby's voice in her words and it hurt to breathe.

"Watching Kate and Adrian together made me smile. He was the type of parent I wished I had; he played games, listened, taught her things and always had time for her. The tour schedule enabled them to spend a lot of time together and she always came before his work."

Adrian lowered himself to his chair.

"The media response to Emily and Adrian's father's accusations was difficult. Adrian was open and honest with Kate, explaining the situation to her and doing everything he could to keep her away from the reporters. I thought taking Kate home with me would give her a break and keep her away from the media, but I was wrong. Reporters followed us to my home and it was my fault Kate was on the evening news."

Adrian shook his head. Libby had taken the whole blame, when none of it was her fault. He knew how tenacious Kate was. He should have allowed her to speak or spoken up himself, but he'd been so scared of the outcome.

"Over the three weeks I spent with Adrian and Kate, I fell in love with Kate. I realize my relationship with Adrian may make my statement appear biased, but let me assure you of this: If at any stage I believed Kate's welfare was in danger, I would be the first to suggest she go to her aunt. However, in my time with them, I never saw anything that would make me feel that way. Kate and Adrian have a bond that anyone would envy. I implore you not to break them up."

Adrian stared straight ahead, not seeing anything. Libby wanted Kate to stay with him. She thought he was a good parent. A vine of optimism threaded through his heart. Maybe she didn't hate him.

George elbowed him and hissed, "No, your Honor."

Adrian shook himself. The judge was waiting for a response. He stood. "No, your Honor." He had no idea what the question was.

The judge's lips twitched upward. "If no one has anything else to say, I will go and speak with Kate."

They all rose as the judge left the room.

Adrian turned to George as he sat. "Why didn't you tell me you'd called Libby?"

"I didn't." George smiled. "Libby called me. Kate emailed her and told her the situation and Libby offered to write a statement. I didn't think it would help much, but I forgot she's a hell of a writer."

"Why didn't you show it to me?"

George glanced at the lawyer. "We decided to leave it aside until we had to use it. We thought your reaction might help the case and we were right. You looked like you'd been punched in the gut. It was obvious you weren't expecting it, and therefore it made her statement more believable."

"But why would she do that after the way I treated her?" He didn't deserve her kindness.

George bumped his shoulder. "You're so stupid. She loves you. Anyone could see that. Heck, the day she came to the rehearsal all the guys started a pool as to how long it would take you to get engaged."

Adrian snorted. George had it wrong. He and Libby hadn't even kissed by then. All they'd done was talk. "What did you bet?"

"Can't tell you yet. It's still open."

Adrian snorted. It didn't really matter. All that mattered in the next hour was the outcome of this case. He checked the time and then checked how Susan was faring. She sat with her hands clenched tightly together, looking straight ahead, her husband next to her.

Another vine of optimism threaded its way through his heart. He might actually win this.

The clock's minute hand moved slowly around the face. The judge had been gone for forty-five minutes. How long was he going to be with Kate?

George leaned over. "Kate's talking his ear off. I bet she's got him wrapped around her little finger."

Adrian laughed. George was probably right. Kate was determined to be with Adrian and she would do all she could to convince the judge.

Finally, after an hour, the judge came back in. He took his seat and smiled at them. "Kate is a lovely girl. I could talk to her all day."

Adrian smiled back at him and glanced over at Susan, but she didn't change her expression.

"It is easy to see why she has two people wanting to be her guardian. She's very lucky that both of you care about her welfare." The judge paused. "From the evidence presented to me today and from the statements I have heard, I see no reason to change the custody agreement already in place. Mr. Hart will continue to be Kate's guardian."

Adrian didn't hear anything else. George whooped and slapped him on the back and finally it sunk in. Adrian slumped down as the relief lifted away his tension. He still had Kate. He grinned so widely he thought his face was going to break.

He stood as the judge left the room and turned to Susan. He felt no animosity toward her. As the judge said, they both wanted the best for Kate. He wanted to make sure she knew she was welcome to see Kate whenever she wanted. Before he said anything, Susan spoke.

"I must apologize, Adrian."

Adrian's eyebrows rose.

"I got caught up in the lies the media told. I should have listened to Libby when she tried to explain it, but I wanted Kate. She reminds me so much of Penny and part of me feels Penny is still alive when I'm with Kate." Tears welled in her eyes. "I only wanted the best for her."

Adrian shuffled his feet and awkwardly patted her on the arm. "I know, Susan. We both miss Daniel and Penny. You'll still see Kate. She and Jemma are never far apart."

"Thank you," Susan said. "You're far more forgiving than me." She met his gaze. "I was going to keep Kate's contact with you to a minimum."

It was a stab to his heart but he kept his tone pleasant for Kate's sake. "Then I'm glad I won."

The doors of the courtroom burst open and Kate rushed in. "We won!" she yelled and hurled herself down the aisle and into Adrian's arms. He picked her up and swung her around before hugging her tightly. He'd faced his demons, fought for her and he'd won.

"We sure did, kiddo." He put her on the ground.

Susan went to walk past them, but Kate put out a hand to stop her. "Thank you for caring for me, Aunt Susan. We'll still see each other. Jem and I decided it would be better to be best friends than sisters 'cause sisters fight too much."

Susan's smile was small. "Maybe you and Jemma are right."

Kate nodded. "We talked about it a lot. I'll see you tomorrow night at Jason's party."

"I'll look forward to it." Susan gave Kate a hug before walking away.

Kate slipped her hand into Adrian's. "The judge told me not to be mad at her. He said I was lucky so many people cared for me."

Her words warmed Adrian's heart. "He was right."

Kate looked up at him. "Let's go celebrate. I'm starving."

"Sure thing, kiddo."

As they walked out of the courthouse, Adrian's thoughts

turned to Libby. Would he win if he fought for Libby? He'd treated her so badly, had pushed her away to protect himself. But he hadn't been able to stop thinking about her, even when he'd thought she'd betrayed him. He loved her and needed to tell her so. Did the fact that she'd written a statement mean she would give him a second chance?

One thing he did know – she was worth fighting for.

"I think this calls for a party," George said as he caught up with them.

"Yes!" Kate yelled.

Adrian grinned. "Absolutely. Why don't you invite your folks around and we'll have a pool party."

"I'll pick up the food on my way around. You guys can set up." George didn't wait for a response as he punched numbers into his cell.

***

As Adrian organized the plates and cutlery they needed for the party, his thoughts kept drifting to Libby. He had to do something, but he didn't know what. He couldn't email her, it was too impersonal, but a phone call seemed wrong as well. What he wanted to do was fly back to Australia, but he couldn't do that either. Kate started school in a week and not only did he have to organize her school things, he didn't want her jet-lagged for her first day.

"I wish Libby was here. She'd love a pool party," Kate said.

Adrian's heart stuttered. Kate was right. He could picture Libby in bathers splashing around with them. "Mmm," he responded, as noncommittal as he could.

Kate glanced up from setting the table, eyes wide and innocent. "Did you thank her for her statement?"

"I'm trying to figure out the best way to do that."

"Why don't you call her?" Kate asked and then grinned as another idea came to her. "Better yet, why don't you fly back to Australia?"

He really wished he could. He held up a hand. "Hold on, kiddo. It's not as easy as that. You're starting school soon."

"You do love her, don't you?" She looked at him. "Like she loves you?"

He didn't know what made Kate think Libby loved him. Perhaps it was just her way of seeing the world. But she was right about him. He did love Libby.

Of course he did. It might have taken standing up to his father and almost losing Kate to make him realize he wanted Libby as a permanent part of his life, but he'd got there in the end. Just remembering the time he'd spent with Libby brought a smile to his face and lightened his heart. "Yes," he said. "I love her."

"You have to tell her. Libby says people often say things they don't mean when they're mad. But if you love someone, you forgive them." Kate paused. "She forgave me when I was mad at her."

It wasn't that simple, but he couldn't explain that to a ten-year-old. "We've got to buy your school things," he said.

"Jem and I are going shopping for that together. Aunt Susan is taking us."

Adrian couldn't ask someone to look after Kate while he went to Australia. Not after he'd just had his custody of Kate confirmed. It would make him seem irresponsible. "If I take you to Australia, you'll be too jet-lagged for school." There had to be some way to make this work.

Kate frowned, concentrating, and then brightened. "I'll be right back." She jumped up and ran out of the room before he could ask her what she was up to.

Adrian got a bag of chips out of the cupboard and poured them into a bowl. In the next room he could hear Kate talking. He stood and wandered toward her voice. What was she up to? He found her in her bedroom with the phone to her ear. "That would be awesome, Aunt Susan. Thanks." She turned, saw him and gave him a guilty smile. "Maybe you should tell him what we agreed," she said into the phone, then thrust it at Adrian. When he took it, she hopped back a couple of steps, her fingers in her mouth.

"What has Kate been saying?" he asked.

"She and Jemma are planning something, but they won't let me know the details," Susan said. "Kate wants to come and stay for a few days so she and Jemma can work on their 'mission'."

His niece was trying to appear innocent and failing

miserably. A suspicion formed. "When does she want to stay?"

"Tomorrow night, and for the next five days. I'm perfectly happy to have her."

Hope and dread tussled for control in his stomach. Would Susan use this as ammunition? He had to be truthful. Walking away from Kate to the lounge room, he said, "I know what this is about. Kate wants me to go to Australia and thank Libby for the statement she wrote."

Susan inhaled sharply. "You haven't thanked her? I'm surprised."

Adrian's defensive side rose. "I didn't know about it until it was read out today and it doesn't seem right to say thank you in an email."

"I think it depends on how you feel about her," Susan said, her voice brisk. "It's obvious she loves you and Kate. If you don't feel the same way, an email is the kindest way." She left the alternative open.

He closed his eyes tightly. "Susan, I can't leave Kate for so long after just reaffirming her custody. It's not right."

"I'm sorry for the hurt I've caused," Susan said quietly. "If I can help to make it up to you by having Kate, I'd really like to. From everything Kate has said, Libby sounds like a wonderful woman." Her tone was earnest.

Hope bloomed in Adrian's chest. "Are you sure you're happy to have Kate for a few nights?"

Susan's voice was the warmest he'd ever heard it. "Of course. It would be my pleasure."

Adrian's heart beat rapidly as they arranged the details. Just before they hung up, Susan said, "I wish you luck."

"Thank you." Adrian hung up and turned around to see Kate hovering behind him. He grinned at her. "You'd better pack your bags if you're going on a sleepover."

Kate threw her arms around his waist and hugged him. "We have to find you a flight first." She raced to the computer and started typing.

***

It was a wet, gray, miserable winter's day. The type of day that made Libby want to stay in bed under the covers and read. She had to force herself up and made herself a coffee and porridge.

Two days ago Kate had emailed and told Libby they had won the custody hearing. Libby was thrilled, but she had no idea whether her statement had been read. She didn't even know whether George had shown it to Adrian.

She told herself it didn't matter either way.

If Adrian had felt anything for her, he would have called her by now. He had never even responded to her voicemail message, but she didn't regret leaving it. She'd done it for herself.

Realizing she had finished her breakfast and was staring out the window at the downpour, she stood, put her dishes in the sink and sat down in her office to start writing.

An hour later she was still staring at the last line she'd written yesterday. Her muse refused to cooperate. It had evidently decided to stay in bed.

Libby sighed and stood, stretching as she did so. Outside she heard the swish of a car going past in the rain. She wandered into the kitchen and turned on the kettle, then flicked on the little gas heater. She rubbed her hands together.

This rental didn't have the charm of her old one, and now that she had the funds, she could look into a different apartment, one where the decor was from this millennium.

The kettle boiled as someone pounded on the front door. Libby glanced out the window at the downpour and hurried to answer it. Whoever it was would be getting drenched.

She opened the door and her heart stilled. She blinked twice, just to make sure her eyes weren't deceiving her.

Adrian stood there, the rain blowing at such an angle that the balcony above gave no cover and water was pouring down on top of him, sticking his hair flat to his head and soaking his blue jacket and jeans.

Libby stood back in shock as she took in every inch of him.

His eyes were serious but his lips twitched up in a hesitant smile. "Hi."

His voice, warm and melodious, thawed her frozen body. She had to say something. "Hi." What was he doing here? How had he found her? She glanced over his shoulder and saw a hire car in the car park but there was no one else in it. "Where's

Kate?"

"She's staying with her cousin for a couple of days." Adrian brushed the water off his face. "She didn't tell me you'd moved. Luckily your old neighbor gave me directions. May I come in?"

The drenched state of him finally sunk in. "Of course. Let me get you a towel." She hurried down the corridor, leaving him to follow. The front door banged behind her, but she busied herself grabbing a couple of towels from the linen cupboard and then showing him into the kitchen, where he could drip all over the linoleum. Why was he here?

Libby thrust the towels at him, not able to look him in the eye as she turned on the kettle again. "Would you like a cup of tea?"

"That'd be real nice."

Libby turned as he dried his hair and her heart hitched. What did he want? Her pulse was unsteady and she turned before he could see her watching him. She poured the two drinks and then, placing one on the table near him, she gestured for him to sit.

Her hand shook slightly and she spilled her tea on the floor. She swore, put the mug on the table and turned to clean up the mess.

"Did you burn yourself? You should run it under cold water." Adrian was beside her, taking her hand and examining it.

His touch was too gentle. Too much. She snatched her hand away. "It's fine."

She bent down to mop up the tea, blinking back her tears, and Adrian stepped back.

The silence was unbearable. "Kate told me you won the hearing," she said.

"That's right."

Libby stood and faced him, unable to put it off any longer. She forced a smile. "Congratulations."

"I wouldn't have won without your help."

"I didn't do anything." Her throat was tight.

"George tells me Piper Atkinson's interview with Emily was your work." Adrian kept his eyes on hers and spoke quietly, almost as if he were trying not to spook her.

"I asked Piper to talk to her, that's all."

Adrian took a small step forward. "The statement you wrote really impressed the judge."

Libby looked away. So he knew about her statement. She had poured out her heart in that document. Had he understood what she hadn't said – that she loved him too? She swallowed. "I'm glad it helped," she whispered. She couldn't look at him, she couldn't get her hopes up that he might feel the same way about her. If she looked up and saw nothing in his eyes, it would shatter her.

"It helped in a number of ways." He moved closer. "It helped convince the judge that I cared for Kate, it helped convince Susan that I wasn't a womanizer and it showed me what an utter fool I've been."

Libby's breath hitched but still she couldn't face him. His hand came up and gently lifted her head. She met his eyes. They were earnest.

"I've treated you so badly," he said. "I was so scared of my feelings for you and of losing Kate that I couldn't see anything else. I pushed you away rather than face my fears."

Tears sprang to her eyes.

He lifted his thumb and wiped them away. "I'm sorry, Libby."

He still hadn't said how he felt. Dare she ask him? "Sorry for what?"

"Sorry for not believing in you, sorry for pushing you away, sorry for not telling you how much I love you."

She'd promised herself she wouldn't love again.

But she hadn't really stopped loving him.

The tears flowed over and she asked, "Do you really?"

Adrian pulled her close, hugging her to him, the dampness of his clothes seeping into hers. "Yes, I do. I love you so much it hurts."

Libby hesitated.

Adrian stepped back, searching her face. "Your phone message gave me the courage to confront my father. You were right, I was letting my childhood rule me. I want to change."

Libby had heard all she needed to hear. She threw her arms around him and kissed him. His scent filled her mind and his taste filled her body.

He broke away, his eyes hopeful. "Does this mean you forgive me?"

Libby laughed. "Of course." Her heart was so big she thought it might explode. "I love you too much not to."

"Thank God," Adrian breathed and pulled her back into his arms, kissing her like his life depended on it.

Libby's mind emptied and she clung on as she lost her heart all over again.

Finally he pulled away and took a small box out of his jacket pocket.

Libby stared at him.

He grinned at her, the lighthearted, mischievous grin she'd missed. He opened the box to show her a diamond ring and took one of her hands. "Libby Myles, will you marry me?"

Libby's free hand went to her mouth. She'd never expected this.

"I don't want to lose you again. These past few weeks have been hell." He paused. "You know I come as part of a package. Kate is part of my life and she loves you almost as much as I do."

"Yes."

Adrian widened his eyes. "Yes, you know, or yes, you will?"

Libby laughed, excitement, relief and love bubbling out of her. "Yes to both."

"Alright!" Adrian picked up Libby and spun her around before pulling the ring out and slipping it onto her finger.

Epilogue

Libby couldn't prevent the tingle of nerves thrumming through her body as they pulled up in front of Adrian's house. It was a red brick house with a high-pitched roof and a big wooden front door. The garden beds out the front were full of flowers and it looked like a family home. Kate would be inside waiting with her Aunt Susan.

"This is home," Adrian said as he turned to her, drumming his fingers on the steering wheel.

She realized he was just as nervous as she was. "It looks lovely."

As they got out of the car, Kate's voice could be heard from inside. "They're here!"

Libby and Adrian shared a grin and seconds later Kate raced out of the door toward them. "You're home!" She flung her arms around both of them.

Libby closed her eyes as she hugged Kate back. With that kind of welcome, it did feel like home.

"Come on." Kate broke away, grabbed their hands and started pulling them toward the house.

"We need to get the bags, kiddo," Adrian protested.

"They can wait," Kate said, not looking back.

Amused, they followed her into the house and into the lounge room.

"Surprise!" Kate yelled.

Libby's mouth dropped open at the room full of people and the homemade banner that said, "Welcome Home, Libby."

She scanned the faces and recognized George and next to him –

"Piper!"

Libby's best friend grinned at her. "You didn't think I was going to miss this, did you?"

Next to Piper were Piper's parents and one of her brothers.

"We thought you might feel more at home if there were some familiar faces here," Adrian murmured to her.

"You knew about this?" she asked, turning to him.

He nodded, his eyes a little unsure as to whether she was happy.

Libby flung her arms around his neck and kissed him soundly on the mouth while the others in the room cheered.

Adrian made the rest of the introductions. There was Aunt Susan, who wasn't the uptight, prim and proper woman she was expecting. She greeted Libby with a hug. "It's lovely to finally meet you." Susan introduced her husband and children. Then Libby met Kate's grandparents and George's parents, Hank and Marla, and one of his sisters, Isla.

Libby was overwhelmed as around her people chatted, each person wanting to greet her and welcome her to Houston. Isla gave her a big hug. "I'm so glad Adrian finally found someone to make him happy. Welcome to our family."

Tears sprang to Libby's eyes. These people didn't know her, but they accepted her as she was.

Adrian walked over and put his arm around Libby. "I hope you're not upsetting my fiancée, Isla," he said, his tone light.

Libby shook her head, unable to speak.

"I was just welcoming her to the family," Isla said and smiled at him.

Adrian pulled Libby toward him, his eyes full of understanding. "It takes a bit of getting used to, but they're your family now too."

Libby's heart swelled and she kissed him.

She was home.

ACKNOWLEDGEMENTS

This book wouldn't be what it is without the help of many people. Firstly to my critique group both past and present; Anna, Teena, Lorraine, Susy, Juanita and Leonie. Thank you for your insightful critique, constant encouragement and good humor. Our meetings always revitalize me.

To the people who helped me with the research for this book: Carla, Rania, Rob, Nicki, Sarah and the members of ROMAUS. Thank you for taking the time to answer my questions. Any mistakes are my own and for the good of the story.

To the 2013 RWA conference team for their encouragement and support. Particular thanks must go to Jennie who did such a great job reading out my manuscript at the submission panel that Joel requested it.

Finally to the wonderful team at Momentum – Joel, Mark, Patrick, and Tara, as well as my editor, Elizabeth, and cover artist, Jon. Thank you for taking the chance on a first-time author, for your patience in explaining the publishing process to me and for helping me make my book shine.

All that Sparkles

The Texan Quartet #2

Imogen Fontaine is living every girl's dream.

She is a fashion designer for her family's haute couture label, lives in a mansion, has a great circle of friends and is the apple of her father's eye. Everything is perfect.

Until the day that Christian, the boy at the center of her childhood heartbreak, walks back into her life.

From there her life starts to unravel, as long-kept secrets are revealed. Imogen learns that her past was built on lies and betrayal, shattering the illusion of her perfect existence. She must seek out the truth if she has any hope of forging a new path for herself and discovering true freedom.

But can she convince Christian that there is a place for him in her new life?

http://www.claireboston.com/books/the-texan-quartet/

Under the Covers

The Texan Quartet # 3

What if the one time you didn't want love was when you truly needed it?

Forced to flee her abusive ex, alone with no support, Elle is determined to rebuild her life and protect her five-year-old son. Not one to take the easy road, she opens a bookshop café, but opening day almost ends in disaster. In the midst of this chaos, the last thing she needs is a man as charming as George Jones getting in her way.

George has always been a sucker for a damsel in distress, and Elle ticks all the boxes. But Elle's not interested in being rescued by anyone, especially not him. She knows her taste in men can't be trusted, but fighting George's charisma is harder than she expected. And George, who is not one to ignore an itch, has found there's something about Elle that's got under his skin.

When Elle's ex turns up to cause trouble, George must overcome his boyish flirtatiousness if he's to convince Elle to trust herself and let him into her life. But can Elle put her past behind her before it overwhelms her present?

http://www.claireboston.com/books/the-texan-quartet/

Into the Fire

The Texan Quartet #4

Piper Atkinson uses the truth as a weapon, but her latest interview candidate is more than just a headline.

Piper wants to be the kind of journalist who makes people sit up and take notice of the issues, and in Houston, Texas, there are plenty to go around. In the city's high-end restaurant world, reclusive Native American chef Taima Woods is discussed in reverential whispers, so when the opportunity to interview him arrives, Piper jumps at it.

But getting to Tai is tougher than she expected. He has a deep mistrust of reporters, and a private life he'd prefer to keep hidden. There are two passions in Tai's life – his cooking and his tribe – and he means to keep it that way. But the closer Tai gets to Piper, the closer he comes to conceding a third.

Through Tai, Piper discovers a world she knew nothing about – a damaged and ostracized community in need of a voice. But the more Piper wants to help them, the more Tai understands that to love Piper is to turn his back on his people.

Will Tai reject the one woman who's ever understood him? Or can Piper show him that hardening his heart helps no one?

http://www.claireboston.com/books/the-texan-quartet/

www.ingramcontent.com/pod-product-compliance
Lightning Source LLC
Chambersburg PA
CBHW031227120726
47905CB00002B/500